I0525634

Always
Lost Souls MC Series
Book 3

Blue Saffire

Perceptive Illusions Publishing, Inc.
Bay Shore, New York

Blue Saffire/Perceptive Illusions Publishing, Inc.
PO BOX 5253
Bay Shore, New York 11706
wwwBlueSaffire.com

Publisher's Note: This is a work of fiction. Names, characters, places, and incidents are a product of the author's imagination. Locales and public names are sometimes used for atmospheric purposes. Any resemblance to actual people, living or dead, or to businesses, companies, events, institutions, or locales is completely coincidental.

Ordering Information:
Quantity sales. Special discounts are available on quantity purchases by corporations, associations, and others. For details, contact the "Special Sales Department" at the address above.

Always: Lost Souls MC Series Book 3/ Blue Saffire. -- 1st ed.
ISBN 978-1-941924-11-2

It's better to reveal what you're ready to deal with than to pull the curtains back on what you're not ready for. In other words, know your measure.

−Blue Saffire

Have you lost your mind?

King

"I'm not too sure about sending Jacky up north. For one, we'd be down a Squad member and Pop is still out there and we have no idea of his endgame. Then we're not completely sure of what we're sending him into," I say to Dad and Brick.

We've been waiting for Gutter to show up to work this morning. I have a few things I want to discuss with him about our problems in New York. If I'm going to send my brother there, I want to make sure it's an environment that he's safe in.

Yeah, I'm still getting used to the idea of Jacky being my little brother. However, the facts are the facts. I'm going to look after him in every way I can.

"Hey, I hear you, but we need to get him away from here until he can reel it in. There's a difference between being a lost soul and a damaged soul and my boy is heading in the wrong direction," Dad says.

Brick stands beside me across from Gutter's desk as I sit behind the desk with my feet up, I looked at him as his phone buzzes and he starts to grunt and huff.

I know for a fact Eva and Misty took the babies out today and Brick is never too happy when she's running around town with his twins. I figure his sudden attitude has something to do with that.

Gutter finally steps through the door. He looks around at where we're all settled. Me behind his desk, Dad in a chair across from me and Brick still stands at my side staring at his phone.

"You're gonna want to see this," Brick says to me and hands over his phone.

I looked down at the screen to find Eva has texted Brick a picture. As I look closer at the screen, my head nearly explodes off my shoulders. I certainly understand the look on Brick's face. It's a picture of Misty sitting in a diner across from none other than Pop, her poisonous father. Where the fuck does she have my son?

"Has she lost her fucking mind?" I roar and jump up from my seat.

I pat Brick on the back to let him know we're leaving. "Dad, let's roll out looks like you're gonna get to put an end to Pop today."

We stormed from Gutter's office; all club business is forgotten. I need to get to my wife and son. We're outside and straddling our bikes before I can think twice. I know exactly where that diner is, and I'm headed straight there.

I don't know what she could be thinking.

Misty

I take a deep breath and remind myself I'm doing this for my family. Pop says he wants to call a truce so that he can be a part of my and my son's life. I want to believe him.

I also want to be able to give my husband this peace. If I can get my father to back off, then that will take a lot of stress off of King's plate.

"You have to make a decision, you can't have a grudge against my brother, husband, and father-in-law and still want to be a part of my life, it's one or the other. You have to give up this vendetta," I say as I sit across from my father.

I'm not really sure how I feel. I want to give this man the benefit of the doubt, but all of my memories tell me that this may have been a bad decision. Anytime someone I love is around this man, they get hurt. He's out to hurt my family, but at the same time, he's my dad.

I want to believe his words from his texts. He says he's changed, and he wants to get to know his grandson. How can I say no to that? He's still my father. A part of me feels like I'm betraying my husband, I know he would wring my neck if he knew I was here.

The bell over the door chimes and all breath leaves my lungs. I don't have to wonder if my husband will wring my neck, from the look on his face as he, Brick, and his father stroll in, I know he's going to strangle me.

Cage and Brick look like they might actually do the job for him. I can understand everyone's hostility toward this man. He's caused us nothing but trouble over the last few months. He's pretty much ruined my life. He's the reason my son will never know his grandmother and the reason why my brother is so angry with life.

I hang my head in defeat as King slides into the booth beside me. He leans into my ear to whisper. "I know for a fact you've lost your damn mind, Mist."

"You have something to say, you can say it to me," Pop says, only making things worse.

"When I'm ready to address you, motherfucker, I will," King says with so much bite I feel like I've been slapped. I jerked my head back as my father frowns.

King's anger is so rich I swear I can taste it. His blue eyes shine with bloodlust. I swear, he's gonna jump over the table and choke the shit out of Pop right here in front of all these people in this diner. However, it's a different pair of blue eyes that makes me the most frightened as I sit here. Cage smoothly slides into the bench seat next to Pop. Like a lion lining up his prey.

A Moment later, Mix walks through the doors of the diner and saunters over to our table. He looks as if he tastes shit. He widens his stance and folds his arms across his chest as he glares at Pop.

"You motherfuckers are looking at me like I owe you something," Pop says.

Cage leans into his face. "No, I'm looking at you like you have a death wish. From here on out I'm gonna be that ghost you forced me to be for six years. And I'm gonna haunt the rest of your existence," Cage hisses in his face. "Didn't I tell you to stay the fuck away from my family?"

"Your family? She's my kid, you fuck. I didn't Force you to do anything. Not like you forced your twin to sit in a jail cell." Pop looks at King. "You didn't know about that, did you? Yeah, your uncle is sitting in a cell all because of your daddy."

"Don't you get enough of spewing bullshit?" Cage says with a grim look on his face. "Kevlar is sitting in a cell because you don't know how to listen and play your position.

"He told you the ATF had a hard-on for him that's why he didn't want to accept that job, but you just had to do it. My brother has something that you don't have. Honor and integrity He wasn't about to let any of our brothers go down for some shit he told *you* not to do. So actually, he's rotting in a jail cell because you don't know how to listen. It's always all about you."

"He could have chosen to get himself out of that situation, it's not all on me," Pop refutes.

"Yeah, he would have had to be a damn rat and send his brothers to jail by rolling on them. He'd rather sit there and do the time than let that fall on the heads of others because you're irresponsible. He's even covering your ass," Cage bites out.

"I should have been named NYC, and Georgia chapter prez once he was gone," Pop says like a whiny brat.

"This… this is your problem and exactly why it didn't happen. The only reason you're still alive after all that is because Kevlar wants to be the one to pull a blade across your throat. One thing I can promise you, it's going to be at Kennedy that ends your life."

With that, King raps his knuckles on the tabletop and stands. He grabs me by my arm and moves out of the booth.

"Let's go," he says in a low rumble.

I get up and look into the eyes of the man that raised me. Mix shakes his head at me. The Disappointment is clear in his gaze. When I walk by, I can see so much pain in his face. I don't know what to say, I really thought that I could help the situation.

CHAPTER ONE

In Too Deep

Misty

Seven weeks later…

As I rest on my knees with my hands cuffed behind my back, I look around the filthy apartment that's now covered in blood. King's going to kill me, but I had to do what I had to do.

There was no way any of us were going to let this continue to happen. I look at Eva. *Shit.*

Brick is going to be next in line to kill me. Eva has a busted lip and a black eye. I smirk. The one who dealt the blows got it much worse.

I sag my shoulders. So much has changed. We're not the girls we used to be. I can see it in Eva's eyes. She's gone too far to turn back. Shit, I feel it in my heart that I have.

I hang my head, not bothering to look at Reap. I already know what I will find there. A look I never thought would belong to me and Eva.

Sad thing is, I know I would do it all again. No questions asked. What is it that King always says? 'No matter if the blood will wash away, Lost Souls will get covered elbows deep for their family.'

I'm elbows deep all right. I just hope my son doesn't have to grow up without me. We got messy.

Eva shouldn't even be here. I'll take full blame for all of this. If I can, I'll save the others.

I don't want anyone else's children to have to be motherless. I got us into this. I should've trusted King to handle it, but he's been busy keeping the club and all of its members safe and alive. Once I found out he took on the entire organization, I know he had so much on his shoulders. I had to do something.

I bite my lip. This isn't the first time I've taken things into my own hands and it's blown up in my face. Nope, this all started with me always taking things into my own hands. It's a nasty habit of mine.

I snap my head up when a rumble I know well fills the air. Brick stands just inside the doorway with his eyes locked on his battered wife. I look to Eva and her lips tremble at the sight of him.

We may have changed, but I know the feeling I see on her face. We still need our other halves. Right now, I know Eva is as scared shitless as I am. The adrenaline is wearing off and reality is setting in.

We're going to jail. We just murdered a roomful of men and we're going to jail. I look at the body of the man that started all this shit and I wish I could kill him again.

"If you don't get those fucking cuffs off my wife," Brick growls.

"I don't know. I think both their asses should go to jail for a few days," King says lazily from the doorjamb where he's leaning.

A tremor runs through me as my eyes lock on those blues. King gives me a glare that could freeze hell over. I know I'm in deep shit. From his expressionless face to his cold blue eyes, I know he's beyond pissed at me.

I left Prince with Rose so I could take care of this. That in itself is going to get me the tongue lashing of all tongue lashings. I nervously lick my lips. I just want to go home to my son.

If there's any chance King can get me out of this, he has to. I want to hold my little boy in my arms. I did this for them, King and Prince. Surely, he'll have to see that. King can't fault me for taking care of our family.

"I'm not going to say it again," Brick says darkly in that drawl of his.

The detective that cleared the place out when he arrived moves forward into the apartment. He uncuffs Eva first, then Reap. When he moves to release my cuffs, King clicks his tongue and shakes his head.

"Nope, not her," King says and folds his arms over his chest. "That one is going to learn a lesson tonight."

"Really, King?" I gasp and knit my brows.

"Really, baby. Getting real tired of you not trusting me. Maybe if you see what it's like not to have me, you'll appreciate what you have."

"King," I groan.

He crosses the room swiftly and bends to get nose to nose with me. "Do you remember how we started? Do you remember me putting my neck out there over how I felt for you?" he says, as if he's in pain. "Do you remember how many times I've come through for you?"

I swallow hard. "Yes."

"Nah, Misty." He shakes his blond dreadlocked head. "I really don't think you do. So, let me remind you."

"Here we go again," Reap murmurs, just loud enough for me to hear.

This is going to be a long night. I squirm on my knees in discomfort as I hold King's icy gaze. Reap's right, I'm in for it now.

CHAPTER TWO

Happy Birthday

Misty

"Happy birthday!"

I look through my lashes while blowing out the candles on the cake. I have my eyes locked on the one thing I want for my birthday. Or should I say who I want. Yes, I know exactly who I want.

King Kennedy, the Lost Souls' prez, the sexiest man walking this earth. I want to climb all six five of his fine ass like a tree. I've been waiting for this day.

King has always been badass, and I've always dreamed of being his badass old lady. We just have one problem. He's nine years older than me and he sees me as off-limits.

To King, I'm just his little sister's best friend. His VP's baby girl. Too young for him to give his attention to. Sure, we're nine years apart, but I know what I want.

King is going to know as well. I plan to make sure of that. I lick my glossed lips after blowing out all of the candles.

He grins back at me and shakes his head as he takes a pull of his beer. He makes the simple act look so sexy. I want to wrap my hand in those blond locks and lick up that sexy throat.

Damn! Pull it together, Misty.

I grin back at him and let my eyes travel over his long, lean, muscled body. King makes his cut look like a cape on a superhero. Superman ain't got nothing on him.

"What you wish for, Misty?" Mix asks, pulling me from my dirty thoughts.

I shrug, not wanting to tell him I wished for just one hot night in King's bed. Nope, not going to tell my dad that one. Not that Mix is my real father.

That's another story for later. I don't want to ruin my day thinking about the bullshit I come from. No, today is a day to celebrate.

"Nothing really," I reply, but keep my eyes on King.

I get annoyed when one of the club bunnies walks over and puts her nasty ass tits on King's arm. He turns and looks down at her. At his towering height, King tends to look down at almost everyone.

I know, I have to crane my neck to look at him from my five-four height. I don't mind though. Looking up into those blue eyes is something I live to do.

"Come on, there has to be something you want, Mist," King croons as he turns his attention back to me.

King Kennedy is mouthwatering. It starts with his blond locks that are the neatest I've ever seen on a white boy—I've heard rumors that his mother was actually Cuban—that would explain the hair and his tanned skin. But those eyes, those eyes come straight from his old man.

King has the same deep blue eyes Cage had. Eyes that will pierce your soul if you're not careful. His lips are full and sexy, just as gorgeous when he's smiling as they are when he's frowning. Not that he gives a real smile to just anyone.

"Maybe, just don't think wishing is going to get it for me," I say.

"Then you should ask for it," he replies.

The corners of my lips turn up. "Oh, I plan on asking all right. No question."

"What you plan on asking for?" Mix says. I turn to find him eyeing me suspiciously. "You still want to take that trip with Eva?"

"That's still on the table. I have a few other things I'm interested in having though."

"Dear God," Eva whispers beside me.

I turn to see my best friend blushing through her pretty brown skin. I'm surprised she's pulled her nose out of her book long enough to realize I'm flirting with her brother out in the open.

"You let us know what you want, Mist. We'll make it happen," King says.

I beam and turn to reply, but he's walking off with the slut that grabbed his attention a moment ago. My shoulders sag and my stomach turns. She doesn't deserve for him to touch her with a ten-foot pole.

I go from disappointed to pissed off in zero to ninety seconds. As I fume, Eva and Dad start to talk about the trip I'm totally not interested in. I'm on the verge of exploding.

I get up and leave the table with the cake sitting on it. Everyone has already started to scatter anyway. I need to clear my head and lick my wounds all by myself.

With my lip poked out, I storm from the clubhouse into the backyard. Brothers are hanging around the picnic tables and in lounge chairs. I avoid them all, rounding the side of the building.

I skid to a stop when I find King alone, leaning against the side of the building. His head is thrown back as he looks up at the sky. He seems to be in deep thought.

I saunter over, pulling his attention. He rolls his eyes over me and my nipples tighten beneath my shirt. His gaze lingers for just a moment before he looks up at my face.

"What you doing out here, birthday girl?"

I can't help but feel a sting from the way he says *girl*. I square my shoulders and move closer. The mixed scent of his cologne with the scent of leather hits me.

"Where'd your friend go?" I reply.

"What friend?" he asks, furrowing his brows.

"The bunny you left with."

He snorts and turns away from me, looking back up at the sky. I can't help admiring his profile. He's such a gorgeous man.

"Don't know what you're talking about, baby girl. I came out here to get some air," he says.

"So did I." I shrug.

"Don't you have a cake you should be cutting?"

I move closer, my breasts inches from his arm just like the bunny did inside. He turns his head, his gaze dropping to my chest again. I bite my lip and smile at him.

"I'd rather tell you what I want for my birthday," I say, looking up through my lashes.

He pushes off the side of the building and turns to me, leaning his shoulder on the wall of the clubhouse. His eyes lock on mine and I almost lose my courage. Instead, I close the distance between us.

"What's going on in that head of yours, Misty?"

I lick my lips, my gaze falling on his mouth. He gives me that smile he reserves for his girls—Eva, Sal, and me. His pretty teeth show and make me want to groan.

"I have a simple birthday request."

"Go on, darlin'. Spit it out," he says.

"I want to fuck your brains out," I say it with a straight face.

Heat fills his eyes, but it disappears so fast I swear I imagine it. He stands up straight and folds his arms across his chest.

"That ain't gonna happen. You're nine years younger than me. Your father would have my balls and rightfully so," he says, his jaw set tight, and his smile gone.

"I'm old enough." I pout. "You said to tell you what I want, and you'd make it happen."

"I was talking about a car, a trip to New York, some shit like that. I wasn't offering you my dick," he replies.

"King—"

"Nah. We're not having this conversation," he cuts me off and starts to walk back the way I just came from. "And Mist?"

"Yeah." I turn and grumble at his back as he retreats.

"Stop coming around here in those little ass shorts and no bra," he tosses over his shoulder.

I beam and bite my lip.

So, he has noticed.

I'll get what I want sooner or later. He can't resist me forever. I always get what I want.

Fake Chris

Misty

Ugh! Why am I here? In theory, this was supposed to be the perfect date. Andy is blond, handsome, and the quarterback of the football team at my college. There has even been talks of him getting drafted.

However, this has to be the most boring date of my life. He's dumber than a bag of rocks. I keep wondering why I've been going on these dates, knowing that I don't really want to date any of these guys. I'm only doing it to piss King off.

I roll my eyes at the stupid joke that Andy tells. He's laughing so hard he snorts. I'm glad someone's amused.

My phone buzzes on the table and I flip it over to look at the screen. I can't help the smile that comes to my face. It's a text from King.

King: *Are you hitting those books?*

Me: *Aye, aye, captain. Hitting them hard.*

King: *I should spank your ass for lying.*

Me: *What do you mean? I'm sitting here with my chemistry book right now.*

King: *That fake ass Chris Evans wannabe doesn't look anything like a chemistry book to me.*

King: *Keep playing with me if you want to. You're gonna learn one of these days.*

I huff and look around the restaurant. Trying to find the Lost Souls that he has spying on me. They're in here somewhere that's the only way he could know I'm on this date and what my date looks like. I'm so sick of King not wanting to pay me any mind but always wanting to tell me what to do.

Me: *Fine, I'm not having fun anyway. I'm going home.*

King

I dial up Teddy, one of the prospects I have watching Misty. That was too easy, I'm gonna need them to keep an eye on her for the rest of the night. She's bound to do something to make me want to wring her neck. I know her too well.

"Yeah, follow her home and report back to me, let me know if anything looks strange. If he gets out of pocket, you know what to do."

"Got it, Prez."

I'm on my feet, heading out to my bike. I could stand to let off a little bit of steam tonight. I push through the doors of the clubhouse and head straight for my bike, pulling off in the direction of Georgia. There's a little woman there that wants some unfortunate soul to learn the lesson.

I'll oblige her wish. Wouldn't be the first time, sure won't be the last.

Misty

We pull up outside my apartment building and I do my best to jump out of the car and leave Andy behind. I look back at him and frown when I hear his car door shut. There's no need for him to walk me to the door. I'm over this date, have been for the last two hours.

I dig in my bag and pull my keys out as quickly as I can, trying to rush to open the front door. One of my neighbors rushes out, opening the door for me. I go to slip inside quickly and shut the door behind me so I can avoid having to say anything else to Andy, but he sticks his foot in the door.

He's a really good player, so I actually have a second thought against slamming the door on his foot in case I injure him. I sigh and let my shoulders slump.

"What's the rush?" he says, causing me to turn.

"I really should have been studying this evening. I need to catch up on everything I'm behind in."

"Yeah, but I've been waiting for so long for you to agree to go out on a date with me," he replies.

"Thanks for the date. I'll text you tomorrow." No, I really won't. I have no intention of putting myself through this torture ever again, at least not with him.

The sound of motorcycle engines catches my attention and they're not too far distant. King comes to mind. I'm quite sure he has a few brothers out there watching and waiting to see what happens tonight.

I've grown hip to him over the last year. This is nothing new, I'm well aware that I'm being watched. It's the reason I go on these horrible dates.

The rev of an engine causes something in my head to snap. If King wants his boys to find a show, I'm going to give them one. I'll give them something to call him and talk about. Two can play this game. I grab Andy by his collar and draw him into me.

Unfortunately, he becomes overeager, cupping my face and smashing his lips to mine. His kisses are sloppy and so unwelcome, I almost gag. I mean, what's wrong with him? Why does he keep moving his tongue like that?

When he removes his hands from my face and reaches to squeeze my ass, I've had it, I knee him in his balls and shove him out the door.

"Good night, Andy. Don't call me in the morning."

King

I stop right outside the college town to fill up at the gas station. As soon as I get the pump in, my phone goes off with a text. I open the text and the video starts to play. That fake Chris Evans is trying to swallow Misty's face. The last thing I see before my vision goes completely red is Misty shoving him away.

"You're mine, motherfucker," I mutter to myself as I finished pumping my gas.

I try to reel my temper in as I send the boys a quick text to let them know to hold that dick there until I arrive. I swing my leg over my bike and head for Misty and Eva's apartment.

It only takes me about ten minutes to pull up. When I arrive, they have him in the parking lot of the apartments where no one can see them and all the lights are blown out.

I have to ask myself, is this even worth it, when I find him shaking in his boots with piss on the front of his pants. This kid is no threat to me, I don't even know what Misty is thinking.

I walked over to him and grabbed him by his neck.

"Do you understand how bad you fucked up? You touched something tonight that doesn't belong to you. Are you always in the habit of putting your hands in places they don't belong? You play for the football team, don't you?"

He nods his head and licks his lips. "Nah, we're talking man to man here," I say. "I'm gonna need you to speak to me in words."

"Y… yes. I play for the team. Please man, I don't want any trouble."

"Stop whimpering and grow a pair. You didn't look scared when you were trying to shove your tongue down Misty's throat, where's all that courage now?"

I release him and take a step back. "Tonight's your lucky night, I'm feeling generous. I won't break your hand this time, but you touch her again, I'ma snap both your arms off."

He nearly trips and falls flat on his face as he tries to scurry away from me and my boys. We all laugh as we watch him run off. I look toward Eva and Misty's apartment and remind myself that's not what I came here for. I head back from my bike so I can take off back to South Carolina, where I belong.

CHAPTER THREE

Troublemaker

Misty

If King thinks I'm just going to slink away and give up, he can forget it. I have a few tricks up my sleeve. I know this attraction isn't one sided. The fact that he interferes with my date tells me it's not.

I've been flirting with him, and he flirts back. I just need to give him a little push. They say out of sight, out of mind. Well, I haven't allowed King to have me out of anything.

I may have started my freshman year at college, but I'm home more than I'm on campus. Which is saying a lot since campus is an entire state away. Tonight, I plan to do more than make sure King remembers me, I'm going to make sure he sees me.

"Misty," King booms across the clubhouse.

I turn to see him with his eyes narrowed at me. I give him a bright smile and sway my way across the clubhouse to his office. He devours me with his gaze, taking in my outfit as I come to a stop on my six-inch heels.

A girl my height can always use a little help. Especially when trying to taunt a giant. He folds his arms across his broad chest when I reach him.

"What's up?" I say as I stand before him.

"Where do you think you're going dressed like that? Why don't you have your little ass at that school we're paying for?" he says tightly.

"I have a date." I swear, I see his eye twitch.

His jaw flexes as he looks me over again. The black liquid leggings are showing off my thick curves and the gold shirt I have on covers my breasts but is cut in strips in the front and back, showing off more of my brown skin than might be appropriate.

"Your daddy know you're going out looking like that?"

"I'm not a baby, King. I can go out on a date if I want, and I can wear what I want."

"Fuck that shit," he huffs under his breath.

"Excuse me?" I say, trying to hold back my smile.

He glares at me for a moment. Suddenly something changes in his eyes, and he grins. Leaning into my ear, his breath fans my skin.

"Don't go trying to give away what doesn't belong to you, Misty," he whispers.

"What's that supposed to mean?"

With his lips still at my ear, he says. "Don't get no one fucked up."

With that, he turns and heads back into his office. I stare after him for a minute before I start to grin from ear to ear. I reach to touch my ear, it still tingles from his nearness.

Yup, this is going to work.

***

Oh my God! This isn't going to work. This date is going to make me claw my own eyes out.

Sexy does not equal interesting or attractive. This guy stopped being attractive about ten minutes into the date. Ugh, why did I do this to myself. His laugh is grating on my damn nerves and if he talks about his ex—One. More. Time. —I'm going to lose my shit.

I've been texting Eva under the table this entire time, trying to get her to send help to get me out of here. She's pissed at me because she needs to study and I dragged her back here to South Carolina. She won't leave her damn books long enough to save me.

Her last text seriously reads…

Are you dying? Are you in danger?

Once I replied no, she stopped responding. I'm going to kick her ass. Just wait until I get back to the clubhouse.

"She always has this way of making me question myself, but I like that about our relationship," my date rambles on.

Shit. This is un-fucking-believable.

"That's nice. I'll be right back. I'm going to go to the restroom," I say.

I need to call Eva. She has to bring her ass down here to get me. I can't take any more of this. It's not worth it.

"Oh, okay," he says and nods.

I wonder if he realizes I've forgotten his name. I duck into the hall between the restrooms and the exit. I dial Eva, but it goes to voicemail.

Rolling my eyes, I stomp my foot. "Damn bookworm. She doesn't even need to study," I huff to myself.

I sag my shoulders and turn to go into the restroom. I need a reprieve from this torture. As I step into the bathroom, the sound of motorcycles reaches me from the distance.

I roll my eyes as hope blooms. What I wouldn't give for those to be the rumbles of Lost Souls' bikes. I'd climb on the back of any brother's bike just to get out of here.

"At this point, I'll walk," I mumble to myself.

I try Eva again after using the bathroom quickly. She still doesn't answer. Just wait until I get back and find her.

Stepping out of the restroom, I have a new attitude. I don't care if I come off rude. I want to go home. This date is over.

I head for our table to tell this guy just that and freeze. King, Grim, Reap, and Axel are all sitting around my date. He looks like he's debating on running for his life.

I look around the diner and take note of some of the other people staring at the group. Shaking the shock off, I walk to the table and place my hands on my hips. King lifts his gaze from his phone to me.

"What are you doing here?" I snap.

"You've been texting Eva. I told her I'd handle it," King says with a smug grin.

I bite back a string of curses. I'm going to kill that girl. I'm seriously questioning our friendship.

"What's going on, Misty?" my date says.

I can't hold back the eye roll. I wasted a good outfit on this guy. This place isn't what I had in mind when he said he was taking me someplace nice.

"You fucked up," King says and pats his cheek. "Stay in your lane next time."

With that, King stands, placing my purse in my hands before he places his palm on the small of my back. My body reacts as if I've been electrocuted. I feel the simple touch everywhere.

It doesn't help that his hot touch is on the bare skin my shredded shirt is revealing. I want to turn and curl into his side, but I refrain from doing so. Instead, I keep my eyes on the door.

"I just want you to know I wasn't with this," Reap says as we step into the parking lot where four bikes are lined up together.

"She called for help," Grim says.

"Not this kind of help." She frowns at him.

Why can't the ground open up and swallow me? This is so embarrassing. Not what I was going for this evening at all. Instead of making King jealous, I've made myself look like an idiot.

"You can do better," King says so close to my ear, I almost jump.

I turn to look up at him and those blue eyes are locked on me. I lose the smart-ass remark I'd planned to make. There's something in his eyes I can't place. Before I can try, he shuts it down and hands me a helmet.

"I thought I was going to ride with Reap," I say.

"You wanted to get those thighs around me, here's your chance," he replies with a crooked grin.

My lips part as images of having him between my legs fill my head. I quickly shut them down before my thoughts show on my face.

"You're a tease."

"Takes one to know one," he says, throwing a long leg across his bike.

I climb on behind him and settle into place. King stiffens for a brief second and I get the feeling I'm not the only one affected here. Wrapping my arms around him, I squeeze my thighs.

King shakes his head, not looking back at me. He starts the bike and we're off. I grin to myself at the thought of being on the back of his bike.

This may not have turned out as bad as I thought.

King

This girl is out to drive me insane. I should've let her climb on the back of Reap's bike. If I were thinking with my head and not my dick, I would've.

Although, when it comes to Misty, I'm never thinking with the right head. I'm twenty-eight. Too old to be lusting after a nineteen-year-old.

Yet, when it comes to that mischievous smile, sassy mouth, her pretty face, and that gorgeous rich brown skin, I can't seem to keep every bit of good fucking sense I have from going up in smoke. I'm still reeling from her words all those months ago.

"Fuck," I mutter as she squeezes her thighs against me and I think of her sultry voice telling me she wants to fuck my brains out.

Misty has filled out like a fucking Coca-Cola bottle. I don't know what we've been feeding these girls over the years, but that shit has my trigger finger twitchy. Where my sisters have no clue how drop-dead gorgeous they are, Misty is dangerous because she knows, and she uses it like a weapon.

"She's going to have my ass in a grave," I mutter as she presses her breasts closer to my back. I shake my head and keep riding.

If I'm honest, all of my girls are a handful. I'm proud of them though. My sisters are good girls. Sal is a genius. Everyone thinks I don't ever hear a peep out of her. That's bullshit.

Sal just gives me a different kind of trouble from her sister. She does what she's told without a problem, but if you don't tell her not to do something, she's going to do it. Trust me, that can cover a whole lot of shit, I'm learning.

Eva and Misty are a different story. Eva never gives me shit, but she finds herself in the middle of it all the time. I wouldn't expect anything less.

Both Eva and Sal are gorgeous girls. Fucking knockouts. Eva just has more curves than one woman should own. I have been praying for years that Sal never catches up to her. Worse part is, neither Eva nor Sal realize how stunning they are.

Misty, on the other hand, well, Misty is a fucking problem. She has been since I started to look at her like a woman and not the little girl of my VP. My little buddy that would hang around to keep me company every now and then.

Mix would have my fucking balls if he knew the thoughts I have when I lie in bed at night. That pouty mouth and those mouthwatering little tits of Misty's have starred in more of my dreams than I would like to admit.

Misty is a stunner. All that thick dark hair that frames her face in soft springy curls, those long lashes, her big brown eyes, and those lips. God, how can you not be drawn in by those lips?

Yeah, her looks are dangerous and the fact that she knows it is what makes her dangerous too. Shit, I've been flirting with her way too damn much when I know I shouldn't be.

"Fuck me."

We pull into the compound gates, and I roll to a stop in my usual spot. Misty lingers for just a second before climbing off my bike. I'm a little pissed off when her heat is gone from my back.

"Thanks for the ride," she leans into my ear to whisper in a seductive tone.

"Keep playing with fire, Mist," I warn. "Getting burned will be the least of your worries, baby girl."

"Not a baby anymore," she says. "Sooner you see that, the sooner I can show you what you're missing out on."

"Good night, Misty."

"Whatever, King," she says, rolling her eyes and turning to enter the clubhouse.

I watch the sway of her hips as she goes. *Damn.* That big ass is going to be the death of me one of these days.

CHAPTER FOUR

Always here

Misty

"Hey, baby girl, what's up?" King answers the phone in his sexy voice.

This part of our relationship is always so easy I can always call him and ask for anything I need. I wish telling him what I truly want was that easy.

"Hey, King, I was wondering if you have any spare laptops at the office. My laptop keeps crashing every time I try to load these brushes and I need them for a project at school," I reply.

"Sure, do you want me to bring it to you or do you want to come get it."

I start to pant on my end as I hear the way his sexy voice drops as he spits the innuendo. This man knows exactly what he's doing.

"I can come get it. I'm ready when you are," I say, trying to keep the sass in my voice and not show him how affected I am.

"Or I can just go online and order you a brand-new one. We could pick it up today."

Just like King, always changing course. Sometimes I wonder if he just happens to forget who he's talking to. And once he has the sudden reminder, the switch flips and he's back to ignoring me.

"A new one that would cost like six grand, you don't have to do that. I only need to get through this project and then I'll look at getting a new one for myself."

He sucks his teeth. "Now when has that ever been a problem? I've spent more on your books for a semester. I have plans to come and get my hair done out your way, it would be nothing to pick up the laptop and drop it off."

"Are you sure?"

"If you need it for school, it's yours. I'm already on the site placing the order. You need anything else?"

"Yeah, but you and I already know that you're going to turn me down."

He chuckles but says nothing else. I start to get excited knowing he's coming here. It's been a few weeks since I've been able to get home to the clubhouse.

Maybe I should cook, I have plenty of time. They say the stomach is the way to a man's heart. I wonder if that will help me get into his bed as well.

I grin, already forming a plan in my head. I haven't been on a date since the last one with what's his name. Maybe I need to step my game up, obviously the dates haven't been working.

"Thanks, King," I say as I come out of my musing.

"No problem, kiddo. I'm always here."

The way he says the words is so heartfelt, I almost change my mind about trying to seduce him through a meal. There was a time where King and I were just friends. We had a really strong friendship going. I sort of miss that.

However, if he were my old man, our relationship would only be that much stronger. My determination kicks back in as I hang up and head for the kitchen to see what we have here. No opportunity should ever be wasted, and this is indeed an opportunity. Once done in the kitchen, with my plan for the evening set. I head to the bedroom to find something to wear.

King

I know my ass is exhausted. I had no business flirting with Misty, but I wasn't thinking straight. I could've easily taken one of the laptops from the office and had it delivered to her by one of the boys, but no, that wasn't good enough.

It's been a few weeks since I've seen Misty, and this is the perfect opportunity to set eyes on her. I'd buy her two new laptops just to see that smile.

The ride there will take a few hours and it will take about two hours to get my hair twisted. I should still have plenty of time to pick up her new laptop and deliver it.

Eva mentioned their air fryer broke. I should pick them up one of those too.

I must be out of my mind. I'm finding any reason these days to try to find myself in the presence of that little vixen. I hiss in impatience with myself. I can't keep going back and forth with this.

However, there was a time where Misty was nothing more than a friend. I long for those days to relax in her presence and have a good laugh. We can get there again, to a mutual place where we're not looking at each other with hungry gazes. As if one is going to eat the other. I think this as I take off for Georgia on my bike.

***

When I arrive at Eva and Misty's apartment, Eva opens the door, and a delicious aroma drifts out of the space. My mouth starts to water instantly. It's been a long day, but I hadn't realized I was starving until this moment.

I step into the apartment and I'm immediately starving for more than the appetizing scent that has risen to my nostrils. Misty stands in a pair of tight-ass jeans and platform heels. The spaghetti strap tank top she has on leaves little to the imagination. Her tight nipples strain against the thin fabric of her T-shirt.

I'm tempted to drop this laptop and air fryer right where I stand and crossed the room to wrap my arms round her and draw one of those tight peaks right into my mouth. If it weren't for Eva standing here watching me, I probably would.

I have to shake my head clear of my wayward thoughts. As soon as Misty smiles, I receive exactly what I've come here for. I need to be good with that. I should turn around now and head back home. If I were working with any of the good sense I was born with, I would.

However, it's a known fact that I'm never operating with good sense when it comes to Misty. One of these days, this obsession is going to set my ass on fire.

"It smells good in here," I say when I realize that I've been staring for much too long.

The little smile in the corners of her lips tells me that I need to pull my shit together. Eva takes the box with the air fryer from me.

"Oh my God, you're a lifesaver," she says excitedly.

I curse myself. I never thought to call to see if Eva needed a new laptop, as well. I was too focused on getting here to Misty. See, never a coherent thought. The right thing to do would have been get them both a laptop, no matter what.

Now guilt is going to ride me all the way back home. They are both in programs that require them to use graphics, she probably could use a new laptop as well. Frustrated with myself and my thoughts, I place the laptop for Misty down on the coffee table.

I turn for the door, knowing I need to get out of here.

"Hey, where are you going?" Misty calls out. "I made dinner for everyone, you can't leave."

"I need to head back," I say, turning to look over my shoulder.

She gives an adorable pout and I already know I'm not going anywhere. Instead of walking out the door, I pull my sister into a hug and kiss her forehead. "Have you two been behaving?"

Eva looks up at me with a frown. "We always behave," Misty says.

"Not from where I'm standing," I mutter to myself.

This causes Misty to give a little evil smile. She turns back for the kitchen, and I groan. Those jeans have to be a second skin. I must be a glutton for punishment.

I follow her into the kitchen to see what's causing the delicious aroma. I find her stirring a pot. Walking over, I place my hand on the small of her back and lean in to look into the pot she stirring. The scent of curry and spices assault me, but it's her delicious fruity scent that grabs my attention as she turns her face toward me.

I'm so tempted to turn into her and take her lips. It takes everything in me not to. Reason number ten thousand and one why I shouldn't be here.

"You're so used to eating out, I figured I could give you a home-cooked meal. Something delicious that will fill your belly," she says in a sexy whisper.

"Who's belly are you really trying to fill? There you go playing with fire again."

I tap her ass and push away. Yeah, that's enough playing for one night. I shut all that shit down as I take a seat at their little table and start a conversation with my little sister. Misty and I can do this sexy banter thing another night. I have club business playing in the back of my mind. This isn't the time for me to be thoughtless and reckless.

CHAPTER FIVE

Intercepted

King

Two years later...

My phone pings on my desk. I pick it up and smile. It's been a while since Misty has tested me with one of these dates she keeps going on. I was wondering when she would start back at it.

I'm headed out this weekend, but I'm still going to keep an eye on this situation. As a matter of fact, since I'm leaving, I'll just nip this in the bud right here and now.

I send a quick text to the brothers watching over her.

King: Don't let him make it to the date. This one ends now.

A part of me feels bad, she actually looks really cute from the pictures they sent. I can tell she put time into this date. Too bad that shit ain't happening.

Should I be ashamed that I have her phone tapped and I can see her texts? Yeah, probably should be, but I'm not. This is the crazy shit she makes me do.

I smile and place my phone back on the desk. This is going to be a wild weekend.

CHAPTER SIX

Drunken Text

Misty

Twenty-one, I'm twenty-one and he's still denying me. I'm so sick of watching those bitches at the clubhouse try to become his old lady. Meanwhile, I'm stuck dating these lames just to get his attention.

Another suspiciously called off date. This time I got the call while in the restaurant waiting for the dickhead to show up. His grandmother broke her hip, my ass. Asshole forgot he told me he lost both his grandmothers around the same time two years ago.

So nice of King to keep playing in my love life. I leave the restaurant and head for the bar across the street. I just want a drink and a good time—dancing, a good laugh.

Eva still spends all her time with her head in her books. Of course, she refused to meet me to kick back and relax. Thank God, we'll be starting our last year at the end of the summer.

Not that school has been hard for me. It's just a pain in the ass to have to go to classes and finish my projects. Should've stuck to my guns and did a two-year program. The things I do for Eva.

"Hey, gorgeous."

Oh boy, and this has been the problem since I've arrived at this bar. No one will allow me to drink in peace. Just because I'm alone doesn't mean I'm looking for company. Ugh. None of these preppie dipshits are my type.

I turn to the blond with his overconfident aura and knock him down a few pegs with just a glare. I slide a gaze over him, making it clear that he's coming up lacking. Without a word, I turn back to my drink and toss it back.

"Can I buy you another one?" His words come out a whole lot less confident this time.

"I'm good. Thanks."

He stands there for a few beats as if I haven't dismissed him. My anger rises with each second. How is it that I can't get rid of guys like him, but King can ignore me like I don't exist?

"Bitch," he says under his breath as he walks away. His cry of pain grabs my attention only a few seconds later.

I turn to see him bent over as Reap's little ass whispers something in his ear. He nods frantically before taking off like someone's chasing him down. Reap turns to me with a grin on her lips.

"I don't even want to know," I say and shake my head.

She shrugs her shoulders and takes the vacant seat at my table. Flagging down the waitress, she orders two beers. No fruity drinks for Reap. Not her style.

"What are you doing in Georgia?"

"How are you going to text me to see if I'm here and then question my whereabouts when I come to hang out with your ass?" she says and rolls her eyes.

"Okay. Point taken. Just curious. Where's Grim?"

"Licking his wounds. Not in the mood to talk about him. Next."

I hold my hands up, ready to change the subject. Whenever those two aren't attached at the hip, there's something wrong. They entered the Navy side by side. They got thrown out together too. I've never seen two people more in love with each other and completely oblivious to it.

"I should've gone home this weekend," I mutter.

"Nah. He's not there," she says. I look at her and blink a few times. "You have to be shitting me. You don't think I know you're hung up on the prez?"

"No comment."

"No comment, my ass. Why don't you just tell him how you feel?"

"Like you told Grim?"

She twists her lips and falls back in her seat. Yup, I hit the nail on the head. She looks away as if that can help hide the way she feels about him.

"It's different."

"No, it's not."

"Yes, it is. King's not your best friend. You're not just one of the guys to him." She turns back to me with her feelings in her pretty eyes.

"He sees you that way because you let him. When was the last time you dressed up to show off that sick body?"

She snorts. "Sick my ass. My tits are too small. I see the bunnies he watches. Have you seen the chicks he hooks up with?"

"You're tripping. I've caught Grim watching your ass more times than I can count. And that's with those baggy jeans and chaps. Besides, your boobs are bigger than mine. You have a good D cup for sure."

"I'm a passable D," she mutters. "Not the triples he drools over."

She plays with the label on the beer the waitress just dropped off. Reap is scary as fuck, but she's gorgeous. I think Grim would lose his shit if she dressed up and showed off the body beneath her clothes.

"Let me dress you up. I bet you'll get his attention."

"And then what?" She frowns. "I'm not losing my best friend over a fucking crush. It's bad enough he's pissed that I want to join the Squad. Things have been different."

I signal for another drink. "Guys are assholes. It shouldn't be this hard to get them where we want them."

"I'm just tired of not knowing where I stand. I'm not going to tell him how I feel. He's the guy. But I'm sick of him thinking he can run my life. Like what the fuck?"

I get the feeling she's going to vent about what's really going on, even though she said she didn't want to talk about it. Her face is pinched as she scowls at her two empty beers. Great, she's here to drink just like I am. I'm starting to feel a little faded myself.

"You're getting further than me," I mumble.

Reap focuses on me. She looks through me with those brown eyes. I try—unsuccessfully—to hide my feelings behind a wall she can't get to.

"You're barking up a tough tree. Prez isn't stupid. He gets you're into him. He just has too much respect for you and your dad."

"Come on, Reap. This is what I'm talking about. I'm a grown woman. Why does my dad have to come into this?"

"It's a brotherhood. You've been around the life. You know the code. Mix loves you like you're his own flesh and blood. Nobody is going to disrespect his daughter.

"The guys are rough with their women. It's not all flowers and pretty roses. They just treat *us* differently. It's what I've been fighting from the beginning. I want to be seen just like one of the guys, not the little princess they want to treat me as."

"Well, that's not working out for you, is it? Grim seeing you as one of the guys is the problem."

She pulls a face at me. Rolling her eyes, she slumps down in her seat. Arms folded over her chest. She mumbles to herself, then to me.

"We're not talking about me."

"We are now. I'm taking it something happened?"

She stares at me as if debating whether or not she plans to share. I sit and wait. I knew Erica before she became Reap. I know there's a girly girl in there who just wants to feel like she has a place to fit in, no matter what she does or says.

"They went on a road trip. You know, one of the ones when they go for new pussy and not those dry ass bunnies at the clubhouse. I got on my bike, ready to roll out. His ass told me I couldn't go this time.

"That shit stung. I've never stopped him from hooking up, no matter how much it hurts," she says, as if in physical pain.

I'm right there with her. The thought of King going on one of those trips makes my stomach turn. I wish I were there to slash his tires and stop the trip. I flex my jaw as the bitter taste of jealousy fills my mouth.

When Reap looks up at me, I see the pain in her eyes. It reflects my own mood. I'm so pissed, I stay silent as she continues.

"I've never lied to Grim until today. I told him it was fine. I had someone I wanted to stay back and hook up with."

"And he believed you? You guys are always together."

"I've been MIA for a bit. Went for a ride to clear my head. I sort of didn't tell him I was going or where," she says and lifts her shoulders. "Fucked-up part, he didn't want me to go with them, but he lost his shit on me when I lied about some dude that doesn't exist. Told me I was irresponsible and I don't give a fuck about anyone but myself."

"What?"

"Yup. Apparently, if I'm seeing someone, I should run it by him. I shouldn't be taking off without him knowing what's going on," she scoffs. "I almost kicked his fucking ass."

I shake my head. Men. So unbelievable.

"I wouldn't have blamed you."

"I'm going to give him some space. That shit hurt. If you ask me, Prez may be doing you a favor. Loving a Lost Soul isn't good for your sanity."

"Did you just hear what you said? We're in love with Lost Souls. We have no sanity." I laugh.

"Good point."

Enough about the men in our lives who drive us insane. I asked her to hang out to forget about men for the night. I want to enjoy myself for once.

"Fuck them. Tonight, we leave all that shit in South Carolina where it can fester. I'm over King Kennedy. May his dick get cooties."

I lift my drink and we both giggle and toast. The drinks keep coming and we forget all about our man problems. I'm glad Reap answered my text. We get each other.

King

"No. Don't bother her. Just keep an eye out," I mumble into the phone.

I hang up and rub my temples. I'm supposed to be having a good time. Me and the brothers are partying hard this weekend.

Things are good for the Lost Souls. We have more legit business than dirty deals, and for the first time in a long time, I don't have to flip my lid over my sisters or Misty. At least I'm not going to allow myself to lose my shit over Misty.

"She wants to drive me crazy," I mutter to myself.

Misty drives me insane. She just does shit to push me to the edge, and she likes that shit. I can't have her, but I'll be damned if anyone else does.

The piece of shit guys she likes to date only serve as stress relievers for me. Beating the shit out of them keeps me from losing my mind and fucking her. No one knows I have it bad for her.

I'm just as possessive over my two stepsisters as I am over Misty. To everyone else, I'm just looking out for the girls who have grown up as my little sisters, Misty included. That's what everyone thinks, except for Misty.

The two of us have been playing with fire for years. It's why I made sure she and Eva went away for school. I needed a fucking break from the little cocktease, but trust me, I have my brothers watching them both.

Misty is one of the brightest girls I know. She knows I'm having her watched, and that's why she continues to date those douchebags. I'm getting tired of hearing about it, but I won't go put a stop to it.

The distance is for the best. That's when I can get her and Eva to actually keep that distance between us. I think they're home more than they're on campus.

"Joke's on me." I blow out a breath and roll my shoulders.

I don't know why I'm on this trip. My mind is totally somewhere else. It's not just on Misty and her date.

Everything around me seems to be going great, but there's something in the air. Something coming that I can't put my finger on or nail down. I've been feeling this way for a while. A part of me wants to be back home watching out.

"You okay, Prez?" Grim asks as he comes over and sits beside me on the back deck of the house we rented for this weekend.

"Yeah." I nod and take a pull of my beer. "What happened to Reap?"

He blows out a heavy breath. "For once, I wanted to get my dick wet without seeing that look on her face. Like I'm a fuckup or some shit. Like she's judging me and every chick I stick my dick in. I lied and told her she wasn't invited."

I let out a low long whistle. These two are never apart. I would never have told Reap she wasn't invited. It feels wrong without her here.

"You're digging yourself a grave," I warn.

"Don't I know it," he says and rubs the back of his neck. "She said she's been seeing someone. She was gone for those few days. It never crossed my mind she was with some guy. The thought of her fucking some dude that entire time. *Shit.*"

"You fuck chicks all the time. What did you think? She's a woman. She has needs too."

"Shit. This is Erica. In my head, she's never supposed to fuck."

"Or is it she's never supposed to fuck anyone but you?"

His cheeks turn red. He runs a hand through his long blond strands. I can see the wheels turning.

"I fucked up. None of those girls in there are what I want. Hearing Reap say she's letting someone else touch her... that shit is fucking with my head.

"I don't know when I stopped seeing her as my buddy. You know I've known her all my life. That shit used to drive me crazy when she would jump her little ass into my fights.

"Now, I feel incomplete without her." He takes a pause to pull a hand down his face. "I can't lose her, but I'll fuck shit up if I tell her how I feel."

I lift a brow at him. "Are you sure about that? What makes you think she doesn't feel the same way?"

"Shit, I thought she was gay. Come on. This is Reap. I wasn't risking my balls to clarify. I've just never seen her interested in a guy."

I burst into laughter. I can't hold it in. He has to be kidding me. He's the only one in the club who doesn't know Reap wants to sit on his face.

"What's so funny?" he asks when I can't stop laughing.

"You need to pull your head out of your ass. You two flirt all the time. Reap would drop her drawers for you any day of the week."

"Bullshit," he snorts.

"All right. Be a blind man if you like. I'm telling you what everyone else knows. Dude, how do you not see how much you two flirt with each other?"

"We tease each other. I... she's not serious about any of that shit."

I burst into laughter again. "Yeah, okay."

He sits thoughtfully. I shake my head again and turn back to stare at nothing. I have my own issues, but I get not wanting anyone else to touch Reap.

I've felt the same way about Misty for the last three years. So much so I have brothers in Georgia reporting her every move to me. I know about every single one of those bullshit dates she goes on. I've gone out of my way to fuck up her love life, even though I know I'll never be able to have her.

It's selfish, but I don't know what else to do about this thing between us. The flirting needs to stop, but every time I'm around her, I can't help myself. Shit, I know one of the reasons I'm out here alone is because no one inside measures up to Misty.

"You think I should tell her how I feel?"

I turn back to Grim. "I don't know what to tell you. It'll come out sooner or later. You're just going to have to ask yourself how far you're willing to let things go with her and someone else before you say something."

He frowns and shoves a hand in his hair. "Shit."

He pulls his phone out and disappears. This should be interesting. I snort and go back to my musing. Misty's date took heed to the warning I sent. That's good. No one has to get hurt.

I frown at my own thoughts. I feel like an old ass stalker. I'm thirty. I need to let this shit go and let Misty live her life.

My phone vibrates, pulling me from my thoughts. I take it out to find a text message from the girl I'm thinking of. My lips turn up.

Misty: *Fuck you King.*

Me: *What's wrong? What did I do?*

Misty: *It's what you won't do. I'm over it. Fuck you and fuck your dick.*

I laugh and call her to hear her tell me this. I know I'm poking the bear. I should let this ride. I just can't.

"Hello," she slurs.

I knew it. She's drunk as fuck. I laugh to myself.

"Hey, baby girl. Why are you so mad at me?"

She snorts. "You know why? I'm not begging you for shit."

"How much have you had to drink, Mist?"

"None of your business. Not like you care anyway."

I start to get a little pissed off. She has no idea how I feel about her. Misty deserves better than me. She definitely deserves better than just a fuck and being tossed aside.

"Since when don't I care?"

"You don't."

"So, I don't care because I won't let you sit on my dick?"

"Yup," she chirps and hiccups.

I roll my lips to keep from laughing. I should know not to take any of this seriously. It's clear she's drunk off her ass.

"I care too much," I say in almost a whisper.

"Bullshit."

"Come again."

"You know how I feel about you, but you just ignore it. I'm tired of being caught up on someone who plays with my feelings whenever he wants. If I'm not good enough for you, stop flirting with me. Stop giving me hope that I have a shot," she yells drunkenly.

I jerk my head back. Yeah, I flirt with her like crazy. I know I do, but I don't do it to hurt her. Caught up? To me, that's totally different from wanting to fuck me.

I work my jaw as I think about what this all means. There are nine years between us that tell me to walk away now. I close my eyes. This isn't a conversation we should be having over the phone or with her drunk.

"Sleep this shit off. We need to talk when you're sober."

"No. We don't have a thing to say. I'm done."

"*Misty.*"

"I'm not one of your brothers. I'm not scared of you, King. I said I'm done. I don't want to talk to you. There are plenty of guys willing to give me what I want. I'll be damned if I keep running after you. You have a good time on your trip, though. Hope you find someone you want."

Fuck. How does she know where I am?

I'm pissed and frustrated now. I have half a mind to ride out to her school and have this chat face-to-face tonight. I look at my watch. I could make it there in an hour at this time of night.

"Mist—" I drag out.

"I'm good. You have a good night."

"You're going to watch how you're talking to me." I pause to reel it in. "I'll call you tomorrow. We need to talk."

The line goes dead. I pull the phone from my ear and glare at it. As much as I know I need to stay away from her, she just keeps drawing me in.

Shit.

CHAPTER SEVEN

Projects & Kisses

Misty

I don't remember a thing from that night I sent King that drunken text. All I know is I woke with a banging headache and a ringing phone. I wasn't human enough to answer the first few calls and that's when King started to text, which led me to find the texts I sent him the night before.

I was mortified. I still am. I haven't returned his calls in a week. Too bad I forgot he's supposed to help me with a school project. I couldn't find another established graphic designer to help me on such short notice. To be honest, King is amazing at what he does.

If he wanted to leave the club life behind, he'd be just fine. Soul Expressions makes great money creating graphic work for major clients. They pay extra to have King design for them specifically.

"Do you really think this is going to work?" Reap asks as she runs a hand over the ponytail I put her hair in.

If I would've straightened her hair, it would reach down her back, but I love her natural blend of 4b/4c curls. Some curl definer and she looks both adorable and sexy at the same time. It's better than the cornbraids and scarfs she usually wears. Either way, she's gorgeous, but like this, she's showing a softer, sexier side.

"Do I think I'm going to get you kicked out of the clubhouse with Grim hot on your heels? Yup."

"Now wait a minute. I live here. I'm not trying to get kicked out," she says, narrowing her eyes at me in the mirror.

"Only one that's going to put you out is Grim. Relax. Come on. We have to finish up. My meeting with King is in twenty minutes. I want to see Grim's reaction before I head to the prez's office," I say, coaxing her out of her seat.

She looks down and tugs on the high-waisted leather miniskirt I dressed her in. I had to fight with her to let me cut the bottom off her Lost Souls T-shirt. I thought the heels would be the biggest fight, but she willingly put the thigh-high boots on over fishnet stockings.

She sucks her glossy bottom lip into her mouth, then looks up at me. Her little nose wrinkled. "Other than the fact the you totally defaced my T-shirt. I think I like it."

I laugh and pull her in for a hug. "He's going to lose his shit. If he doesn't come for you after this, move on. Trust me, it's not worth the heartache."

"You still giving up on Prez?" She pulls away to ask, searching my eyes.

I shrug. "What's there to give up on? He doesn't want me. I'm moving on. It is what it is."

"If you say so."

"What's that supposed to mean?"

"Nothing," she chirps. "Come on. You have a project to do, and I have a man to figure out."

I roll my eyes. "There's nothing to figure out."

"We'll see about that. I just might lose my best friend before the night is over."

I sigh. She's been nervous about this since I got here. While Eva took off for her room to bury her nose in a book, Reap snatched me into her room so I could dress her up as promised.

There's a party tonight. It'll be the perfect opportunity for her to break out the new look without it being out of place. Grim still won't know what hit him.

"It will be f—"

"Misty," King's voice booms across the clubhouse as we step out into the common area.

"Oh, shit. You may be done with him, but he's not done with you," Reap sings as she saunters away.

I fold my arms over my chest and glare at King from a distance. He rolls his gaze over my ankle boots, tight leather pants, and cropped T-shirt. I see his lips move, but the words don't reach across the clubhouse. He narrows his eyes at me and turns back into his office.

I follow the unspoken command, wanting to kick myself for my obedience. I look at my watch. I still have fifteen minutes. Looking back over my shoulder, I find Reap at the bar.

All eyes are on her, but no one's crazy enough to move toward her. Grim isn't anywhere in sight just yet. Maybe I can get this over with and still catch his reaction.

I stroll into King's office and to my surprise, he closes the door behind me. I jump, a little startled. Turning, I find him in front of the door with his arms folded over his chest.

"Why haven't you been answering my calls and texts?"

"I've been busy. Look, are you ready to help me with this project? If not, I can find someone else."

He closes in on me and gets right up in my face. "I'm getting real tired of you telling me you'll replace me."

I fold my arms under my breasts. "Your problem. Not mine."

He drops his eyes to my lips. A loud rumble comes from his chest. He stalks toward me, causing me to back up until the backs of my legs bump against his desk.

"You're so damn stubborn. It always has to be your way. This can't be your way."

"That's funny. Aren't you the one always telling me to go after what I want?"

His eyes turn dark and narrow. "You know what you get when you're in my bed? It ain't nothing nice, little girl. You're not ready for a man like me, Misty. Stop with all the fucking attitude."

"Get over yourself. I'm not fighting with you. If you're not interested… whatever," I say the words with as much strength as I can muster.

He scoffs and a look of pain crosses his face. "I'm not interested? Yeah, okay. The shit I'd do to you."

I snort. "Big talk. You can keep that shi—"

Before I can get the words out, he has his lips on mine. I'm stunned silent until he grasps ahold of my ass and groans into my mouth. I wrap my arms around his neck and kiss him back. It's even better than I've ever dreamed.

When he breaks the kiss, we're both panting. He has his lust-filled blue eyes fixed on me. I stroke his jaw, leaning in to kiss him again.

"Fuck, we can't." He shakes his head and steps back.

"Seriously?" I push at his chest. "You're an asshole."

"This ain't right, Mist." He runs his hands over his dreads. "Shit."

I turn away from him. I'm completely crushed. I don't know how much more of this I can take.

"I'll just ask my professor for an extension. I'll find someone else to help me with this."

His body heat seeps into my back as he moves closer, standing so near, but so far. He places a hand on my hip. "I've got everything you need set up. I'll help like I promised."

His deep voice sends chills through me. My first instinct is to melt into his comfort, but I push that feeling away. I shake free from his hold.

"Don't. You may see me like a little sister, but I can't see you that way. I'm tired of this. We've been playing this game for three years. I'm tired."

"You really think I see you like a little sister? I don't kiss or hold either of my sisters like that. Come the fuck on, Mist. You're hearing what you want."

"I told you that we can't, not that I don't want to. *We. Can't.* Period. It's not what I want, it's what has to be," he says tightly.

"If we can't, then don't touch me and don't kiss me," I snap.

He throws his head back and shoves his hand in his dreads. "You're right. Listen, I can email you all the shit for your project. We don't have to be in the same room together. I want you to get your grade."

"Thanks," I murmur down at my shoes.

"One more thing," he says, causing me to lift my head. "If I'm never going to get to do this again, I need this."

I don't get to respond. He crushes my lips with his, and this time, he deepens the kiss. It tastes of need and goodbyes. At least, he thinks he's saying goodbye. The way he kisses me and has my toes curling in my boots, it changes everything for me.

King wants me.

Knowing this is a game changer. I'm just going to take my time to get what I want. I've waited this long. He'll break, eventually.

CHAPTER EIGHT

Disrespectful

Misty

I can't pull my eyes away from the man standing across the yard. His white wife beater shows off all of his tanned muscles and tattoos. His jeans hang low on his hips. He has his locks pulled up on top of his head, showing off his strong jawline.

It's been two months since he kissed me in his office, and I still can't get it off my mind. I should move on, but I haven't. Not really. I've let him try to put distance between us. As much distance as he can, every weekend I come home.

Still, that's not enough. I've caught him giving me heated stares and little smiles before he catches himself. I think that kiss has remained on his mind as much as it has mine.

"Ugh," Reap and Eva groan, pulling my attention.

I turn to see Laney walking out of the clubhouse with a few of her friends. I. Can't. Stand. This. Bitch. Laney makes my ass itch. There isn't anyone more annoying and vomit inducing in the world. I don't know what King sees in her.

She's a twit. I roll my eyes as she flips her long, blonde hair over her shoulder. She starts for King, but he grabs his beer and starts for me and the girls. I want to laugh my ass off as Laney follows the move with her eyes, the smile falling from her red-painted lips.

"Did you get your grade back for that project?" King asks me once he gets over to us.

I take a sip of my beer before answering him. His blue gaze fixes on my lips. I lick them when I pull the bottle away. The lust in his eyes is so intense, I feel it in my bones.

"I got an A." I shrug.

"Good." He turns his attention to Eva. "How are your classes going?"

"Great. I need to find an internship soon."

King nods. "I got it covered. Don't worry about that." He turns back to me. "Do you need an internship too? You can come work for me."

"I'm good. I'll find what I need," I say and turn back toward Reap and Eva.

Before I can start a conversation with the girls, King leans into my ear. "Don't let our shit fuck with your future. If you need my help, say it," he whispers.

I fight to ignore my nipples tightening in my bra. His cologne and the smell of leather wrap around me, the scent of beer on his breath is more alluring than it should be. I want to turn into him and taste the bitter flavor from his mouth for myself.

Instead, I turn to look him in the eyes. "My future is just fine. I think someone's looking for you." I nod toward Laney, who has stopped a few feet away.

She has the nerve to glare at me. This bitch has a slick mouth when King isn't around. She's one step away from me popping her in it.

"I'm talking to you. I don't care who's looking for me. Get me what you need me to fill out for your internship. Business has been increasing. We can use your skills," he says, not taking his eyes off me.

I sigh and nod. Before all of this, I truly did want to work at Soul Expressions. Not just because of King. It's a great opportunity as a graphic designer.

King pays his designers great money. The employee turnover is little to none. Everyone loves to work there. Although, quite a few are brothers. Their loyalty to the club keeps them with the company regardless.

"Good," he says and runs a hand down my arm.

I can't suppress the shiver that runs through me. Unfortunately, since Laney has been watching us like a hawk, she sees it too. She makes a sour face and thins her eyes into little slits. Ignoring her, I go back to my friends and my beer.

"Reap," Grim bellows from across the yard.

We all turn to find him shirtless, with his long blond hair hanging loose and damp. He's dressed in jeans and black leather chaps. Grim is a fine ass man too. I can't blame Reap for being head over heels for him.

"What?" she calls back.

"Babe, get your little ass over here."

"Fix your own damn bike. You wouldn't listen to me, now figure it out."

"Woman," he barks before stalking over to us. He stops before Reap, grasping her neck with his grease-covered hand and kisses the shit out of her. "I finished with the bike. Now I need a shower, so do you."

Plucking her from her seat, he tosses her over his shoulder and starts for the clubhouse. I smile at the two, as well as the fact that Reap has on a pair of little black leather shorts. I don't think she has worn baggy clothes since the first time I dressed her up.

"Hey, are we leaving tonight? I want to get back and go over my presentation one more time," Eva says, grabbing my attention.

"Maybe," I reply. My focus is on Laney hanging off of King.

He looks down at her and says something that makes her pull a face. In the next second, he takes off into the clubhouse. I can read in his body language. He's frustrated.

"You're driving back, so you might want to slow down on the beers if we're leaving tonight," Eva says, oblivious to everything else going on around us.

"Maybe the morning is better," I mutter.

The only reason I agreed to go to summer school is because we'll get to graduate a semester sooner as long as we complete our internship. Eva, on the other hand, would rather be in school than be here anytime.

"Look at you two. Aren't you grown up?" Laney says as she stops in front of us.

I turn to look at her. It's the condescending way her words come out that causes me to glare at her. She shoots ice back at me with her blue eyes.

"Hey, Laney. What are you doing here?" Eva asks as if just noticing her arrival to the cookout.

"Hey, Eva. I'm here checking in with your brother. I'm about to head out. Just wanted to come say hi to you guys."

"Oh, okay. I'm going inside. It's hot and I want to finish my book. See you. Let me know what we're doing, Mist," she replies and gets up to go into the clubhouse.

Laney stands with her arms folded over her boobs. I tilt my head at her, not sure why the hell she's still here. She rolls her gaze over me and her face pinches.

"You're a pretty girl, but King is way out of your league."

I stand up from my seat. I might be shorter than her, but I don't care. I ball my fists at my sides. "You, occasional booty call, don't make me whip your ass. Why are you even here? Don't you usually show up after dark when he can't find anyone else he'd rather fuck?"

Her cheeks turn red, and her lips turn into a flat line. She steps forward like she plans to do something. One of her friends grabs her arm to hold her back.

"Bitch, I wish you would. You're lucky I haven't told King some of the shit you've said to me in the past. Stay out of my face, Laney. I'm gonna fuck you up."

"Whatever."

"Whatever my ass, slut."

I see the n-word on the tip of her tongue. King doesn't play that shit. I've been waiting for her to cross that line. He'll banned her from the club for life. Too bad her friends tug her away before she makes that grave mistake.

I watch her go and my mind is made up. She's never getting her stink ass in King's bed again. I'll make sure of that shit personally.

King

I needed to come inside and clear my head. I haven't forgotten that kiss. I can't forget it, but I have to.

Misty is a smart girl. She doesn't need my fucked-up ass making a mess of her life. Still, I can't get her off my mind. I never should've kissed her.

Beer's not going to do it. I need something stronger. I don't like where things are between me and Misty.

"Knock, knock." I turn to see Mix at my office door. I groan internally. He's the last person I want to talk to. "Got a minute to talk to an old man?"

"You're always welcome," I mutter despite my mood.

I have a deep respect for this man. Not just as my VP, but he's been like a father since I lost my own. It's one of the reasons I can't go there with Misty.

I don't know how Mix would feel about the way I feel about his little girl. Shit, I'm not sure what I feel anymore. I want more than a fuck with Misty. However, I know I'm not right for her.

"What's on your mind? You sent Laney away. Must be deep."

Shit, this dude doesn't miss a thing. Laney popping up is one more thing to annoy me. She wasn't invited and I just don't feel right having her here with Misty around. Shit, that never used to come to mind before I kissed Misty.

Honestly, I haven't stuck my dick in a pussy since that kiss. Whenever I look at someone else, I see her face. Those sexy lips and big brown eyes. I'm so fucked.

"Just not in the mood. You know how I get when they start inviting themselves to shit."

I miss Jane's ass. She was my go-to when I needed to get my dick wet. We had an understanding. I didn't have to worry about petty shit with Jane. We fucked and she got lost when it was over. Yet I don't think I would want her either if she was still around.

"I hear ya," Mix grunts as I pour him a glass of whiskey and hand it over.

He takes a seat on the couch in my office, and I move behind my desk to kick my feet up. We drink in silence for a bit. I try to push thoughts of Misty out of my head.

"You're taking off next week?" I say to distract myself.

"Yup. Need to make a run. I'll be gone for a bit. Need to make a few rounds up north."

"Checking in on Kodak?"

"Of course. It's been a while. Want to make sure she doesn't need anything. The kid never asks for much."

I'll admit that I miss Sal. My little sister is a big part of the organization. I never asked why she wanted to take off and live somewhere on her own. I just made it happen.

"She's a good girl. I think she's content in her own little bubble," I say.

"That she is. Eva and Misty will be coming home soon. Since Reap moved out of the clubhouse, maybe we should consider getting them an apartment. They'll probably want to live together," he muses.

I've been thinking about this myself. I can't have Misty living here again. Now that Eva's all grown up, it's not a good idea for her either. A lot of things need to change.

"I'll talk to them and see what they want to do. If Brick hires Eva after the internship, she may not be coming back this way. Not sure what Mist will do after that."

I had already set in my mind to get Eva's internship with Brick once she mentioned it. It will be a great opportunity for her and there isn't a brother I trust more to make sure she learns and gets the job of her dreams.

Mix knocks back his drink and pours another one. "It will all work out. Shit always does around here."

I hope so.

CHAPTER NINE

Not Tonight

King

I am fucking hammered. Been this way all day. I've been in my thoughts for weeks, which has had my ass in a bottle every night. I'm tired of fighting this shit with Misty.

I sigh in relief, knowing that this week she and Eva aren't going to show up here to drive me nuts. Eva wanted to study for her finals, wherever Eva is, Misty is. Something I'm grateful for. I don't have to worry about that little doll showing up here for once.

Although, this ache in my chest makes me question if that's a good thing or bad. This girl has my head fucked up. I need to wash my brain of Misty before I do something stupid.

"Hey, daddy," Trixie, one of the club whores, purrs at me.

Trix has been around for a long time. She gave me my first blow job. Believe it or not, she still looks good after the years she has put in around here. I know she would love to take a place as an old lady, but that ship has sailed. Damn sure ain't happening with me.

"Hey, Trix," I say with a drunken grin.

I'm on the right side of feeling good and horny as fuck. I look down at Trixie's inflated tits and consider sampling what she's selling. It's been a while since I had a good fuck.

"Like what you see?" Trix says with a saucy smile on her red lips.

Something about that smile turns me off, but I need to get laid. I look around the club. My annoyance rises. These sluts are as disloyal as they come. Jane was as close as I could get to a loyal lay and she's long gone.

Club bunnies like Trix and the vultures around me think nothing about becoming clingy and trying to start up some shit. The thought makes my dick soft, and I change my mind. I don't have time for the drama.

"Nope, not tonight." I shake my head and turn for another bottle of whiskey.

"You sure, King?" she purrs at my back. "I can do things these girls wouldn't dream of doing."

"I'm good, sugar." I snort. "Go take care of my boys."

I stagger to my room with my bottle in hand and a smile on my lips. I may not want to fuck any of the offered pussy out there, but I have a go-to girl I plan to give a call. I pull my phone from my pocket and send her a text before I pass out.

Misty

I'm supposed to be in Georgia. We have finals coming up. Eva was hell-bent on staying on campus to study. I have other plans.

It looks like I pull up just in time too. I park my car, blocking Laney's way as she heads toward the clubhouse. She stops and scowls at me. Climbing out of the car, I close the distance between us.

"Get out of my way," she snarls at me.

"Get back in your car. Your visitation has been revoked."

She snorts. "By who? King sent me a text to come over." She turns her lips up into a smug smile.

"By me. I don't give a fuck what King texted you. Trust me. Once he and I have a conversation, you're banned for life."

"Get out of my way, little girl. He doesn't have time for a little bitch like you and neither do I." She reaches to push me.

I lose it. I grab her arm and commence to whipping her ass. All that tough talk goes out the window as she tries to duck away from me while squealing at the top of her lungs. I pop her in the mouth.

"Shut up," I hiss. "Take this ass whipping. You've been writing this check for years. Now cash it like a woman, you skank."

"Get off me."

"Not until I finish stomping some respect into your ass." I hold on to the side of my car as I stomp her.

She hits her head against the car and crumbles to the ground. I give her one last kick, sending her halfway under the car. I've been waiting a long time to get that one out.

"Who's your black bitch now?" I grumble.

Yup. I could've had her banned a long time ago for the shit she's said to me in the past. I've just been waiting to hand her this ass whipping.

With her forgotten, I head for the clubhouse. If King sent her a text, he'll be waiting for her. I lift my head as I march inside to give him a piece of my mind.

Everyone's drunk off their ass. No one's paying attention to me as I make my way back toward King's room. My old room is in the other direction. If anyone were paying attention, they would know I'm headed for the wrong side of the clubhouse.

I dodge everyone, making my way down the long hall to King's room. I give a knock and wait. After a few beats, I press my ear to the door and can hear King's loud ass snores coming through.

Reaching out, I test the doorknob. When it turns and opens, I smile. I push my way in, stepping inside before I close and lock the door behind me.

I find him spread out on his king-size bed, still fully clothed. He's so damn beautiful. Even in his sleep.

I came to talk, but now I have another idea. I bite my lip as the thought comes to life. I squeeze my thighs together in anticipation.

Before I can chicken out, I tug my T-shirt over my head and kick off my shoes. He grunts and bends his right leg, planting his foot in the mattress and swaying it from side to side in his sleep. I pause for a moment until his snores get loud again and he settles. Wiggling out of my jeans, I kick them aside and crawl onto the bed.

King has told me for years to go after what I want in life. I don't think he was talking about this back then, but I'm sure going to apply it to now. Here goes nothing.

King

I'm groggy when I feel small hands tugging on my zipper. A smile creeps on my lips. Laney must have gotten my text. I sleepily move my hands behind my head.

Laney can give some good head and I love pulling on her long blonde hair. Her tits have a nice bounce to them as well. Me, I like a nice average pair. Enough to fill my big hands, but they don't have to spill over.

I should know something is off the moment those soft, full lips wrap around my cock. Instead, I groan and kick my boots off. I keep my eyes closed as the alcohol courses through my veins. Damn, I drank a lot tonight.

"Mmm, *fuck*," I hiss as her tongue twirls around my length. Laney isn't her usual aggressive self, but I fucking love what she's doing.

I buck my hips up into her face as she really starts to bob up and down on my shaft. I reach for her hair and that's when my eyes fly open. My hand isn't met with the silky golden strands I expect. Instead, it's met with thick springy curls my palm has no business knowing.

"What the fuck?" I growl as my gaze meets with a big brown one.

When my dick pops free from her full lips, it's the sexiest thing I've ever seen, right down to the string of saliva that hangs from her bottom lip before breaking and slapping onto her chin. I want to tug her back to my cock to finish what she started, but I restrain myself from doing so.

"Misty, have you lost your mind?" I bite out. My face burns with rage as I take all of her in. She's dressed in only a gold bra and matching thin, little lacy panties. The gold makes her rich brown skin look like it's glowing.

Her medium—more small than large breasts taunt me—along with her thick brown thighs. My cock grows harder at the sight before me, and my brain starts to short-circuit. I have to draw a deep breath to regain focus.

"What are you even doing here?" I grunt when she still hasn't given me an answer.

Misty bites her lip as if thinking of her reply or her next move. She shocks the hell out of me when she reaches behind her back and unclasps her bra, tossing it quickly and straddles my hips.

"Misty," I warn.

"King," she whispers in that sexy, sultry voice. "I'm tired of you pushing me away. You say I'm too young, but I have more sense than the whores you let into your bed. I want you and I know you want me too."

I lift my sleep and alcohol sluggish body up, coming nose to nose with her. Her hot pussy is burning into my lap, but I try like hell to ignore it. This kid is driving me fucking insane.

"You don't know what you want, little girl," I say hoarsely. "You come in here and suck on a grown man's cock like it has no consequences. I told your ass. We can't do this. I respect your dad and you don't need a fuckup like me in your life. Go back to that school we're paying so much fucking money for and put your nose in your books."

"I call bullshit, King," she hisses in my face. "You and the boys have run off every guy I've tried to date. I know it's you. If you can't have me, no one can. Is that it?

"Well, if you haven't noticed, I'm not a little girl anymore. I want to be touched, I want to be fucked, and I want it to be by you, but if you don't want to do it, I'll find someone else to."

With those words, she tries to climb off my lap. Again, with threatening to replace me. I start to let her go like I know I should, but then her ass comes into view with the gold thong disappearing between her cheeks.

That kiss in my office plagues my brain and her words sink in. I turn into a raging beast.

I move into action, reaching for a handful of her short curls and tug her back into my chest as I move to my knees. I bring my lips to her ear, licking the shell. She smells so fucking good.

"You have played with me for the last time, Misty," I growl.

I'm tired of this. It's not the first time we have confronted each other with feelings that shouldn't exist. The girl drives me fucking nuts.

When Misty stepped to me on her eighteen birthday to tell me she wanted to fuck my brains out, I almost forgot who she was. The little shit did it with such confidence, I almost caved right then. I shut her down, but my mistake has been flirting with her after. Teasing, we're always teasing each other.

It finally hits me that my agitation has come from her unwillingness to keep things where they were. She's changed the game we've been playing for the last three years, forcing me to deal with this. Forcing me to admit to myself she's mine.

"I've never known you to talk so much, Prez," she purrs and wiggles her big ass against my throbbing erection.

"Fuck," I hiss before tugging her mouth to mine.

I'm blinded by my desire for this little feisty kitten in my arms. None of the women I have slept with compare to Misty.

If she were at least five years older, I would've claimed her ass a long time ago.

She whimpers in my mouth and reaches a hand up for my dreadlocks. I groan as I watch her chocolate hand wrap around my blond locks. Damn, I never let women put their hands in my hair, but Misty's hand looks like it belongs there, and I won't dare stop her. She tugs harder as I deepen the kiss.

I reach for her perky breast and cup it in my large hand. I pull back so my blue eyes can lock with her big brown ones. I'm in a spell that only this girl can weave around me.

I want her in ways I shouldn't. For years now, I've had everyone thinking I see this girl as just one more of my little sisters. That I'm overprotective of her, just like I am Eva and Sal.

In reality, I would kill a motherfucker for touching Misty because she has always been mine. I have just been too stubborn to give in to what my heart, body, and mind know.

I kissed her again. Her taste bursts in my mouth, her tongue dancing with mine. As I take her lips in a rough, possessive kiss, I'm floored by the tether that forms between us. I have never felt anything for the women I've slept with. However, I know that I'm going to be destroyed after tonight.

Oh yes, I'm going to fuck her brains out. There's no going back now. She has tempted me for the last time. Misty will think again the next time she shows up at this club in short shorts and tight tank tops with no bra on.

"King," she cries out when I reach between her legs and flick her clit over the thin fabric of her panties. I love the sound of my name on her lips. "Please."

"Please what, Misty? Hmm, baby, what you asking for?"

"Please, make me yours." Her words come out of those pretty lips and ruin me.

I have taken down some bad motherfuckers in my life and here I sit, letting the words of this pint-sized woman tear me to pieces. My need for control has me ripping her thong to shreds.

I shove Misty's upper body down, so she's on all fours. I love the bounce of her ass as it lifts in the air. I reach for my top draw for a foil packet. Shoving my pants down lower, I roll the condom over my still glistening dick.

I'm so hard it's painful. I don't know or do gentle. It's one of the reasons this little girl needs to stay away from me. I'm not going to play nice with her little twenty-one-year-old pussy.

I'm going to destroy her chocolate ass. Misty will never want another man after tonight. I'm going to teach her pussy to sing my name.

I stroke her folds to find them soaked for me. Images of her sucking my cock blasts me and that's the end of my restraint. I grab her hips and thrust my unbelievably hard dick into her wet canal.

"Fuck," I bellow out as she screams my name.

I pause with my chest heaving. Her tight pussy feels so good around me, I swear my eyes cross. She clinches around me, and my spine starts to tingle. There's no way I'm coming like I'm fifteen all over again.

I tighten my grip on her waist and grit my teeth. Misty has melted into the sheets. Her face is in my mattress, ass in the air. Her round brown ass looks amazing next to my paler complexion. My tanned abs and waist have nothing on her beautiful skin, but together we look perfect. I've never seen a more beautiful sight.

"This ass is mine, Misty," I grunt, as I finally have my body under control and I start to move inside her.

I pound her pussy like I'll never get my hands on her again. Misty's groans, moans, and mewls can be heard filling the room even with her face pushed into the sheets.

"King," she sings out my name.

"Is this what you wanted, baby girl? Does that feel good?" I hiss out as I grind my hips into her. Her ass bounces with each thrust, driving me mad with each ripple. "Speak up, Misty. Where's all that sassy mouth now? I want to hear you, baby."

"Fuck, King, I can't," she whimpers, I chuckle darkly.

"What happened? I know you're not scared of a little dick, baby. You've been talking shit for going on four years now. You want to be my woman, show me. I need my old lady to fuck me right," I grunt and grin, knowing she's drowning on all ten inches of my thick cock.

Misty growls in frustration and takes me by surprise. She wiggles free from my hold and turns to face me. Cupping my face in her hands, she then kisses me. I devour her sweet pouty lips, but this time she gives back as good as she's getting. She reaches between us, slides onto my length, and wraps her legs around me.

I palm her lush ass and start to drill into her core. She gets into it this time, riding me like it's her one and only job. She locks her hands in my dreads and her pussy clamps around me as she grinds her hips.

"Like that, Prez?" she purrs. She rocks, swirls, and grinds her hips. I growl. "Yes, yes, yes. Your dick is anything but little, but I can handle it."

I smirk as I look into her twinkling brown eyes. "I hope you can. We're just getting started, darlin'. You wanted in my bed, good luck getting back out."

CHAPTER TEN

We Fucked Up

King

I lie here staring at the ceiling. That was the best sex I've ever had. Shit, each round just got better. It did fuck with my head to find blood on the spread. However, Misty shrugged it off as no big deal and hopped her ass right back on my dick.

She's fucking crazy and I'm in trouble. We've never talked about that night when she drunk texted me. I know she has feelings for me.

Truth is, I'm in love with her. Always have been. I need to fix the colossal-sized mess I've made.

"What are you thinking about?" she murmurs into my chest. "You want me to leave and don't know how to ask?"

"Shut your little ass up," I snort, squeezing my arm around her. "If I wanted you out of my bed, I would've thrown you out already. I'm thinking about how I'm going to explain this to your daddy when he gets back. We fucked up, Mist. I should've told Mix that I wanted to claim you."

She lifts her head. "Claim me?"

I push her head back down on my chest, missing the comfort of her pressed against me. "What do you think this is, baby girl? You're no bunny and you're not one of my wait arounds. This is what you wanted. Now you've got it."

"Are you saying I can spend more time in your bed?" The mirth is clear in her voice.

"We have to be careful. Mix won't be back for months. We can't go public with this until he's back and I talk to him. But I want you in my bed every damn chance we get," I murmur, stretching one of her curls in my fingertips.

"Um, I don't know. You seemed to have a problem with my age. I don't think we should get into anything too serio—"

I slap her ass. She lifts her head again to scowl at me. I smile, lifting to take her full lips in a kiss. I love kissing her. I'm hard as fuck and ready to have more of her. I can't get enough.

However, now that I know she was a virgin, I force myself to hold back. Shit, I've gone months now without sex, I think subconsciously. I decided a long time ago I was going to go after Misty. Her coming to me first just caused me to make the conscious decision.

Deep down, I knew I was going to have a talk with Mix sooner or later. I just wish I'd manned up and done it sooner. Now, I look like a fucking coward betraying his brother.

"I should probably head back," she murmurs.

I can hear the sleep in her voice. I'm not letting her drive all that way exhausted, but she should be on her way out of my room before the clubhouse comes to life. I look at the clock and groan. She should be creeping out right about now, but I don't want to let her go. This isn't going to be easy.

"You're not driving until you get some sleep. Head to your room. Get some rest there. Then you can drive back," I say, reaching for her chin to bring her lips to mine.

"I'll be fine. I can head back now."

I slap her plush ass again. "Did you not hear me? Take your little ass to your room and sleep. I mean it, Mist."

"Fine," she mumbles against my lips.

"Don't make me have to come check on you. I'll have the brothers block your car in," I warn.

Her mouth falls open. "That was you that time? I knew it."

I take her full, swollen lips in a deep kiss. "I don't know what you're talking about." I suppress a laugh.

"Unbelievable."

"Get your ass out of my bed before I spend the day fucking you and you can't go anywhere until tomorrow."

Her eyes light up. "So tempting. If I didn't have assignments to finish." She licks her lips.

I laugh and slap her ass, beginning to love that bounce against my palm. I have to fight not to keep her in my bed for the rest of the day. I think about my brothers getting curious as the day goes on and decide against it.

She straddles my waist. That hot pussy burning into my stomach. I drag my gaze from her breasts to her eyes. I love the way they light up as she looks down at me. I lift, coming nose to nose with her.

"Just one more kiss before I go," she whispers.

How can I say no to that? Locking my fingers in her soft hair, I nip at her lips before sliding my tongue into her mouth and consuming every inch of her warmth. Her moans and my groans mix together, driving me crazy.

"Shit," I breathe as I break the kiss. "I don't know how I'm going to keep my hands off you. Last night shouldn't have happened."

Her smile melts into a pout. I kick myself for thinking out loud. That didn't come out the way it should've. I peck her cute little nose.

"You know what I mean. I don't regret us. I just wish we held out until I did this the right way."

"I'm grown, King. I grew up here. As much as I'm around, I was bound to fal… to get involved with a brother."

I growl before I can think better of it. The thought of any of the brothers trying to claim her or fuck around with her digs right under my skin. She cups my face and kisses me. The calm I feel from her kiss is something I've never felt before.

I slide my palms down her back to cup her fat ass. I'm so tempted to slide back inside her warm, wet heat. I nearly do, but my phone goes off.

"Damn, get to your room."

"Bossy," she mutters, climbing from the bed to get dressed.

I can't take my eyes off of her as I take the call. I only half hear the brother on the other line reporting in. Yeah, this is going to kill me.

CHAPTER ELEVEN

MC Camping

Misty

The chapter is going for a ride. After some debating and a few arguments, King and I decided I would go. Eva was reluctant to come, but I need her as my cover.

Once we hit the mountains, everyone will camp out. The brothers and their old ladies will be so lit no one will notice once King and I decide to slip away. It's risky, but we both want to spend time together. No, we need to spend time together.

"Who are you riding with?" Eva asks looking a bit uncomfortable.

"I was going to go with Jacky, but if you want, you can ride with him, I'll see if Reap's okay with taking me."

"Nah, I already asked her she's riding with Grim. I'm thinking about asking Sugar."

"Cool, let me know."

I checked my bag one more time for all the items I plan to take, including a little nightie I plan to slip into once I'm in King's tent. A girl has to be prepared. I'm nearly bouncing with excitement when I hear the bikes start to rev. I remember these trips from when I was younger.

They were always so much fun, like a huge family reunion. Volleyball games, tossing frisbees, food, lots of food and for the adults more liquor than one should consume. It's been years since I've gone to one of these.

Back in the day. Sometimes other MCs would meet up with us. It was like a time to celebrate their truce and the gains from working together instead of fighting among one another.

All that was a long time ago, I don't know how the other MCs are interacting with the Lost Souls these days. A lot has changed after Cage. Although King is just as good a prez as his daddy.

"Let's roll out," King booms.

I turn toward him and catch one of the bunnies as she slides up to his side. It looks as if she's going to attempt to ride on the back of his bike. I glare at King, letting him know that shit ain't happening. He winks at me before he laughs and throws his head back.

He says something to the skank and her face falls. Next thing I know, King throws his long leg over his bike and pulls to the front alone. My heart aches because I'm supposed to be on the back of that bike. I'm almost tempted to walk to the front and climb on, but I don't want to make a scene.

"You coming, sis?" Jacky says, sounding all grown up.

When did my brother become a man? I wouldn't tell him that I see him as one. I don't want him getting any ideas and deciding he's old enough to run off. I give him a nod, toss my bag on my back and then climb on his bike behind him as he fixes his long hair into a ponytail and puts his helmet on.

Jacky has hair women would kill for. He keeps it long on the top, seriously long. I'm talking, hanging mid-chest. The sides are always shaved low and if you're ever near enough to him, you'll notice that his strawberry-blond locks always smell like strawberries from his shampoo.

It's the same brand my mom used on him as a little boy. I think it's a comfort for him. Something I've never tried to take away.

I settle on the back of my brother's bike and wrapped my arms around his waist. And soon he pulls right into the formation. There have to be at least a hundred bikes and other vehicles making this trip.

The closer we get to the campsite, the more nervous I get. I know we made a plan for this, but I'm still so worried that someone's going to catch us. The last thing we want to do is play our hand too early. We still have a few more months before Mix makes it back.

We make a pit stop along the highway for everyone to fuel up and use the bathroom if needed. Some of the brothers have little ones who need the rest.

I head into the store as Jacky fuels up. Grabbing some fruit snacks, a ginger and pineapple drink, and some peanuts, I head for the counter. As I wait in line, King walks by me and brushes his arm against my ass as he passes by.

I turned to look up at him and he sends me a wink. I stiffen, but give no other reaction. He's playing dirty, it's so not fair.

My body heats from the simple touch. I know my chest is heaving from anticipation. If anyone's paying attention to me, I've given myself away because I can't help reacting to him.

When It's my turn to pay for my things, I step up to the counter.

Suddenly I feel heat at my back, I look over my shoulder to find King pulling out his wallet. He pulls out a few bills and hands them to the clerk for my things.

"Keep the change," he says to the clerk.

I get ready to make a smart remark, but Eva walks up at that very moment. She places her things on the counter and King pulls out a few more bills and pays for her things as well.

After, he dips his head to whisper in my ear. "See, nothing out of the ordinary. I'm just taking care of my girls, as always. You need to relax, it's going to be fine."

He then turns to the clerk. "Let me have two boxes of MAGNUMS."

I purse my lips and toss him a glare over my shoulder. He snickers and shakes his head as he goes to pay for his purchase. I'm wondering if this trip is such a good idea after all. I may give us up by being nervous as hell. While King is acting as smooth as a cucumber.

King

Maybe this wasn't such a good idea. Misty is too damn nervous. The goal was for us to act normal, it's not like we haven't been friends in the past and hung out together. However, whenever I get within inches of her, she freaks out.

This is going to be a long weekend. We finally make it to the campsite and I help to delegate where everyone should set up. I, of course, decide to put my tent as far away from everyone as possible with this much tree covering is I can find. It's not out of the ordinary. My tent can get pretty loud, so I usually stay away from the brothers and their kids. They won't be blaming me for the sex education their kids get.

I don't plan on having a quiet tent this trip either. As a matter of fact, I'm counting down the hours until Misty can maneuver her way into my tent without anyone seeing. I have plans for those boxes I picked up on that pit stop.

I'm grabbing a beer from the cooler when Sandy, one of the bunnies, pops up at my side. Before we left the compound, she was flirting as if I was going to offer to let her ride up on the back of my bike.

Wasn't happening, even before I noticed Misty watching. That seat is reserved for two fat brown cheeks alone. Misty didn't have to worry about that.

"Hey, Prez, you plan on getting into anything tonight?"

"I plan to play some volleyball and maybe get in a game of basketball with some of the brothers," I reply.

She snickers. "Prez, you and I both know that's not what I'm talking about."

"So, it's obvious to us both that that's not where my head is at."

I open my beer and take a sip. Sandy narrows her eyes at me. I'm not interested, but because she's cool, I don't tell her to fuck off like I want to.

"Something is different about you. I know you've always been selective when it comes to us bunnies, but lately it seems like you're pulling back from everyone. At first, I thought it was because of Jane, but now I'm starting to think that's not quite it.

"You know she left because she fell for someone outside the club, don't you?"

"You know, that's not my problem, do you think I really care? Jane was free to do whatever she wanted to do and so she did."

I know exactly what happened with Jane, she told me before she left. I had no problem with it, we weren't serious or anything. The way club bunnies come and go, if I got attached to every one I messed around with, I'd be one sorry soul.

"Whoa, save the attitude, Prez. I'm not your enemy. I was just making a statement to prove my point," she says as she squints her eyes at me. "Yeah, I think you've gone and fallen in love on us. Another one bites the dust. Damn, there were a lot of us hoping we'd be able to snag you as our old man."

"There are a lot of you who should know that was never going to happen. Most of you should have that understanding."

"Ouch," she says and giggles. "I'll give you one thing, you've always been straightforward. I've always known my place when it comes to you. A lot of these brothers sell dreams, not you, King."

"I ain't got time for that shit. What you see is what you get." Yep, I'm as raw as I look. I've never bitten my tongue and I don't plan on starting now.

The sound of more bikes approaching pulls my attention. I turn to see a few Falcon bikers arriving. At the head is the Falcon VP and my childhood friend, Trip. A smile breaks across my face.

Our bond was sealed when a few Devils tried to toss his ass over a bridge when we were in middle school. Shit was rough back then. Rival MCs wouldn't be caught dead together. Hell, Trip's father once pulled a gun on my old man.

It was only after I saved Trip that his dad and mine called for a truce. Those were the old days. I get the feeling the Falcon's new prez doesn't much like me. Not that I give a fuck.

"Brother," Trip croons as he closes the distance between us.

"Hey, Trip," I reply.

He stops before me and pulls me into a one-armed hug. Trip is as tall as I am. His gray eyes hold that killer instinct. He's come a long way from the little punk that was cornered and dangled over that bridge.

He releases me and looks around. He squints his eyes and snaps his fingers. "Is that your little buddy?" he asks, then whistles.

I follow his line of sight. Misty and Eva are by the grills, pulling too much attention.

I want to tell him to roll his fucking tongue back into his mouth. I reel it in and respond.

"You stick to the bunnies. She's off-limits."

"Well, shit. You finally planning to give her the time of day?"

"What do you mean by that?"

"Bro, she's been trying to get your attention for years. You have to know that."

"Whatever," I mutter.

"So selfish. You won't let me ask out that fine ass Eva, either. Come on, you know I'm a good dude," he says with his signature sly smile and a wink.

"It's because I know your ass, you need to stay away."

"Ah, why are we standing here talking shit. I need a beer and some tits. Where's your southern hospitality?"

I roll my eyes and lead him to the cooler. Once I get him hooked up. I won't see him for the rest of the night.

"if I didn't think my daddy would roll over in his grave, I would come over to the Lost side," Trips says.

"Trouble with your backyard?"

"Same bullshit. Different day."

"I feel you."

CHAPTER TWELVE

King

I look up at the sky as I sit on one of the camping tables. The party started to die down a while ago. I've showered since my last game of basketball.

All in anticipation of this evening. I was expecting Misty to make her way toward me by now, but I haven't caught sight of her for a few hours.

The last time I saw her, she gave me a death glare, and I have no idea why. It's only been a week into our relationship, we can't be fighting already. I haven't done anything to begin with.

I drain the rest of my beer and throw the bottle into the trash. I've had enough of waiting. I stand and look around the campgrounds. That's when I spot Misty, standing around a small fire with Reap and Sugar.

I saunter over to their group and toss an arm around Misty's neck. She stiffens at my side and gives me that glare again. I pull her beer from her hand and finish it off too.

"If you ladies don't mind, I want to have a talk with Misty for a minute," I say to Sugar and Reap.

"Be our guest, Prez," Reap replies knowingly.

I give her a grin as I tighten my hold on Misty and drag her away with me. I give a quick look around as we approach my tent. Seeing we're all clear. I wrap my arms around her waist and tug her inside the opening, and quickly zip it shut.

"What do you think you're doing?"

"What was taking you so long? I thought we agreed you would be in here by now," I respond.

"I didn't want to interrupt you and your bunny," she hisses at me.

My temper starts to rise. "My what?"

"Your bunny, the one that's been in your face all day since before we left the compound, that's what."

"Yo, baby, you're tripping. I've been waiting all day to get my hands on you."

"Didn't look that way to me. Every time I turn around, Sandy is in your face."

I closed the space between us and bend until we come nose to nose. "We barely get time together, I don't want to spend the time we have arguing. You know this isn't the ideal situation, you're going to have to check that temper and realize that I can't just brush off everyone else because it'll look suspicious. Number one priority as my old lady is to trust me."

I don't give her a chance to respond, I cup her face and crush my lips to hers. She laces her fingers in my locks and moans into my mouth. I palm her ass and drag her body into me.

I break the kiss and place my forehead to hers. "Why are you so crazy?"

"Hello, kettle," she replies. "I saw you pull that brother aside back at the clubhouse this morning. All he did was say hello."

"All you saw was him saying hi. You didn't see the way he turned and gawked at your ass."

She lifts her brow at me and places her hands on my hips. "So now that you have me here, what do you wanna do with me, Prez?"

I give her a wolfish grin. Gliding my hands down her sides to her lush ass, I capture her lips once again and devour her. I groan at the flavor of beer that's coating her mouth.

She reaches for my length and squeezes it through my pants. I growl and grab her throat, spinning her until her back is to my front. I lean over her and capture her lips again, biting, nipping, and sucking at the plump flesh.

She pants heavily as she brings her hand up to the one I have around her throat. I give a gentle squeeze and move my lips to her ear.

"I should punish you for getting mad at me for no reason," I breathe against her ear, sending a shiver through her.

"Or I could leave and go find your friend and flip her ass to show everyone to stay away from you." She reaches back between us and squeezes my cock again. "And I'll just leave you to handle this situation by yourself."

I apply a little more pressure to her neck, tilting it farther to the side and bite the exposed skin. She moans loudly and I smile. All that trash talking is about to end. Reaching around her body, I pop the button on her jeans and stick my hand in.

I'm not surprised to find her dripping wet. However, I do groan as I feel how silky it makes my fingertips. I finger her with ease as I continue to suck on her neck. I release her throat and move my hand to cup her breast. She moans and widens her stance, allowing me to get better access.

Her little sneakers are tap dancing against the ground in no time as she tries to lift on her toes and ride my fingers at the same time. It's been a week and I didn't get my fill the first time.

Impatience takes over. I grab her jeans and tug them down her thighs. Then I begin to fumble with my belt. We tumbled to the ground on top of my sleeping bag. Misty trying to pull her jeans farther down her legs as she moves around in front of me. I just barely managed to get my jeans under my ass.

"Get on all fours," I command.

She does as I say, pushing her ass into the air. I grab my shaft and thrust right into her heat.

"*King,*" *she screams out.*

I bare my teeth. It's all I can do to keep control. Placing a hand in the center of her back, I lower her torso all the way to the ground. Lifting back to my feet in a crouching position, I start to pound into her roughly.

She sobs out my name repeatedly, her pussy taking me and holding me tightly as she drips all over me. I reach for her clit and start to massage it. No mercy given.

She gasps and pants as she claws at my hands that I have tightly gripped to her hips. However, the way I have her penned, there's nothing she can do but take it. I drive down into her, letting her know who she belongs to and that she's the only one I desire.

Yeah, it's a good thing I made sure to be far away from everyone and covered in the trees. We're probably still going to get strange looks and complaints in the mornings.

As she gets louder, I palm her mouth and wrap a hand around her throat. All that planning, just one person needs to recognize her voice and that's it. Cover blown. Game over.

"You're mine, baby. You like the way I fuck you? Can you take that cock? You want more?" I grunt.

"Holy shit, yes. You're fucking me so good. Please don't stop, please."

And I don't.

CHAPTER THIRTEEN

Spend Some Time

Misty

Two weeks later...

I rush into the clubhouse, searching out King with my gaze. It's been an entire two weeks since the camping trip. I'm tired of the texts and the calls. I want to be able to set my eyes on him in person.

He doesn't come into view right away. Although, the clubhouse is busy. I know I have to be careful about this, so I'm trying not to make it obvious that I'm seeking him out. The sound of pool balls knocking together draws my attention. I turn toward the game room where the pool tables, the arcade games, and jukebox are.

Arched over a pool table with a cue in his hand is King. His hair hanging in his face and around his shoulders. I can't help but stare as his T-shirt stretches over his biceps and along his torso. His jeans hanging low with bike chains hanging from them. His feet are clad in tan construction boots, not his usual black riding boots.

The man can make anything look sexy. I reel in my excitement and saunter over to the game he's playing. The moment I stop beside him, he lifts to his full height, sending his cologne wafting through the air. I have to bite my lip to hold a groan back. Memories from his tent blast my brain.

He takes me in with those sparkling blue eyes. I stand up straighter, confident in the denim shorts romper I have on. My red heels the kiss of death this outfit needed.

He lifts a brow at me and curls his lips up into a grin. He bites his lip after taking a quick look around the clubhouse. With his grin in place, he reaches to tug me into a headlock, as he has done a million times over the years.

My heart sinks for a second as I think he's taking us back into the friend zone. That's until he breathes hotly in my ear.

"We're getting out of here. I've missed you. My bike is around back. Meet me there."

I stifle a moan as he lets me go. I look back at him over my shoulder, through my lashes. He drops his eyes to my ass and mouths *now* before he nods toward the back.

I sashay through the clubhouse to the back, waving at a few friends here and there. I make it through the back door and look around to see if anyone's outside before I moved to King's bike. It doesn't take long for him to follow me through the exit. Coming over to hand me a helmet before he swings a long leg over his beast, then holding out his hand to help me on behind him.

I wrap my arms around him and bury my face into his back. When I squeeze my thighs around him, he places a hand on my knee. It's like coming home, this is where I belong. I inhale deeply, letting the anxiety of the last two weeks fall away.

Without a word, King starts his bike and pulls out of the compound. I get the feeling that he's moving so quickly so that no one will catch sight of us. Not that I care at this very moment, I snuggle into his back and hold on tight.

About thirty minutes later, we pull into his apartment complex. I haven't been here in years. King hardly ever stays at his place anymore, not since he became prez.

He pulls to a stop in his parking spot and cuts off the bike. I remove my helmet as he gets off the bike and I look up at him. He gives me a sexy growl before grabbing the back of my neck and capturing my lips. He kisses me so deeply my toes curl in my red heels.

"You look amazing," he says against my lips. "Come on, I want those heels around my neck."

I'm not complaining. It seems we want the same thing. I hop off the bike and follow him upstairs. When he opens the door, he steps back so that I can pass. The moment I crossed the threshold, he slaps my ass.

"I've told you about those tiny shorts in the clubhouse. Trust, now that you're my old lady, that's going to stop."

I turned to him and wrinkle my nose, lifting a brow. "Really?"

"Come on, Mist. You can't keep coming by the clubhouse dressed in those little shorts with no bra in those fuck-me heels. I'm not responsible for what I do once someone looks at you wrong, and I lose my head. You feel me, baby?"

His last words melt any fight I have left. Hearing him call me baby and not baby girl in a friendly way makes my heart flutter. I'll dressed up like a mummy if that's what he wants.

He closes the gap between us. I reach up and grab his cut, drawing him into me. He places his hands on my waist and dips his head, the passionate kiss he gives me is dizzying. His mouth is sweet, anybody that knows King knows he has a sweet tooth, he was probably eating a candy bar before I showed up at the clubhouse.

He possessively squeezes my ass and drags me into his erection. I groan and pant for him. This is exactly what I need. I need to get my hands on him. To know that this is real, not something I dreamed.

I reach for his length through his jeans, causing him to hiss. Next thing I know, he has his long fingers creeping into my romper from behind. He sucks in a sharp breath when his fingers are met with my bare, drenched pussy lips.

"Ah, you're so wet. You came to the clubhouse like this?"

"Yes," I purr. "I was coming to see my man."

He growls and grabs my face, nipping and licking at my lips as he walks me back toward his couch. He sets me down gently before him on the soft seat. I perch on the edge and look up at him.

He unzips his jeans and pulls himself out. "Finish what you started," he commands.

I drop my gaze to his gorgeous length. It's pulsing and twitching with need, a need that I can provide. I take him in my palms and he's so smooth and hard at the same time. Not wanting to disappoint, I fill my mouth with saliva and spit on the tip. I start to glide my hands over the lubrication, but it's still not enough. So I lean in and start to lick the underside.

His groans and moans fill the room and my chest with excitement. When he drags his hands into his dreads to hold them up on top of his head as he drops his head back, my confidence is boosted.

I wrap my lips around him and start to bob up and down his length. He hisses out a curse, freeing one hand to place it behind my head. My confidence shoots through the roof and I let go of all my inhibitions, taking him to the back of my throat, making sure that he's nice and wet and slick to help my hands twist as I slide them up and down. Working him until his voice is the only thing in the room heard above my slurping and sucking.

"Fuck," he bellows out tightly.

I meet his hot blue gaze and smile up at him as I look through my lashes. His mouth is open, and he has a sexy smirk on his lips. I move back as I spit on his crown. He bites his lip, and before I know what's happening, he has me on my back with my legs over his shoulders.

Even though my romper is a snug fit, he somehow manages to push it to the side to get his mouth on me. After only a few licks, I'm trying to wiggle my way away from his mouth. However, he grabs the top of my thighs and pins me in place. I'm left to scream for mercy and plead his name.

"Mmm, you taste so good. I've been wanting to do this all week, be still."

I'm a whimpering mess as my legs shake around his head. After a while, I couldn't move if I wanted to. My stomach caves and I pant for water, a lifeline or a raft to safety. For the next two hours, I allowed King to have his way with me. It wasn't a dream after all, this is my man. I finally have the prez.

King

From the moment she walked her ass into that clubhouse, I wanted to devour her. From the little outfit to her red heels. Everything about her is sexy. She has some type of product in her hair that's making her curls pop and that red lipstick is like a siren call. As I said before, Misty knows exactly what she's doing. She had my dick harder than granite from the time I stood up from that pool table.

I should be worried about whether or not someone saw us leaving from the clubhouse, but I intentionally left through the back gate, knowing that no one really pays attention to the garage and exit. Not unless it's a brother on watch. Gutter happened to be the brother on watch today, but just as I thought, he turned his head to mind his own business as usual.

It's going to kill me to sneak around like this for the next few months until Mix gets back. I play with one of the springy curls in her hair as she lays across my chest. We never made it to my bedroom, I ended up pounding out her tight pussy right here on this couch.

I can't get enough of her, and I can't keep my hands to myself. This is a recipe for disaster. However, as she starts to wiggle on top of me and I tighten my arm around her, I know that losing her isn't an option. We're at the point of no return.

CHAPTER FOURTEEN

A King Thing

King

I'm on my way to a mall in Georgia to meet up with Misty. I feel like a teenage boy again sneaking around behind my father's back to get my dick wet. I haven't had to sneak around like this in years.

Not since that one time when Rose found me in the garage with an older woman who happened to be one of her friends at the time. I smile at the memory.

However, I'd do anything for the opportunity to spend some time with Misty. So here I am, taking a day off from work to see my girl. She promised that she didn't have anything serious going on in school and she could take the day, so we're meeting each other halfway.

It's my goal to take her shopping, get her something to eat, do normal boyfriend shit. It's as normal as I'm ever going to get. At the end of the day, I'm still prez. I still have two chapters to look after and a ton of club business, not to mention running my own design company. Soul Expressions has a lot on its plate at the moment.

It seems like my mind is never still, it's always moving with thoughts of the future, of how I want the club to change for the better. Some of the shit we're into is going to get someone hurt. We've been doing this too long, someone's bound to become complacent when they're comfortable with how things are done. It's time to change things up before it causes a problem.

I know this and Mix knows this too. Some of the other brothers that are heading up the other chapters agree with me and we've been doing all we can to make changes. It's not like the Lost Souls aren't filled with wealthy businessmen. We could probably run the chapters off our businesses alone. I've taken it upon myself to show everyone just how that could work out for us.

We don't have to lose respect by losing our footing in the black markets. I think we could earn more respect by turning this lifestyle around and making it successful. Too bad not all the brothers see it that way.

Eventually, I'm going to have a fight on my hands. Bless the ones who want to take that fight on. I'm not one to lose. It has never happened and I don't plan to start now. Being a leader is in my blood. From my daddy to my uncle, we were born Lost Souls.

"Hey, baby," Misty squeals as she runs toward me.

I'm waiting for her in the food court. It is the easiest location for her to find me. As always, she looks stunning. A simple black

T-shirt and light blue jeans, with a cute little pair of sneakers on her feet. I guess she's prepared for shopping because usually Misty will have on six-inch heels.

My first reaction is to grab her by her jaw and kiss those luscious lips. I feel like I've been denied enough. So, I kiss her until she's breathless.

She pulls away and looks me over with a smile. I didn't get to make it back to the clubhouse to change out of my suit after my morning meeting. She reaches for my black tie to straighten it and runs her hands over the lapels of my tailor-made black suit.

"Phew, my man is putting a hurting on this suit," she says.

Her man, I still haven't gotten used to hearing that, we're in a relationship. I kiss her forehead and wrap an arm around her waist.

"Come on, let's go shopping. Any place in particular you want to go?" I ask as we turn for the stores.

"I was thinking about a new purse and maybe some shoes, other than that, nothing special," she replies.

"We can do that. No problem."

"How was your meeting?" she asks as she snuggles into my side.

I tighten my hold on her. "It was great we got the Commission. I'll be doing a few billboards for a couple of major hotel chains."

"I knew you would kill it."

I can't help that my heart swells at the sound of pride in her voice. Misty has such confidence in everything I do. In all actuality it feels good to have someone I can talk to about my day and someone I know will have my back. In this life that's not something common to find. Someone to keep your bed warm, sure, someone to safely share your deepest thoughts with, not so much.

The more we date, the more I'm starting to see a future together. I'm becoming anxious to have that talk with Mix. There are times I wish I would have talked to him right after that kiss in my office. I think I knew then and there that I was going to pursue Misty on a more serious level. Although, I hadn't consciously given myself the green light.

My phone buzzes in my pocket and I frown as I pull it out. I grind my teeth as I answer, and I loosen my tie. I already know this call is going to irritate me.

I pull my wallet out in take out my bank card. Nodding toward the store, I hand it over to Misty.

"The pin is your birthday. Get whatever you want," I say and press a kiss to her forehead before she turns and walks away.

Turning my attention back to the phone, I answer, "Yo, this is King."

"Hey brother, this is Toothless. I need to know if you have some time to have a talk with me? We're in a bad way down here, we could use some of your help. Things have gotten real bad for business and if it ain't legit, it ain't moving. You feel me?"

"I feel you and I'm gonna get on top of that mess as soon as I can. I've been looking into all the options. Sounds to me like you guys need to rebuild from the bottom to the top. That's gonna take a lot more focus than I can give at the moment, I need you to give me some time," I reply.

"Sure, sure, brother, just trying to make sure this chapter doesn't fall through the cracks. Things haven't been what they used to be. However, your chapter is thriving, and I just want us to follow in that example."

"I've got you, brother. I won't fail you, just give me some time, that's all I ask."

"King, I'm not trying to overstep. Just hear me out. Your daddy was the mother chapter prez. There were more of us that wanted you to take that role than you know. Still do."

"I hear you. I do, but I have enough on my plate. Mix and I agreed Uncle Kelvar would step in when he gets home."

"Shit, the chapters could all fold by then," he grumbles.

"I'd never allow that to happen. I'll come that way in a few weeks, brother."

"Thanks for your time. Looking forward to seeing you."

This is something I've been trying to avoid for a very long time. Becoming the organization's prez is a heavy undertaking. That's more men to oversee, more chapters to make sure are thriving. And now that I have Misty in my life, I'm not sure I want that risk or stress.

I sigh and head into the store where Misty is shopping. Her little ass has more than a purse and some shoes. I smile and wrap my arms around her from behind.

"You good?"

"Yeah. Thanks. Is this too much?"

"Nah, not at all. Don't think about it. Get whatever you want."

The beaming smile on her face is worth any amount of money she spends. I'd buy out the entire store to see that smile every day.

Looking into Misty's eyes, I can't help but think back to that call. While South Carolina is the mother chapter, I felt like I was too young to take on fifteen chapters when my father died. Now, with all the good I know I can do and the future I want to build, taking on the other chapters may be what I need to do.

Misty reaches up to brush her finger across the center of my brow. "What are you stressing about?"

"Nothing, just some club business," I reply.

"Ugh, is this really my life?"

"What's that supposed to mean?"

"It's club business," she mocks. "You wouldn't understand, it's a King thing."

She chuckles. I pinch her side. I ignore my phone for the rest of the day as I get lost in my woman.

CHAPTER FIFTEEN

Misty

I roll my eyes at Eva as she heads toward the library. It's Friday, you would think she would take at least one day off from studying. The girl hasn't failed a class in her life.

I shake my head and turn for our apartment. I've been trying to talk Eva into going home to South Carolina this weekend. She has some exam next week so I don't think that's gonna happen.

However, I'm missing King like crazy. I think he picked up on how much this morning when we spoke on the phone. His voice changed when he heard how bummed out I was that I might not be able to see him this weekend.

He's been so busy with club business, and I've had a lot on my plate with school assignments. I thought we would find time for each other by now.

As I turn the corner and my apartment comes into view, my jaw drops as I see the man I was just thinking of posted against his bike. He's dressed in all black with a red rose in his hand and his head bent. There is a perplexed expression on his face, as if he's thinking deeply over his actions.

His expression clears the moment he lifts his gaze to me. A smile spreads across his face and he stands up straighter. I can't help but run toward him and jump into his arms. I kiss all over his face as he catches me.

"Hey, you. I'm so happy to see you," I say. "I thought you said you wouldn't be able to get away."

"I had to make it happen I didn't like the way you sounded this morning." He looked me in my eyes. "We good, baby?"

"Yeah, we're good. But you do know Eva will be home soon enough?"

"Which is why we're going out. Take your things upstairs and pack an overnight bag."

I stare up at him with a goofy smile on my face. I can't believe he's come all this way just because of the sound of my voice. The more we're together, the more I'm falling for him. It's the little things that mean so much.

He gives me a pointed look and I shake myself from my musing to rush upstairs and put down my schoolbag and get a spend-the-night bag ready. I can't help but wonder where we're headed.

King

I'm falling for this girl so hard. I have a ton of shit to do back in South Carolina, but the moment I heard how sad she was this morning, I knew I wouldn't be able to do anything but bring my ass to Georgia.

So, I booked us a night at a place I know. We'll be able to be away from prying eyes and have some time to just be alone together. I'm doing my best to make this work. As long as she's happy, I'm happy.

I thought about the risk I was taking coming here like this, Misty and Eva are always attached at the hip, but I was willing to take it. Mist has become a priority for me.

I've been trying to figure out when that happened. Especially as I stood here waiting for her to arrive. When did I become willing to risk it all?

Honestly, I've always belonged to Misty. It's just time for the rest of the world to know, but am I ready for that? That's the question.

An hour later, we pull up to a beach house. Misty is vibrating with excitement at my back. I cut the engine and she hops off the back of my bike. I had a feeling she would love this beach house.

It's what she deserves and a million steps up from the hotels and motels we've been going to. I know I've gotten it right when she starts to jump up and down in place. Shaking my head, I lift from my bike and head for the beach front rental.

It's so fucking hot today. My T-shirt is sticking to my back. I head straight for the main reason I chose this place. The large infinity pool in the back. For a guy as large as me, it's hard to find a swimmable pool, one deep enough to dive into and long enough for me to swim laps. This pool is perfect.

I strip down until I'm naked and dive into the pool. I cut through the water smoothly as I do a few laps. This is the most relaxed I've been in weeks. With each stroke, all the tension seems to fall away.

With more and more brothers coming forward, trying to push me into the position of organization prez. I've had a lot on my mind. Mix isn't around for me to talk to, and it's not like I can go and see my uncle. Uncle Kevlar is… different, so I'm not able to get his opinion on the situation either.

I do a few more laps before I come up for air mid-stroke and see Misty headed my way with two beers in her hands. I make it to the edge of the pool and come up out of the water. she freezes in her tracks, a look of awe comes over her face.

I can't help taking a moment to take her in, in her bra and panties. Knowing Misty, those panties are nothing more than a thong. I love how her thick thighs kiss as she walks toward me. All those hips announcing the truckload traveling behind her. I can't help but bite my lip in anticipation of seeing her turn around fully.

"What?" I ask and tilt my head to the side as my gaze returns to her face.

Misty

This. Can't. Be. Real. I'm very aware that my man is gorgeous. However, in this moment he simply breathtaking. His body is so lean, yet muscular. I had no idea that he was completely naked out here.

I try not to drool all over myself. His blue gaze is fixed on me as water droplets fall from his long, full lashes. It's enough to cause envy. What does he need with such long lashes and perfect brows? The man is simply beautiful.

"You take my breath away," I say with a goofy grin.

His gorgeous smile grows, he resembles the big bad wolf as he reveals his perfect white teeth. He crooks his finger at me. It's like he's massaging my pussy with the motion. I move toward the edge of the pool.

Plopping down on my butt right in front of him, I have to wiggle back and forth on my cheeks. The ground is superhot. As a matter of fact, it's just hot in general. Sweat is building on my upper lip and my forehead.

"I grabbed these beers so we could cool off," I say and hold out one to him.

He takes it and gives me a wink. "Thanks."

He drains half the bottle before he sets it on the side of the pool and reaches for my thighs to gently pull me closer to the edge. I lift my hips so my bottom doesn't scrape the ground. Once he has my legs wrapped around him, I settled back on my seat and rest my hands behind me.

He moves his hands to palm my cheeks, absorbing some of the heat from the ground. I take a long sip of beer as he watches me. As soon as I pull the bottle away, he captures my lips.

I'm caught off guard, but I managed to put the beer down and lock my fingers in his dreads, holding him to me. He deepens the kiss.

He kisses me with such passion and hunger. I can't help but moan into his mouth. It's the only thing I can do to keep from melting into a puddle and sliding into the pool.

He groans. "I've missed you so much. I've needed this, I have so much on my mind I just need some time to clear my thoughts."

"Anything you want to talk about?"

"I don't want to talk about anything but me and you," he replies.

He takes my lips again, but this time he doesn't linger. He makes a trail to my chin, down to my collarbone. I take in a breath when he plays with the strap of my thong, gliding his hand between my cheeks.

"King," I whimper as he pulls my bra cup down and captures my nipple.

He sucks and nibbles on it. The sensation shooting straight to my core. Meanwhile, his hands are everywhere, heating my already warm skin. His moans and groans only heightening my excitement. He sounds like a man enjoying his meal.

If you told me a year ago that I would have King Kennedy feasting on my body like this, I would have called you cruel. This was all once a fantasy I never saw coming true. Now I'm completely consumed by the reality of that fantasy and I wouldn't trade it for the world.

I cry out and start to shake as he pumps his fingers in and out of me. His mouth is still working my tight peak. I can't help rocking my hips, I'm greedy for more. I drop my head back and plant my palms on the ground, lifting to grind on his hand.

"Oh Mist, baby. Do you hear how wet you are? I need a taste."

Before I can register his words, he lowers and scoops my legs over his shoulders. I anchor myself by the roots of his hair and ride his face for all I'm worth. I don't even care what the neighbors may think when I scream out my release. It's too good, too mind-numbing for me to wonder about anyone else.

At least, that is, before someone blows an air horn on the other side of the fence. I nearly jump out of my skin. When I look at King, rage and lust fill his face.

"Come on, let's take this inside," he says, lifting out of the pool in all his naked glory.

I'm too busy salivating to move, so he bends and lifts me onto his waist and carries me inside. When we enter the large master bedroom, everything in here is white, from the curtains to the bedspread. It's like a tropical Oasis.

He places me gently on the bed. Then he grasps ahold of my neck in a choke hold as he reaches to peel my thong off while keeping his eyes on mine.

King

Not for the first time, I drop my gaze to Misty's cute pink-painted toenails as she pulls her knees back into her chest, spreading herself out just the way I want her. I settle my body between her legs and palm her thighs to hold her where I need her to stay. Then I eat her pussy as I work her clit with my thumb.

"King," she screams, as if scolding me for making her come so hard. With a smile, I lift up, lick the palm of my hand, and stroke my cock a few times. Then I line up with her entrance and enter her in one smooth thrust. Her slick walls suck me right in.

I keep my hold on her throat as I dive into her tight pussy. Misty rolls her eyes back in her head. She cries out nonsense. *Oh fuck* is the most I can make out.

She gasps. "Shit, King, you're so fucking deep."

"Yes, baby, you just keep coming on that cock."

And she does. Over and over again. And I'm supposed to give this up? Yeah, fucking right. In this moment I decide that everything must change. I'll be whoever I need to be to make sure Misty is by my side indefinitely.

Misty

I can't get rid of the smile on my face as I wake up and stretch, my body still sore and throbbing from earlier. I miss him already and want more. Sex may be rough with King but, it's amazing.

I would never ask him to change a thing. I smile as he tightens his arms around me and kisses the side of my face. I snuggle my butt against his growing erection.

"I didn't give you enough?" He chuckles.

"Not nearly," I purr.

I burst into laughter. "What?" he asks.

"They blew an air horn at us."

We both start to laugh. "If I wasn't so distracted by you, I would've jumped over that gate and ripped someone's head off."

"Good thing you were distracted."

He snorts. "What time are your classes tomorrow?"

I groan, not really wanting to talk about classes or school or anything else. "My first class is at noon."

"Don't get too comfortable, you still have to ace your classes before I even think about making you an offer to work at Soul Expressions."

"Who says I want to work for you?" I pout.

He pecks me on my lips. "Who the fuck else you think you're going to work for?"

"I don't know, but I think I should explore my options. Especially if you're gonna be this bossy and we're only dating."

He starts to tickle my sides and I burst out laughing. This is exactly what I needed. All of the anxiety and depression have slipped away. My man is pure perfection.

CHAPTER SIXTEEN

Stealing Time

Misty

I giggle as the stubble on his face tickles my neck. The sound turns into a gasp when he sucks my skin into his mouth. I lace my fingers in his locks as he presses me to the wall in the hotel room.

We've been sneaking around for weeks now. I've crept into his bed on weekends when I drag Eva back home. When I can get away during the week, we've met halfway to spend time together. Sometime getting a room, other times just going out to eat.

Tonight, we met halfway and went to a movie. We made it to the middle of the movie before he leaned into my ear and told me to get up in a low, sexy growl. Anticipation coiled in my belly as I followed him in my car, wishing I could be on the back of his bike.

"I couldn't wait a moment longer to get my hands on you," he says as he thrusts into me.

I cry out and throw my head back. He feels so good. He always feels so good. I cry out as he pounds into me hard, knocking my back into the wall behind me.

Sweat pours down both of our faces as he pushes us both to that place of pure bliss. "King."

"Fuck yeah, Misty. Come on that cock."

The sound of his panting, my whimpers, my back knocking against the wall, skin slapping, and his belt buckle clinking become a chorus around us. He crushes my lips with his and I can taste the sweetness of the candy he had in the theater. I swirl my tongue in his mouth.

I'm getting so close. His fat dick inside me swells, letting me know he's not that far behind me. I can't help wishing there was no barrier between us. I'd give anything to feel those thick ropes of cum inside me.

I hit my peak and he pulls out, lowering me to my feet. He tears the condom off and looks me in the eyes.

"Come suck it out," he says. The look on his face is so hot, I obey without thinking about it.

I have my mouth wrapped around the fat head, teasing him as soon as my knees hit the carpeted floor. He still has on all his clothes—his T-shirt and cut untouched, his jeans around his ankles, and his riding boots still on his feet. My pants are tossed somewhere, and my thong is ruined and torn to bits around my waist.

I moan around the mouthful I'm focused on draining. King rocks his hips forward, pushing me to take more as I soak his silky-smooth flesh. "Mmm."

"Fuck, I'm coming, baby. That shit feels so fucking good."

Proud to please my man, I put in a little more vigor. He locks his hand in my hair and moves his hips jerkily. I look up at him through my lashes.

His eyes are fixed on me and it's so hot. I reach for his balls and he narrows his blues. His lips part slightly and moments later, he spills into my mouth with a roar that vibrates through me.

I take every single drop. Swallowing with a smile on my lips. I savor every moment I can with King. I know he still has concerns about how we did things.

Sneaking around like this isn't making that any better. Mix is going to be pissed. So, yeah, I savor these moments because our future isn't guaranteed.

"Damn, baby," he pants, helping me to my feet. He wraps his arms around me and holds me against his chest. "Stay the night with me. I don't want to head back tonight. I'll get us some shit to eat, and we can crash here for the night."

"I'll have to text Eva to let her know I'm not coming home."

Placing a searing kiss on my lips, he says, "Do that. Give me your car keys. I'll be right back."

I turn in a circle to find my forgotten purse. It's lying on the other side of the room. I have no idea how it made it that far when we never did. I go to grab it and fish the keys out to hand to him. He has his pants back up and fastened.

He takes the keys in one hand and runs his other through his locks that have fallen in his face and hang loose around his shoulders. As I look up at him, those three words rest on my lips. I've been in love with him for years, but this is something different.

I bite down on my lip to keep from letting my true feelings slip. I don't want to ruin getting to stay the night with him. Things have been going great just the way they are.

"Anything you're in the mood for?" he asks as he pulls me in close.

"Pizza?"

He smiles. "One nasty ass pepperoni and pineapple pizza coming up."

"You know you love it." I laugh and poke him in the ribs.

He has teased me for forever about how I like my pizza. However, I talked him into trying it once and he has tried to pretend he doesn't like it, but my pies always seem to shrink faster than I can eat them. "That shit hits the spot when you're drunk and starving."

"Whatever."

He kisses the top of my head and starts out of the door. I stare after him dreamily, still throbbing from our fucking. I stroll into the bathroom to take a shower.

I stare at my phone, wanting to tell Eva the truth. I'm in love with her brother and we've been sneaking around, having sex. However, telling Eva would be risking Mix finding out before we have a chance to tell him.

Instead of taking the risk, I send her a text message.

Me: *Won't be in tonight.*

Eva: *Who are you with? Do you have an address or something?*

I wrinkle my nose at the message. I hate this part. I used to always tell Eva what guys I go out on a date with and give her all the details in case of an emergency. I can't do that tonight.

My brain totally farts. I have no idea what to tell her. I pace the bathroom, trying to come up with something. I chew on my lip some as I deliberate.

Me: *Hooked up at a bar. Will text you the address of the hotel.*

I roll my eyes. Everyone thinks I'm a big slut. All because I'm addicted to King and have lied about dates to make him jealous and now I'm lying about dates to sneak around with him.

Eva: *Be safe. Call me if you need me. Love you.*

The knife twists. I feel so guilty. I sag my shoulders as I reply.

Me: *Love you too.*

I put the phone down and jump in the shower. I'll be so glad when Dad comes back.

CHAPTER SEVENTEEN

Hard Head

Misty

Senior year…

I'm so damn excited that we're at the end of the road. After this semester of classes, we start our internship and we're out of here.

I'm tired of sneaking around and searching for stolen moments with King. I want to be able to spend more time with him. The calls and texts aren't enough. I miss him. With this being our final semester, it's getting harder to run home for the weekends. Not to mention King has been busy with club business.

He told me not to come home this weekend because the clubhouse would be busy, and he wouldn't have time to spend with me. After talking to Reap, I decided that's some bullshit.

It's the first weekend in a month that I've had time to go to South Carolina and I'm going.

"What's your rush?" Eva murmurs from the passenger seat as she looks over at the speedometer.

"No rush."

"Ha. You've been speeding since we left campus. Is there a party at the clubhouse or something?"

"Actually, there is," I reply.

I'm pissed as fuck. King said things would be busy. He didn't tell me the brothers are throwing a big party.

My question is why? It's not like I've never been around for a Lost Souls party before. Why is this one different?

Things have been going good. At least, I thought they were. If he's tired of me, he better tell me to my face.

I'm not going to play games with him. If we're through, I'm a big girl, I can handle it.

I floor it as our exit comes into view. The party should be in full swing by now. If I'm going to catch King on some bullshit, it would be around now.

This is when the guys start looking for their hookup for the night. Or should I say, this is when the bunnies start going after the bed they want to spend the night in.

Those bitches still don't know King and I are together. He's fair game as far as everyone is concerned. I want to see how he plans to handle that.

"Um, Misty," Eva says. "The guys party all night. I don't think you're going to miss anything."

"I have to pee." I lie. I'll be at the clubhouse in five minutes if I can help it.

What the hell are you hiding, King?

King

"Hey, Prez."

I look up to find Sandy standing in the doorway of my office. I frown. I'm not in the mood for this shit.

I just finished up a deal I wish I didn't have to get involved in. It's times like this I wish my plans were complete already. I'm tired of these little pockets that could unravel everything.

"Will that be all, Prez?" Striker asks as he hands me the duffel bag of money he just finished counting.

"Yeah, go on and enjoy yourself."

I wish I could enjoy myself. It killed me to have to tell Misty not to come home this weekend. Once the meeting location changed to the clubhouse, I couldn't have her here. If something went wrong, I wanted her to be as far away from here as possible.

"You looking for some company?" Sandy asks, reminding me that she's still in the doorway.

"No, darling. I'm fine. You should find someone else to give you a good time."

She ignores my words and takes a seat in front of my desk. The little bra top she has on shows off her big tits and her little skirt leaves absolutely nothing to the imagination. I mean, nothing. I can see her red panties as she sits before me.

"I'm not going to bother you. I heard you say no. I'd just rather be in here," she says, making herself at home.

"What's on your mind, Sandy? You only come in here like this when you're thinking."

"You know, I've been around here since I was a girl. Followed in my mama's footsteps. Thought I'd snag a brother by now. This shit is getting old." She huffs.

"So, what's the plan?" I ask, leaning back in my seat.

"I want to take some classes. Maybe get into doing hair or something," she says and begins to chew on her lip.

I lift a finger. "Hold on, darlin'."

First things first. I need to handle business. I grab the duffel bag of money to place it in the safe. I return to my desk and grab my laptop. Rounding the desk, I sit in the chair beside her.

"Here's a school for cosmetology."

She gets up and sits on the arm of my chair. "Yeah, I'm interested."

"How about you take some day classes and start working at the bar, Soul Elixir. You can make some money there for your supplies. We'll take care of your tuition."

She nods, tucking her dark hair behind her ear. "You guys are the fucking best. I've come across girls from the other clubs and they're treated like trash. The brothers at their MCs keep them high and fucked up. I appreciate this, King."

I look up at her and smile. "It's what my daddy would've wanted. You girls are welcome to make a living anyway you like. If this is what you want, we'll take care of it. Get signed up and let me know what you need from me."

She cups my face and kisses my cheek. Just as she does, all hell breaks loose and my night turns to complete shit.

Misty

The party is in full swing when we arrive at the compound. Guys are outside shooting dice. Some are hanging around the bikes, making a ruckus, laughter spilling into the air.

Eva rolls her eyes and groans as we make our way to the clubhouse. I keep my eyes open for King as we go. He's not out here. I purse my lips as I note that fact. Most nights when King's not in the mood to party, you'll find him out here working on a bike while he jokes around with the guys.

That's if he's not inside with some chick on his arm. That used to be his MO. I grind my teeth as we push through the front door. The party is lively, but there's still no sign of King. I want to storm into his office to see if he's there, but one: I shouldn't be here and two: I don't want to draw attention to us.

"Wow, there have to be at least two other chapters here," Eva says as she looks around.

"Naw, just one," I mutter as I look around at the familiar faces. "The other bikers are the Falcons. Not our boys."

However, the Georgia chapter is here. I recognize most of the guys. It's pretty rowdy in here. Much more than usual.

"Let's put our things in our rooms," I say as I confirm King is nowhere in sight.

We get halfway down the hall to our rooms, but Striker, one of the newer brothers, comes up behind Eva. He grabs her boobs and starts to suck on her neck. I'm stunned at first as Eva yelps and drops her bag.

"Get off her," I shout and push at him, but he doesn't let go. I drop my bags and try to pry him off, but between his height, weight, and the fact that he's piss drunk, I can't get him to budge.

I turn to run for King's office, that's only a short distance away. If anyone can reel this boy in, it's King. I shout his name as I make my way to the door. There's music blaring, drowning out my cries for help. When I get to the cracked door of his office, I push in and freeze.

Sandy is sitting on the arm of the chair King is sitting in, with her boobs in his face. She looks at him adoringly. She has his face cupped in her hand as she leans in to kiss him. I see red. The only thing that keeps me from fucking them both up is the squeals of Eva.

"King," I snap. "Eva needs you. Striker won't let her go."

King turns to me with a look of surprise on his face. I bet he is surprised, fucking asshole. I don't wait for his response. I turn back for my best friend, to help her. I manage just a few steps before King bellows from behind me.

"Have you lost your fucking mind?"

Everything in the clubhouse comes to a standstill. The music turns off and everyone's attention turns to King, Eva, and Striker. Striker releases Eva like fire has been set to his palms.

Striker starts to stammer as King charges at him. "Brother, I—"

He's eating a face full of King's fist before he can get the words out. King knocks him on his ass. Striker lies on the floor out cold. I'd probably be turned on if I didn't just find him cheating on me.

I go to snatch up my bag and grab Eva's hand to tug her back out of the clubhouse. King grabs ahold of my wrist to stop me. He keeps a firm grip as he keeps his eyes on Eva.

"You all right?" he asks her.

"Yeah, I'm fine," she whispers.

"Somebody get his ass out of here. His patch is mine. He's banned. Any brother ready to vouch for him, I can drop the gavel tonight and both your asses can be out," King growls out to everyone else.

"Can you let me go? We're leaving," I say, looking down at my wrist pointedly.

He glares at me. I know he's not going to make a scene in front of this crowd. Reluctantly, he loosens his grip, but doesn't let go. Instead, he tugs me a few steps away from Eva.

"We need to talk. I know what you're thinking. It's not like that," he says low and tightly.

"I don't care. I'm taking Eva back. We're good on this place for now."

"You shouldn't have been here tonight as it is. I told you not to come down here. Your hardheaded ass always has to do what you want. I have reasons for telling you shit."

My nostrils flare as I glare back at him. "Don't worry about it," I hiss back. "We're getting out of here and out of your hair. You can go back to doing whatever it is you didn't want me to know about."

"Misty," he growls in warning.

"King," I say and lift a brow. I cast my gaze around purposefully. We're drawing attention.

He releases my wrist completely this time. Turning on my heels, I grab Eva and leave all the bullshit behind.

And this is why I should've never chased after him. There's not one married brother here that hasn't fucked around on his wife.

Guess I'm getting out just in time.

CHAPTER EIGHTEEN

Play too Much

King

Misty has been pissed as fuck at me and I just haven't had the time to go running after her to straighten things out. She makes me so damn furious. She's been ducking my calls and shit.

I'm tired of it. We need to get this shit straight. She didn't see what she thought she did.

If she would've listened to me, we wouldn't be going through this shit right now. I'm going to spank her little ass for this shit she's trying to pull. Of course, I have my boys watching over her. Just because I know Misty so fucking well.

She's on a date with some asshole to make me jealous. That shits only going to get someone hurt. I rode all the way out here to Georgia to handle this shit myself.

"Get up," I say to the dude sitting across from Misty in this swanky ass restaurant.

His bewildered expression is hilarious. Here I stand in jeans and my cut, my arms folded over my chest, demanding he get his ass up from the table. Murmurs rise around the restaurant from the other tables. I could give two shits.

"Sir, I'm going to have to ask you to leave," the hostess says nervously behind me.

"I'll be gone when I'm ready, darlin'. You go tend to your business. This doesn't concern you."

"Sir…" she repeats defeatedly, letting her sentence trail off.

"I told you to get your ass up," I say to Misty's date.

"Why. Are. You. Here?"

"You know this guy?" The dark-haired asshole asks.

"She more than knows me, pretty boy. Now get your ass up before I drag your ass from the table," I hiss, glaring down at him.

His mouth flaps. I lean over the table, placing my knuckles down on it. I let my muscles flex. His eyes nearly pop from his head. He slides from his seat slowly. Keeping his eyes on me.

"Unbelievable," Misty mutters under her breath. "Pussy."

"You pick 'em that way," I say to her, not taking my glare off her date. He pulls his wallet out to pay.

"She doesn't need your money. Get the fuck out of here."

He clutches his wallet and stumbles for the exit. I take his seat and fold my arms over my chest. The hostess is still standing, staring at me as she bounces from foot to foot. I take out my wallet and toss a few hundreds on the table. More than enough to cover the bill.

Seeing this, the hostess's shoulders sag and she hurries away from us. I snort and shake my head. Fuck these people. I'm here for my girl.

"You really want to test me on this shit, Mist?"

"What are you talking about? You wanted to be free to do whatever you want, Prez. I'm just making it easier on you," she says, then mirrors my posture.

"You walked in on me helping Sandy find a school. There was nothing going on between us."

"Sure, didn't look like nothing to me." She glares at me.

"It was. She thanked me for helping her and kissed my cheek. That was it."

"Whatever."

I grind my teeth. She can be so damn headstrong. I have half a mind to throw her over my shoulder and storm out of here.

"So, what is this?" I lift my hands and gesture around the restaurant. "Payback?"

"I'd have to care for this to be payback."

I growl. The woman at the table next to us gasps. Old ass prude needs to mind her business and finish her meal.

"You're trying me. I want you to think about that hard. Are you sure you want to do that?"

"Why couldn't I come to the clubhouse that night if it was all innocent?" she snaps, her lips trembling.

"I had business coming in, baby girl. You didn't belong there. If something went south, I needed to know you were nowhere around that shit."

She stares at me for a long moment, searching my face for the truth. I stare back, not backing down in the least. Misty is the first to turn away.

"You could've told me that," she murmurs.

"Bullshit, and you know it. It was club business. You want to be my old lady, Misty, your ass is going to have to start trusting me."

She turns her gaze back on me. I can see the war happening inside her. She bites her lip and starts to fidget with her hands in her lap.

"It looked bad," she says.

"I'm sure it did. You came looking for something and found what you were looking for because that's what you had your mind set on."

"That may or may not be true."

I snort. "We agreed you wouldn't stop your little dates and shit, so no one would get suspicious. We also agreed you would tell me when you went on these bullshit dates. I knew nothing about this one, so imagine my surprise when I found out *my* woman was out on a date."

"Stop having your boys spy on me and you wouldn't have to find out things like this," she huffs.

"That mouth of yours is going to get you in a world of trouble, baby girl. Let's go. This place is getting on my nerves."

I stand and wait for her to do the same. She does reluctantly after a few seconds of staring up at me. I lift a brow when her tight red dress comes into view.

I lean into her ear. "You love playing with fire, don't you? We're going to see how much of it you can handle. It's going to be a long night for that ass, Misty. A very long night."

Misty

The moment I cross over the threshold to the hotel room, King grabs the back of my dress and tears it open. I had a feeling he didn't like the dress from the way he looked at it, but I didn't think he would destroy it. He grabs a handful of my hair and tugs me into his body.

The air conditioning from the room makes me shiver as I stand in only my bra, panties, and heels.

"Let's get one thing clear. I belong to you, and you belong to me. Neither one of us is free to give any parts of us away to anyone else," he says next to my ear. "Now climb on the bed, lie on your back and spread your legs for me."

I spin on my heels and look up at him defiantly. The gleam in his eyes tells me he was hoping I would be defiant. He backs me up against the post at the foot of the bed. Placing a hand around my throat, he then holds me in place. He licks the fingers of his other hand before roughly shoving them into my thong to cup my heat.

"Why don't you listen? Isn't that why you're in trouble now? I plan to teach you a lesson, Misty."

I pant as he breathes the words in my face. My defiance begins to drain away as he works his fingers in and out of me. I'm not even sure what I was so upset about anymore.

Gently he pulls me away from the bedpost and tosses me on the bed. This time when he commands, "Spread your legs for me." I obey.

I climb on the bed and pull my knees into my chest, placing my hands behind them to hold myself open for him. He drops to his knees on the bed, hovering over me. His shirt is the first thing he tugs off and tosses behind him. In one swift motion, he lowers himself and starts to nibble across the back of my thigh to my apex. The first sting comes, sending a vibrating clapping sound through the room.

I glare at him, only earning myself another slap to the opposite cheek. He soothes the sting away with openmouthed kisses as he rubs at my smarting flesh.

"Are you still in the mood to defy me?" he says as he pushes his two fingers into me.

I have no words to offer him as I approach my peak, ready to explode. He pulls back just as it's within my grasp and slaps my butt cheek again.

"If I'm telling you something, it's for your own safety. Don't ever show up at the clubhouse again if I tell you not to. I don't care what you think is going on," he demands. "Do you understand?"

"Yes," I cry out.

"Yes, what?"

"Yes, King."

This time, he uses his hand and his mouth to bring me to a full climax. My legs are shaking, my heart is pounding, my throat is raw, and he hasn't even penetrated me yet.

He kicks off his boots and suits up with a condom before he slowly sinks into me with his gaze locked on mine. I sob in pleasure as he stretches me.

Ever the tease, he starts to pull out, then slowly sinks back in repeatedly. I bite my lip as tears start to blur my eyes. If this is my punishment, I need to make him mad more often.

Three hours and a ton of withheld orgasms later, I have a smug grin on my face. My entire body is sore. King made good on his promise. Not an inch of my body remains untouched by him or free of his scorch. I don't know how I thought I was going to live without him.

Not just my body, my soul and heart cry for him and his attention. I've come so close to telling him that I love him all night. Keeping the words trapped in feels like it's causing physical pain. Still, I don't know if we're there. It will kill me if he laughs in my face or goes running for the hills.

"What's on your mind?" he asks as that blue gaze stares intently at me.

He's lying on his stomach beside me with the pillow cradled in his strong arms. I go to pull my thigh from over his legs, but he reaches down behind him to lock it in place. His rough palm glides up my skin, sending shivers through me.

"Nothing."

"Bullshit." He turns onto his side and lifts to look down at me.

His dreads are loose around his shoulders. Reaching up, I finger them. He's such a gorgeous man. I could spend hours just looking at him.

"How do you think my dad is going to take this?"

He sighs, placing his warm palm on my belly. His face turns thoughtful, his brows drawing. "I don't know. Mix can be unpredictable at times. I think he'll be more pissed about how we did this."

"Maybe it should come from me," I say and bite my lip.

He's already shaking his head. His locks sway with the motion, a few falling into his eyes. He lifts his hand from my stomach to brush them back. I miss the contact instantly.

"We're doing this my way, Mist. I don't want you pulling any of your shit. Let me handle Mix. This one's on me," he says firmly.

"Okay, fine."

He grins down at me. "I'm looking at places."

I furrow my brows. "What do you mean?"

"After we settle shit with Mix and you move back home, we're not going to live in the clubhouse. My apartment sucks. It's for a single motherfucker.

"I'm not single. We need a place. I was thinking of giving Jacky my old place as a graduation gift."

I think my heart jumps out of my chest. I stare at him in awe. He didn't just say he's looking for a place for us.

On top of that, he wants to give my little brother his old apartment. I know for a fact I'm in love with him. I cup his face and search his eyes. I'm just astonished.

King has done so much for Jacky. He and Mix have made sure he's always taken care of. Even after he got his ass kicked out of that fancy school they sent him to.

"Seriously?" I breathe.

"After that Striker shit, I hardly want any of you at the clubhouse anymore. That fucker is lucky he's still breathing."

"Yeah, that was kind of crazy. I don't know if I can say I'm surprised, though. I've never interacted with him much, but that look he always used to get in his eyes."

I shudder.

"You're telling me…" He pauses, his expression becomes distant and thoughtful. "Hold that thought, baby."

He turns for the nightstand and shoots off a text. I can feel the tension coming off of him. His instincts are at play. I've watched him get like this hundreds of times over the years.

I reach for him to trace the reaper on his back with my fingertips. Such a beautiful man with so much power and danger lurking within. I won't fool myself into thinking King is a saint. He has changed the club a lot, but he still does what he needs to do to keep things going.

"Lost Souls for life," I murmur. Just like the ink on his back, this lifestyle isn't going anywhere.

"What?" he says over his shoulder.

"Nothing."

This is what I signed up for. Soul deep.

CHAPTER NINETEEN

Let's Ride

King

I've been missing Misty like crazy. Mix surprised her and Eva with tickets for a trip to Vegas to celebrate Misty's birthday. I had plans to spoil her for a few nights away myself, but she called me squealing about the carrier dropping off the gift from Mix.

I can't be mad at my brother for taking care of our girl. It's just been two weeks since I've seen her. I miss her little ass like crazy. I don't think I'm going to be able to keep my hands off her when they arrive this morning. We certainly can't stay around here.

I don't have it in me to pretend she means nothing other than a little sister to me. Misty is so much more than that. She's become my peace. When I'm with her, I can rest my head. I don't know how I'm going to deal with one more semester of her away from me at that school.

"Hey, Prez." That sultry voice rolls through me and raises the hairs on the back of my neck.

I grin as I still the wrench in my hand. When I turn to look over my shoulder, there my girl stands. She looks so fucking gorgeous.

Her skin has a glow to it, which tells me she and Eva spent a lot of time out in the sun while in Vegas. She has on a sundress that gives her a sweet and innocent look. I know that's bullshit, but I like the look on her anyway.

I drop the wrench and stand. She saunters her little ass over to me, placing her hands on my chest when she stops. I brush my fingers across her cheek, when all I really want to do is devour her mouth. Dipping my head, I take her lips, not giving a fuck.

She's only been here for two minutes, and I already can't think straight. I break the kiss as I struggle for sanity. She looks up into my eyes with a dreamy gaze.

"Let's go. We need to get out of here," I say, grasping her hand and leading her over to my bike.

I've been working on one of the other brother's rides as a favor. He won't be back for it anytime soon. His old lady has been giving him shit about spending so much time at the club now that they have a baby on the way. His bike can definitely wait.

I want some alone time with Misty, and my cock isn't in the mood to wait around for her to slip into my room tonight. I need my woman in my arms badly.

We jump on my bike and take off before anyone can see us. It's still early in the morning. Most of the brothers haven't even turned over yet, after the party we had last night.

It feels good to have Misty at my back. Her thighs around me and her arms holding me tight. I should've just gone to a hotel, but I want something more intimate. Although this ride to my cabin is about to kill me.

The longer she's wrapped around me. The harder I get. I need to get my hands on her in the worst way.

When I make a stop for gas, I can't help taking her lips after she takes her helmet off. "I missed you," she whispers when I release her and place my forehead to hers.

"Not half as much as I missed you, baby girl. Let me pump this gas before we give these people a show."

I wink at her and go to pump the fuel. The machine won't take my card, so I have to go inside. It's a good thing I do. I wasn't thinking about condoms, and I know I don't have any at the cabin. I purchase a box as I pay for the gas.

"Hey, where are we headed?" Misty asks as I place the plastic shopping bag in my saddle bag.

"The cabin."

I have a cabin up in the mountains that no one knows much about, except for Mix, Brick, and the girls.

"Oh, I forgot about that place. I haven't been there since I was... wow. I don't even know. Rose and Cage took me and Eva up there. We had so much fun."

"Yeah, I haven't been in a while myself. I go up there to think sometimes." I peck her lips. "Get your helmet on."

We take off again and the tension between us only grows more. What seems like two days later—only two hours in reality—we pull up to my cabin in the mountains. Lacing my fingers through hers, I lead her into the house to collect a blanket. With the blanket and the plastic bag with the condoms in it, I take her out back and spread the blanket down in the grass by the lake.

"It's so beautiful here. More beautiful than I remember," she says as I wrap my arms around her waist.

"Happy belated birthday," I murmur against her lips.

"Aren't you going to ask me what I want for my birthday?"

I pull back to look at the twinkle in her eyes. The mischievous grin on her lips gives her away. I know what she wants already. I want the same thing.

I take her lips in a kiss that feels like it will burn through to my soul. It hits me that I missed her more than I thought. I lock my fingers in her hair and hold her to me as I devour her mouth, those sweet lush lips move with my demand.

I travel my kisses down to her neck and worship the sweet skin there. She moans that cute ass moan I long to hear every time she's near. I love it almost as much as I love her smart-ass mouth.

Teasing the strap of her sundress down with my fingertips, I taste the smooth skin of her shoulder. I'm starved to be inside her. Lowering our bodies flat on the blanket, I suck and kiss at the tops of her breasts.

She slides her hands under my shirt and locks her legs around my waist. I drag her dress up to reach between us to her center. She releases the hold her legs have on me, allowing me better access to her core. I find her dripping wet, pulling a groan from my lips.

I've tried to be softer for Misty, but how the fuck am I supposed to do that when she's turning me on like this. I release my belt and work to free my cock from my pants. I need inside of her, and I need it now. Her plea seals the deal.

"King, please. I need you now."

Misty

The rumble that comes from his chest should make me afraid of what's to come. Instead, it excites me, causing me to gush in anticipation. The crazed look in his eyes as he reaches for the plastic bag he came out of the gas station with says a million words.

I grin when he retrieves a box of condoms. He tears them open and bites into a gold packet. Then he sheaths himself the fastest I've ever seen. I part my lips and my breath whooshes past them as he pushes into me. It seems like forever since the last time I felt him inside me.

"King," I say breathlessly.

"You feel so good," he groans.

I arch my back off the blanket as I stare up at the open sky. He drives into me so deep. I cross my legs behind his back again as I grow slicker by the second. With each pass, I can feel him growing harder as my walls cradle him and ease his passage more and more.

"Yes," I whimper.

"You want this? Show me how much," he commands.

I pull him to me by his locks and devour his mouth. Squeezing my walls around him each time he pushes into me. It causes his body to shiver over mine. He pulls back, eyes wide and dark with lust.

"Keep doing that shit. Damn, this tight pussy makes me want to lose my fucking mind. Fuck, Mist."

He nips at my chin, then tugs the top of my dress farther down to expose my breasts. When he sucks my nipple into his mouth and swirls his tongue around it, I explode. I lose control of the flex of my pussy. I'm reduced to a quivering, shaking mess.

"That's what the fuck I'm talking about," he croons as he plows right through my orgasm.

He lifts his torso, placing my legs together in the air. His thrusting continues, building me to my next climax. I grasp onto the blanket and hold on for dear life.

I tilt my head back, my eyes fixed on the clear blue sky. My mouth is open in a silent scream. He's so deep. I feel him everywhere and still I want more. I want him deeper.

"Yes, yes, shit, King. Yes. Please."

"I love it when you call my name like that. Fuck, baby."

I lower my gaze to meet his. He licks the back of my calf before biting down hard. His eyes are on me the entire time. He pulls out and I know exactly what he's about to do. I brace myself because the ride is about to get wild.

King's tongue game is sinister. He's guaranteed to put my ass to sleep. The first lick tells me it's going to be one of those. He's out for my life.

King

"Should we start to head back?" Misty asks once I've let her come down from her orgasm.

I chuckle. "We're not heading anywhere."

Our bodies are too spent for us to take that ride back and I wanted more time with her. "I haven't seen you in two weeks. I'm in no rush to take you back," I say.

"Fine with me."

I lie there for a few moments to catch my breath and to regain use of my limbs. So I can lift her in my arms and drag us back into the cabin to my bedroom.

"I could get used to this." She giggles as I carry her.

"Yeah, me too," I murmur, more to myself.

I mean it too. Being alone up there. Just the two of us. It feels right.

CHAPTER TWELVE

Time Cabin

Misty

I open my eyes to the morning sun shining in my face. Reaching out to my side, I find the bed next to me empty. Taking a deep breath, I think I know exactly where King is.

With a smile, I rise up out of the bed. Seeing his T-shirt on the foot of the bed, I pick it up and bring it to my nose, inhaling deeply. My heart swells as I take his sent in. Darn near dancing, I pull the shirt over my head.

Happily, I pad my way to the kitchen where the aroma is coming from. I find King at the stove, he's scrambling eggs and frying bacon. He turns to face me with a piece of bacon hanging out of his mouth. A smile comes to his face. He pulls the bacon from his mouth.

"You hungry?"

"I could stand to eat something."

"Have a seat," he says and gestures toward the stool in front of the island with the pan in his hand.

He leans over the counter to peck my lips. I beam at him and snatch the bacon from his hand, popping it into my mouth. I chew and groan. I guess I'm a lot hungrier than I thought.

He sets a plate before me before placing a second one next to me for himself. Rounding the island, he then takes the seat beside me. I turn to him and smile, in return, he cups the back of my neck and devours my lips in a toe-curling kiss. I can't help wiggling in my seat as I think of how he woke me last night.

I start to dig into the food on a plate before me. I shouldn't be surprised that it's so good. King has always been good in the kitchen. He used to cook for us all. Just one more thing to endear me to him. Knowing he's willing to cook just for me.

"What are we doing today?" I ask.

"Honestly, baby, I thought we could just chill and de-stress."

"Sounds good. Do you want to talk about it?"

He shakes his head. "No, not really."

I look at him and draw my brows at the way he said that. It's like he doesn't, but he's going to anyway. He confirms the vibe when he opens his mouth to continue.

"There's a lot going on with the club. You know my daddy was the Prez of all the chapters. South Carolina had been the mother chapter when the Lost Souls started. That means I was supposed to inherit all the chapters, not just South Carolina and Georgia. Mix and I decided I was too young to take on that responsibility. So, I've only been overseeing South Carolina and Georgia.

"Now quite a few of the other chapters have gone to shit and there're a whole lot of brothers looking for me to step up and step in. I've been waiting for Uncle Kevlar to come home so he can take that role, but there's no telling when that's going to happen and with the ATF breathing down the necks of so many chapters it looks like I am going to have to step in. There's just so much on my shoulders at the moment. I wish my dad were here to tell me what he would want me to do," he says.

"I think your dad would tell you to do it. You're a great prez, all the brothers have so much respect for you. I'm sure you can turn those other chapters around just like you did the ones here," I reply.

"If only I had as much confidence in myself as you do."

"What do you mean? I've never seen you lack confidence," I say.

He twists his lips to the side and rolls his eyes. "Mist, you do realize I had two teenage girls dropped in my lap, as well as two MC chapters? I haven't known what I've been doing for six years, most of the time I'm winging it. Look at how royally I fucked up the shit between us."

"How could you know I was going to show up in your room that night? That was all on me."

"I could have stopped it all from happening. I knew Mix was headed out of town for a few months. I could have stopped and waited to have a man-to-man conversation with him. Choices, we always have choices. I'll admit that I haven't been making the right ones. Which is why I'm not sure if I should step into the role as prez for all the chapters. It's a heavy responsibility and with the shit show that's going on, it's going to take a lot of finesse from me.

"I already have plans to change some things, but this is going to be an even bigger undertaking. Lost Souls ain't nothing nice. If the world got wind of who and what we really are, a lot could change and not for the better. With the damage done to the other chapters, I don't know if we even want to be affiliated with most of them anymore. It's a lot to think about."

I looked down into my plate as I fidget with the hem of my burrowed T-shirt. I wonder if he regrets being with me. It sure sounds like he does.

Now I sit with my own trepidation. I want to see him straighten out things with the club. However, I wonder if I'm in the way of all of that.

"Enough about all that crap. Want to take my chopper for a ride?

"As in me driving?" I ask, both in surprise and excitement. "Hell yeah!"

"Let's shower and get dressed."

I look up at him with sad eyes, I really want to have the opportunity to ride his bike. He lifts a brow at me as he searches my face.

"What's the matter?"

"We came here with no luggage and no change of clothes."

He gives me a wink. "Don't I always have you? I stepped out to get some things when I went out to get ingredients for breakfast. Everything's in the bathroom."

I hop up and rushed to the bathroom to get ready. King doesn't let anyone touch his bike, but he's going to let me ride it today.

Wow.

CHAPTER TWENTY-ONE

Avoiding

Misty

"Oh my God, what's that smell?" I gag as I come out of my bedroom.

Eva pulls a face as she looks at me. "What's wrong with you? It's nachos from that place you love," she replies.

"Well, is the sour cream rotten or something?"

I could smell that disgusting smell all the way in my room. I've never hated the sight of a nacho so much in my life. I'm tempted to take the whole carton and throw it in the garbage.

"No," she grumbles.

My stomach roils. Everything has smelled so repulsive to me lately. I rub my temples. This headache won't go away either.

"Hey, I'm making a list to go shopping do you need deodorant or pads or anything like that? I'll pick everything up on my way home after school tomorrow. I only need your list."

The room freezes. It's like all the air has been sucked out. I narrow my eyes at Eva as I think over her question. When was the last time I needed a pad? As a matter of fact, I should be on my cycle now.

I start to chew on my lip. This can't be possible. However, it would explain the extreme nausea. King is going to have a fit.

As if he can sense something is wrong, my phone starts to ring. I look and see that it is indeed King calling. Instead of rushing off to my room to answer right away, as I normally do, I send it to voicemail.

First, I'm not sure of anything yet. Second, I need to confirm and since I suck at lying to King, it's best that I just avoid him. I say a prayer of thanks that Eva never pays attention to much outside of her books.

Only me. I swear I'm a magnet for shit. I just step right into it.

King

"Hey, this is Misty leave a message."

I pull the phone from my ear and frown at it. She never sends my calls to voicemail. Something in my gut tells me something's off, so I shoot a text to my brothers to see if she's been out and about and what's going on.

The last few times we talked, she has sounded a little off. I let it slide at first, she has finals and graduation coming up so I didn't want to put any extra pressure on her. However, now I need to know what's going on.

I get a text back and I open it quickly.

Turf: *She's home boss.*

I grind my teeth and work my jaw. Dragging a hand through my dreads, I scratch my scalp. With my thoughts spinning, I dial her once more.

Again, it goes to voicemail. "What the fuck?" I bite out.

I remember the look on her face when we talked about me stepping up as the organization's prez. I hadn't missed the change in her body language. Is she that concerned about me taking on so much? Is that what all this is about? Whatever I choose to do, I will always have her best interest in mind. Before I can call again, my phone rings.

"Yo," I call into the phone.

"Hey brother, the streets are talking. It looks like you have some problems coming your way. Just wanted to give you a heads-up. Keep your eyes open and your mind clear."

I bite my fist to keep from tossing my phone.

"Thanks, brother."

My head is ready to explode. Why the fuck do I have outsiders calling to warn me of shit? Trip is a good friend, but he's in a rival MC. He's the last person who should be calling me to tell me what's going on at my back door.

At least, I know I'm not crazy. I've had a gut feeling that some shit ain't right. I'll have to deal with Misty later. Instead of calling her back, I shoot a text to my Squad members to make sure they're alert. Shit is about to hit the fan.

CHAPTER TWENTY-TWO

Why Me?

Misty

This can't be happening. This really, really can't be happening. I'm in a shitload of trouble and the only one I have to blame is me.

I started this. I couldn't stay away. I force the tides that have us drifting in this sea of shit.

If I would've just listened. If I would've just stayed away, I wouldn't be going through this all now. I am scared shitless. This has the potential to not only destroy my life, but the lives of the family I have grown to love.

Things will never be the same in the Lost Soul's clubhouse after this. At best, King is going to kill me and start a war, at worst he'll embrace this and get himself killed while starting a war. Either way, this is bad.

I sit here in this bathroom weighing my options. I could run, but that won't work. King will hunt me down and demand to have answers.

I belong here with Eva. King has made sure of that. His girls are always where he can find us. He would have the head of every brother he has assigned to keep an eye on us.

Sure, he still doesn't admit to having me watched, even though he knows I know. Eva may be in her own bubble when it comes to the club, but I've never been. I have always paid attention. It's what has me in this mess now.

I paid attention to the truth and not what I was told. Which leads me to the option I know is my only one. I have to tell the truth. Anything less will have me standing in the way of a two hundred and forty-five-pound bull.

If I've learned nothing else through the years that I've known King Kennedy, I know for a fact he's a force to be reckoned with. It is what has drawn me to him since I have been able to walk. To be honest, I had a hard start to life.

I am no stranger to danger. I sort of crave it. My dad was a drunk and an abusive husband.

My biological father, Pop, and my dad that raised me, Mix, had been best friends. That is until the night my father beat my mother to death on the side of the road while my brother and I sat in the car crying.

Jacky was only five at the time. I was nine. Dad had always claimed that Jacky and I weren't his kids, that mom had messed around on him.

Honestly, while I have my dad's chocolate brown eyes and chocolate skin only a few shades lighter than his, Jacky's hazel-green eyes and light skin were a dead giveaway. Mom had light hazel eyes and hazelnut skin but nothing as light as Jacky's eyes and complexion.

The night Dad snapped was the night mom opened her big mouth. She loved to taunt him until he cracked and beat her ass. It was a sad sick game I had to watch one too many times. That night mom told him she did fuck around on him, and she wasn't sure if either of us belonged to him.

"Uncle Mix. We need help," I whispered into the line.

I called him on the special phone he gave me for when my parents lost their minds and forgot about me and Jacky. He always came to the rescue. He was just too late this time.

Dad had pulled the car over to the side of the dark road and he beat mom until she stopped breathing. By the time Uncle Mix and Uncle Cage got there, it was way too late.

"Please, baby, come back to me," my father had sobbed, holding Mom's battered body.

Uncle Mix lost it on him. I never saw my real father again after that night and Uncle Mix became my dad. The only father I have ever truly known. Despite him treating me like a princess, I still crave the edge, I crave danger.

Well, danger is what my ass has now. Mix still hasn't returned for King to talk to him and now this.

I never thought I would change all of our lives forever that night I beat Laney's ass. Mix is going to lose his shit. *Shit*, I'm going to pay for it all. Hell, I already am.

I lift my phone and stare at it. I know what I have to do. With a big sigh and a deep gulp of air, I forge forward.

Here goes nothing.

King

Misty's little ass has been avoiding me again for weeks now. Shit has just been out of control at the club and my business. I have too much shit going on.

I had to travel repeatedly for two months, then I've been too busy for the last few weeks to get down here to get to the bottom of the problem. I thought we were good after I stormed in on her date.

Since we've started, she's found any reason she can to get her ass back home. Every chance she gets, she's been sneaking her pretty ass into my bed. Now, I can't get her to South Carolina to save my life.

I still haven't come clean with Mix. I never meant for this shit to happen, but now I crave Misty like air and I'm going to handle all this shit to breathe.

I want Mix to be the first to know things have changed between me and Misty, and I want him to hear it from me. I owe my brother that respect. I know Mix is not Misty's real father, but he has been the closest thing she has ever had to one, and he takes that shit seriously.

He'll be home soon, but first I need to get to the bottom of what has Misty dodging me. In my head, there is no doubt that Misty is my woman.

It took me a while to decide to come here. I miss Misty's thick brown legs tangled with my long white ones. My hands itch to hold on to her curves, but I know the moment my sister figures out that I'm sleeping with her best friend, things are going to get ugly.

Coming here could be a problem. Not that Eva will have a problem with it. I'm just not sure she'll keep her mouth shut long enough for me to have a talk with Mix. I may be the

President of the Lost Souls, but Mix has been the VP since I was in diapers. He and my father ran shit together until the day my daddy died.

I wanted Mix to take the reins. I would have been happy as his VP. However, the votes didn't go that way and Mix was at the head of the pack nominating me to take things over. He has been right at my side ever since, just like he would have been with my old man.

I heave a sigh as I swing my leg off my bike. Only Misty is worth this drama. I smirk as I think about the day after she slipped her sexy ass into my room. I wondered what happened to Laney that night. She usually showed up whenever I sent her a text.

Apparently, she did show up. She showed up to an ass whipping. Misty cornered her in the compound parking lot and commenced to beating her down.

I watched the club surveillance and laughed my ass off. My baby girl has a temper. I'm not even sure she planned to beat Laney's ass at first. When I asked her about it a few months ago, she dropped to her knees and shut me up. Something I'll only allow Misty to do.

I get pissed off all over again when I think about her lips wrapped around my cock. I desire her now, so I have been going through a bit of withdrawal since she's been avoiding me. I've been horny as fuck and only Misty's pussy will do.

My phone rings in my pocket as I approach Misty and Eva's apartment building. I pull it out and look at the screen. I groan as I see Eva's name light it up.

I know she went out on a date with some little shit tonight. Benny and Turf were watching the place when she left. Once

Benny told me Eva went out, I decided to chance this visit to Misty at their apartment, instead of luring her out.

From what the boys say, Misty hasn't left the place in a few days. Another red flag that had me on my bike to come see my girl. Misty has some answering to do, but first I have to see what my sister has gotten herself into this time.

"Hey, baby girl, what's up?" I ask as I put the phone to my ear.

"King, I'm so sorry, but I need your help. I went out on a date, and he told me he forgot his wallet at his place. When we got here, he started drinking and got touchy-feely. I had to lock myself in the bathroom. He's beating on the door, and I just want to go home," Eva rushes into the phone, her voice quivering.

Fuck, I knew it. Eva just can't seem to stay her ass out of trouble. Well, at least this time Misty isn't caught up in the middle of it with her.

I look at the building where my woman is hiding from me and calculate my options. When Eva yelps and I hear the shitbag in the background, I growl into the phone.

I get ready to head back to my bike, but my other line beeps in. I look at the phone and see its Misty. My brows draw in as I wonder why she's just now deciding to call me back. I sigh, letting the call go to voicemail.

"Listen, baby girl, I have some club shit I need to handle. Besides, I wouldn't get there fast enough. I'll call a brother I can trust to get you out of there," I say into the phone, already knowing who I'll call.

I'm annoyed with myself for telling her a half-truth, but I shake it off. I don't trust many with my baby sisters. I'd kill for those girls.

I know I can trust Brick. He's like a real brother to me and he's one big motherfucker. He won't be having any problems getting Eva out of there safely.

Brick is one of the last people I would usually call for something like this. I reserve him for heavy shit. The pussy trapping Eva in will probably piss his pants, no matter who I send, but this is Eva.

Like I said, I don't just trust anyone with her. Half the brothers in the club lust after her when they think I'm not looking. My girls being black never shielded them from a damn thing. My old man ran off all those who had a problem with his black old lady and her children.

Our brotherhood is mixed with all races and brothers from all walks of life, but we used to have a few in the ranks that had narrow minds. Not anymore. If my little sister bothered to bat a lash at those goons, they'd all drool all over themselves to get to her.

Eva saves me some grief in that department. I have never seen her interested in the opposite sex. I once thought she was asexual or something. When I mentioned it to Misty, she laughed in my face. I still don't know why.

"I'm sorry, King. Thank you," Eva whispers into the phone.

"It's what I do, baby girl. We'll talk about this later. Let me make that call," I reply.

"Okay, love you." Eva sighs.

"Love you too," I say before I hang up.

I quickly pull up the number I need and dial. He picks up the phone groggily on the third ring. I smirk because if there is anyone that can be gruffer than me, it's Brick.

"What's up, Prez?" Brick grumbles.

"Need a favor. Eva's gotten her ass into a bind. I have some business to handle. I need someone I can trust to get her out of there," I reply.

Sounding more alert as he shifts around on the other end, Brick replies with a growl. "Where is she? What happened?"

"Locked in her date's bathroom. I have a tracker on her phone. I'll text you everything you need to know. I just need you there fast," I rumble as I head back for the apartment building.

"I've got you, brother. I'll take care of it."

"Never doubted it. Take care of my girl and make sure you get in and out without unnecessary problems, you feel me?" I say.

"You're not talking to a rookie, King. It's been a long time since I've been a prospect. I did more than earn my patch." He chuckles. "I'll handle this like a pro."

"Thanks, brother. Good to know I can still rely on a good few." I laugh back.

"Call you later," Brick says before disconnecting.

I'm at Misty and Eva's front door when my phone rings again. It's Misty again, which has my curiosity piqued. With a smile, I pick up.

"Hello, baby, open the door."

CHAPTER TWENTY-THREE

Consequences

Misty

My entire body tingles as his voice comes through the phone. It takes me a few seconds to absorb his words. I push up off the bathroom floor and rinse my mouth out. Flinging the bathroom door open, I rush for the front of the apartment.

When I pull the door open, there he is. All six foot five of my solid wet dream. Those full lips look as good as they taste. Trust me.

He's wearing the fuck out of a tight gray T-shirt with his cut over it. His jeans hang low on his tapered waist, begging for me to drop to my knees to worship what lies beneath. I just want to trace my tongue over the tattoos I know are hidden under his clothes.

He lifts his arms over his head to hold on to the frame as he looms over me. I follow the moment with my lust-filled gaze and I swear my panties become moist. I can never focus around him anymore.

"Are you going to let me in or are you going to just stand there staring at me?" he says with a smirk.

I stumble back to widen the door and give him room to enter the apartment. Although, I'm not sure this is such a good idea. I was just barely brave enough to call him. I should've known he would show up on my doorstep soon.

I knew I wouldn't be able to hide forever. Only buying as much time as I could get. I look at the floor, trying to buy a little more. It's useless as King closes the door behind him and crowds my space.

He cups my chin in his large hand and tilts my head back. His intense blues burn into me. He's searching, probably trying to find the answer to why I have been avoiding all contact with him. I'm not sure what he finds, but whatever it is causes him to crush my lips with his.

I moan into his mouth as he grabs ahold of my ass with his other hand and lifts me into his hard body. His arousal presses into my belly. My body starts to hum for him. I don't know how I've made it this long without him.

He reaches for my T-shirt and rips it over my head. He groans when my breasts bounce freely into his view. Dropping to his knees, he pulls me closer and starts to place kisses up from my belly to my breast. He latches his hot mouth onto my right mound, and I cry out from the shock to my tender nipple.

It's like ice water is thrown on me. "King."

He looks up at me with narrowed eyes. It's now or never. I have to get this out before I chicken out and let him take me right here, everything else be damned.

I cup his strong jaw in my hands and take a deep breath. "King, we need to talk," I start.

He narrows his gaze further. "You going to tell me why I haven't seen you in three weeks or are you going to tell me why you've been avoiding my calls?" he grunts.

"Both," I reply and wet my lips with my tongue. "I'm pregnant."

There… I said it. I've lived a good life. If he kills me now, I can say that I have loved and been loved. I wait with bated breath for him to respond.

King

Am I hearing shit, or did she just say that she's pregnant? I had a lot of things running through my mind that she would say when I got here, but being pregnant damn sure wasn't one of them. I'm stunned speechless as I sit on my knees before her.

I haven't doubted my feelings for Misty since that night in my room at the club. I've even stopped sleeping at the clubhouse overnight as much. Hell, I've been looking to change a lot of things in my life to move forward in this relationship. Mix will only allow the best for his baby girl and that's all I want for her.

I blink a few times as it all settles in. I'm going to be a father. Fuck, I know exactly when it happened. The weekend after her birthday. When we went up to the cabin.

I spent hours driving between her legs like I'd lost something in her pussy. When I wasn't inside of her, I ate her sweetness until I had my fill. I can still feel the sun at my back as I slurped and sucked at her juicy flesh.

I'd used up every condom I bought by the time night fell. Our bodies were too spent for us to take the ride back and I wanted more time with her. So, I lifted her in my arms and dragged us back into the cabin to my bedroom.

I remember reaching for her in the middle of the night with such need, I hadn't thought about a condom. I can never get enough of her. I pushed into her from behind and the feel of her wet, tight folds parting for me and sucking me in whole was so amazing, I got lost in thrusting into her.

I'll be honest. Knowing I was inside of her raw, drove something inside me. I never in my life came so hard, even after emptying my balls into her numerous times that day. I didn't even care or think to ask her if she was on birth control.

In my mind, Misty is mine. I don't give a fuck if she's on the pill or not. A baby is just one more way the world will know she's property of King.

Misty

I think I hold my breath the entire time after the words slip out of my mouth. I watch as a range of emotions cross over King's face, but I can't get a read on any of them.

So many women before me have tried to trap King. I don't want him to think I'm one of them. This was an honest mistake. I'd had to change my contraceptive method. I never thought anything of it. King always uses condoms.

That night at the cabin, I was so groggy when he woke me by thrusting into me from behind, I hadn't thought about or cared about whether or not he was wearing a rubber. It had felt so good, and it didn't dawn on me he hadn't worn one until he spilled his hot seed deep inside me.

I bite my lip as I try to come up with something so King doesn't lose it on me, but I quickly think against talking when I watch his blue eyes light up. King slides his hand into the back of my little shorts, squeezing my cheeks as he looks up into my eyes. I'm so small next to him he doesn't have to look too far up, even on his knees.

"My baby," he murmurs, almost to himself.

He dips his head, placing a kiss on my stomach. I feel the tears well in my eyes. I'm so in love with this man it hurts. Sometimes I feel like I can't even breathe.

King stands, lifting me with him by my ass that he's still gripping. He captures my lips and devours my mouth in a searing kiss. I moan into his mouth and tangle my fingers in his locks.

King is the first to break the kiss as he growls. "Mine, my woman, my baby, don't you ever try to hide my baby from me again."

"King, this is —" he pecks my lips, cutting me off.

"No, I'll take care of it," he says, as if he knows what I'm about to say.

"But you have to—" I start again.

"I said I got this. I'll handle this shit. You're mine, Misty. You feel me, baby? I'll take care of everything," he demands as he takes us into my bedroom.

"I feel you," I whisper as he sets me on the bed and climbs over me.

"Ain't shit coming between us, Misty," King says as he kisses first my nose, the corners of my lips, and then my chin.

"This is my fault. I should've never come to your room. I forced you to do things wrong," I whimper.

King moves back to hover above me and looks me in my eyes. "You already know that's bullshit. Nobody forces me to do shit. Would I have liked to talk to your daddy first before I knocked you up? Yeah. Would I have liked to have his blessing before I made you mine? Hell yeah, but what's done is done and there's nothing we can do about it now."

"King, I'm—" I try.

"No, baby, not tonight. I've been starving for you for weeks. We can talk later. Right now, I need to remind you of what's mine," he says as he sits up on his knees and shrugs out of his cut. He tosses it aside, then pulls his shirt up over his head.

He throws his shirt into the corner of the room and reaches for his belt. I sit up to help him release his zipper and unbutton his jeans. I watch in awe when his fat, thick erection springs free from his pants. My mouth waters and my pussy floods with desire.

Between his work of art abs and the steel between his legs, my stomach is already quivering in anticipation. I've missed him so much, my need has me blinded to anything else.

We should talk about the consequences we're facing. This isn't going to just blow over with my dad. Lost Souls live by a code. There are rules and King has bent more than a few. If Dad wants to, he can call for King's patch, gavel, and a pound of flesh.

King places his fingers under my chin once he removes my shorts and panties. He looks deep into my eyes. "I'll take care of it, Misty. You and the baby have nothing to worry about. All you need to worry about is where you want to wear my brand, baby. You've been wanting me for a long time. Now you have me," he says against my lips.

With that, he takes my mouth once again and kisses me thoroughly. I gasp into his mouth when he starts to sink into me. King growls as my warmth sucks him in. It's been a while and it feels like the first time all over again. Only this time, I can tell King is being gentle with me.

He moves into me inch by inch until his entire length is covered in my silky folds. I breathe through my nose and lift my legs to wrap around his back. King bands one of his thick arms around me, cradling me to his chest. He kisses his way to the crook of my neck and starts to suck on the flesh there.

"So fucking good," he groans against my skin.

I wiggle a little beneath him and he takes the hint. He starts to thrust into me, slipping an arm under my thigh and pinning it back. He's deep and his thick shaft rubs my clit with each pass. My eyes roll back, and I start to scream his name.

I'm so wet, the sound of my soaked pussy under his powerful thrusts fills the room along with his heavy grunts. I grip the sheets in one hand and claw at his back with the other. I am already so close to the edge.

"You like that, baby? You miss me?" he grunts.

"Yes, I missed you so much," I cry out.

King looks me in the eyes and grins. His blues are the color of midnight oceans, they come to life and gleam at me. He dips his head and pulls my taut nipple into his mouth and that's all she wrote. I come so freaking hard my heart starts to palpitate.

King reaches between us and flicks my nub and it's over. I black out with a huge grin on my face. I love this man.

CHAPTER TWENTY-FOUR

Check-In

King

Misty is right. I wouldn't let her say the words, but she's so right. We did this wrong and now I'll have to pay for that, but I won't let my woman or my baby go.

I never even knew I wanted a baby. Now I can't keep my hand off her belly. Just the thought of my son or baby girl growing inside her has me beaming from ear to ear.

I should be asleep after last night, but my mind is full of plans and things I need to handle. I need to get Mix back home so we can sit down and talk. This could go south if I don't do things right from this point forward. I fucked up enough as it is. I may be Prez, but we live by laws and there are codes I have to follow.

I need to get Misty back home with me as well, but from what she told me last night, she's not ready to ride on the back of my bike for a trip home. She's sick more often than not. My little baby in there is already raising hell for its mama.

I pinch the bridge of my nose while my other hand continues to caress Misty's stomach. Eva isn't going to ignore me living here until I can take Misty back home with me.

That's when it dawns on me. I reach for my phone to check the time. I never heard Eva come in. Brick didn't text me either.

My heart starts to race with the thought that he never made it to her. I would never forgive myself if something happened to Eva or Sal. My father left them for me to look after.

I open my phone and dial Eva's line. Tension builds as her phone goes to voicemail. I dial her again, twice more. Her voicemail comes on each time.

I call Brick and wait for him to pick up so I can drag his ass for not calling to check in. The line rings until his voicemail picks up. I dial him again. My jaw is tight as I hold the phone to my ear.

This time he picks up, grumbling into the line. "Hello."

"Where the fuck is Eva?" I growl. "She's not answering her damn phone."

"She's with me. She was shaken up last night, so she came to my place."

I sigh in relief. She's safe. That's good.

The wheels start to turn. This may be a good thing. I'm still not sure Eva knowing about me, and Misty is for the best. A plan starts to form in my mind.

I'm irritated with all of this. It's not like me and I don't like it. Frustration fills me as I become unfocused for a moment. I'm desperate to protect my family and relationship. It starts to sink in that I have no idea how Mix is going to take all this shit. I've dug a hole and it's just getting bigger.

"I need a favor. She can go to the apartment to pack a few things, but I need you to keep her with you until I can smooth some shit over," I say before I can change my mind.

Brick doesn't say anything at first. I can hear him moving around. A door closes and that's when his voice comes back to me, sounding as if he's ready for war.

"What's going on? Some motherfucker have a death wish?"

I sigh and shake my head. "No, brother, this shit is on me. I don't want to involve Eva in my shit," I start to ramble as my thoughts race.

"I just need some time. I know this is asking a lot, I need a few weeks. I don't need to complicate this any further. Trust me, when I wrap my head around it, we're going to need to have a few beers together."

I run a hand through my locks. This all could unravel at any moment. My thoughts become distant.

"You know I have your back, brother," Brick says, drawing me back to the present. "She's good with me. I'll take her to the apartment before I head into the office. I'll just have to move some things around."

"Thanks, brother." I remember Eva's internship interview. "Make sure she gets her ass up for her interview and gets there on time. I don't want her thinking things are being handed to her.

"I spoil her and Sal enough. The women in my life drive me fucking insane." Just then, Misty jumps up and runs for the bathroom. "Listen, I gotta go."

I hang up without another word, rushing to follow her into the bathroom. Well, isn't this morning starting off great.

CHAPTER TWENTY-FIVE

Reality Hits

King

I think I held my breath the whole time I watched Misty empty her stomach this morning. Not because of the smell, but because I was going out of my mind watching my baby girl and not knowing how to make it better. She wasn't joking about her morning sickness.

I managed to take her out to breakfast while Brick brought Eva over to collect some things to stay at his place for a while. I swear, Misty didn't take two bites before she was off to the bathroom again.

I want to take off for South Carolina, but that's not going to happen anytime soon. Being on the back of my bike isn't the issue here. Misty can't stay out of the bathroom long enough for the trip back.

I'm pretty much fucked. I'm not leaving her, and I can't keep skirting the truth. The shit I'm doing is starting to sound like a lie to my own ears.

It's ten at night and this is the first time all day Misty hasn't been bowing before a toilet. She looks so peaceful in her sleep. It's also the first time I've been able to think all this through.

I run my hand over her scarf-covered head. I can't believe I'm going to be a father. This shit is still working its way into my brain.

Well, none of this shit is going away, so you might as well deal.

Misty's eyes flutter open and I sigh. She didn't nap that long, but I guess that's kind of hard to do when you feel like shit. However, as soon as her eyes open, they droop right back closed. She releases a soft sigh and settles back in.

I get up to go pace the living room. This is such a clusterfuck. Staying here with Misty will bring up questions.

I'll have to lie about where I am or ask a brother to lie to cover for me. None of that's my style.

I pull out my phone and pull up Mix's number. It would probably be best to just come clean. Still, this ain't some shit you tell a brother over the phone. I blow out a breath and run my hand through my locks.

There has to be a middle ground. Misty is supposed to start her internship with me next week. I have some clients that are here in Georgia.

I can give them some face time and make this more personal for them. Misty can work as my assistant as far as the office staff is concerned. Staying with my sister while I do that won't seem out of the ordinary. No one other than Brick knows Eva's not here.

I can make this shit work.

I'll get Teddy or Sugar to bring me a few things. I can get most of my shit done from here. Yeah, I have a plan.

My phone rings just as it all starts to gel. I bare my teeth. I've been waiting for this call. Some things just ain't sitting right with me.

"Speak," I bark into the phone.

"He's gone, brother," Axle replies. "Not a trace left."

"Call Vault. Make sure nothing's coming down the pipeline. Let's switch things up for a bit. Nothing happens on home territory. Wash everything and then we'll keep a clean nose for a while. Hand our work over to some friends," I command.

I'm known for my killer instinct. I haven't lost a brother to a jail cell yet. My gut is telling me this is one of those times when we need to cool things down for a minute.

"Got it. Do you want me to keep digging?"

"No, I don't want to stir anything up. Leave the gate open. If he pops up on the grind, I want to know," I say.

"Got it."

I hang up and stare into space for a bit. I've been getting that feeling again. Something is lurking in the wings. It's been too quiet, which is why I need peace in the ranks.

My phone rings again and this time I stare at it for a few beats before I pick up. "What's up, Mix?" I answer.

"Hey, kid. Have you talked to Eva or Misty?"

"Yeah, what's wrong?"

"I talked to Misty, and she sounds… off. Have they been home?"

"Not in a few weeks."

I stick as close to the truth as I can. I know I should say something, but this just doesn't feel like a conversation we should be having like this. Although, the words are right there on the tip of my tongue.

"I'm worried about her. She's a tough kid, but she's still young. She makes irrational decisions that put her ass in a bind every time. Do me a favor. Check in on her."

His words hit me in the chest. Misty is young. Nine years younger than me. She can do some irrational shit at times. Hell, she can be downright reckless.

Guilt starts to set in. What if he feels I'm one of her irrational decisions? Misty could do a hell of a lot better than me.

"I'll take care of it," I reply.

"I know you will. Thanks, King. I'll see you on that side soon, brother."

I hang up and feel like shit. Pinching the bridge of my nose, I close my eyes and groan. I love Mix like my own father. I hate this shit with a passion. If I could turn back time, I'd do this right.

I'd still be with Misty. I just would've gone to her old man first. It was coming. I was losing the battle with resisting her long before she found her way into my bed.

"Everything okay?" Misty asks.

I turn to find her leaning up against the wall, staring back at me. She's so small. Not being a hundred percent herself makes her look even smaller.

"I'm fine."

"That was my dad, wasn't it?"

"Yeah." I nod tightly. Not wanting to talk about it, I change the subject. "You need anything?"

She shudders. "I'm afraid to do more than drink water."

"You have to try to keep down something. I can go to the store and get you whatever you want."

Misty

The sincere concern in his eyes makes me love him even more. I don't want to eat a thing but for him, I'll at least try. I smile and tilt my head at him. He looks so stressed.

I didn't miss that he changed the subject from my dad. Our talk was brief, but I realized after I hung up that I may have tripped his suspicion. I'm not cut out for this hiding shit.

"I'll have whatever you're having. You didn't eat, did you? You've been watching over me all day. It's late. You should have something too. I can cook us something," I say.

"*You* cook?" He gives me a sexy smile and lifts a brow.

"Whatever, King." I laugh and start for the kitchen.

He follows me, wrapping his arms around me as I look into the refrigerator for what we have in there. Spotting cold cuts, I grab them with some bread and cheese. King rumbles with laughter.

"Making a sandwich isn't cooking."

"Say that after I feed you," I toss back.

Moving out of his arms, I plug in the grill before starting to make the sandwiches. Once I have the gooey sandwiches prepared, I place them on plates, and we go to sit at the small dining room table.

"This shit is good," he says after his first few bites.

I just grin at him. I nibble on my sandwich quietly. Halfway through his, King takes pause. His gaze is on me, causing me to look up. I give a weak smile and he drops his eyes to my plate.

"Come on, Mist. You have to try to eat more than that, baby."

"I'm trying. It just takes a little longer if I plan to keep it in. If it were junk food, I'd devour it. I swear, candy bars have been my saving grace," I say.

He frowns. "You need more than a bunch of sugar. Maybe you should just rest tonight. I'll go shopping in the morning. I'll pick up some healthy snacks and more food."

"So you plan to cook for me?" I smile wider at this.

"You already know my daddy taught me to cook. It was just us. He made sure I knew how to take care of myself. In the MC life you never know when it's your time." He frowns as those last words slip from his mouth.

They have an effect on me as well. Club life is hard. We've both seen the harsh sides of it. Not just the club shit, but even the ride itself can change things in the blink of an eye.

"I remember you cooked for all of us that one time when we were all on lockdown. I thought for sure you hired Bobby Flay to come cook for us." I laugh.

He narrows his eyes. "Yeah, I remember that. I also remember you and Eva giving me those puppy eyes to get seconds. Damn, that was so long ago. So much shit has changed. My dad was crazy about Rose even then. Eva might as well had already been my sister. She was at our place enough."

"I know, right? I miss your dad. Sometimes I look at your office door and I swear he's going to come out barking orders and calling me Squirt," I say and smile fondly.

"Yeah, tell me about it. Some days, I feel like I shouldn't be sitting in his chair. I wish he'd show up and lift some of this shit off my shoulders."

His eyes go distant. King has never thought he should have taken Cage's spot. I know we all thought Cage was invincible.

"You're doing a great job as prez. I think he would be proud of you."

He snorts and shakes his head. His blond locks move with the motion. "Nah, I think he'd have a few things he'd think I could do better."

"You mean us?"

"Among a few things."

"Don't do that."

"Do what?"

I look down at my sandwich and pick at it. I've been thinking about how *I* feel about all of this. I'm in love with King. I'm happy to be having his baby, but I don't want to feel like some burden to him.

"I… I'm in love with you regardless of my age or how messed up things are because we did this wrong. Please don't make me feel like my love is wrong," I whisper.

His silence greets me. I slowly look up at him. His blues are blazing back at me with so much heat in them. My mouth falls open when he lifts from his seat.

He moves around the table to me and squats. Turning my chair until I'm fully facing him, he drags me into him by my thighs and reaches to brush a finger across my lips.

"Say it again," he chokes out.

"I'm in love with you, King."

He leans in and presses his lips to mine. He kisses me so deeply it hurts. Still, you couldn't pay me to pull away.

"I love you too," he says against my mouth when he finally lets me come up for air. "So fucking much. I've been in love with you for a long time. If our love is wrong, then we're going to be a whole lot of fucked up together."

He goes to kiss me again, but his phone rings. Pulling it from his pocket, he frowns. I slump down in my chair when he stands to take the call.

"Speak," he barks.

Just like that, our moment is gone. I get it. He has to take care of club business.

He moves to the next room as he rumbles into the phone. Something becomes very clear by the second. I'm bringing a baby into a dangerous world. This is seriously nothing new, but its reality based now.

All of the lockdowns growing up, the random brawls I've seen both my dad and King get into, the way people tend to shun us when we ride out as a family. They're all taking on a new meaning with a baby on the way.

Maybe I really, really did mess up. King has been trying to phase out a lot of the extras the club is into. I have heard the murmurs about it all. I know he's been worried about Eva and Sal being targeted because of the life. Especially Eva, she's the sister everyone knows. It's hard to miss how close they are.

But what if he can't? What if the club takes him from me and the baby before he gets the chance to see this all through? What if someday he starts to crave the thrill of getting a little dirty every now and then?

King is crazy smart, but all it takes is one distraction, one miscalculation and I could lose my world. That's what King has become. He's my world. I love him so much.

Maybe he was right all along and I'm just not cut out to be his old lady. I'm already folding, and we haven't had our first real sign of trouble. As the tears prick the backs of my eyes, I talk myself down.

I'm emotional because of the baby. I take a deep breath. King would never let anything happen to me or the baby.

I stare at my phone. I want to call Eva, but I don't know how to tell her all of what's going on, without telling all of what's going on.

Ugh, I am so frustrated.

King said to rest, but I can't. Not with all these thoughts running through my mind. I get up and head for my bedroom.

I pull a duffel bag from my closet. I might as well pack. I know we're leaving. Judging from King's tone, I wouldn't be surprised if we end up on lockdown just as we were reminiscing about.

I pause in my packing. King's voice has turned into a murmur in the other room. I sit on the edge of the bed and hold my hand over my belly.

I have a little person in here. Was club life really so bad for me?

"I don't know, little one, but I only want the best for you." I sigh. "I want to talk to your Auntie Eva. She would know just what to say."

I slump where I'm sitting, because reality truly hits hard. I'll be wherever King is. I'll be the old lady I have always dreamed of being.

You want to know why? Because I've belonged to King Kennedy from the day I was born, just like I've been a Lost Soul from that very same day. I don't know anything else.

I'm frustrated with my own wishy-washy thoughts. These hormones are kicking my ass. I pick up my phone again, longing to speak to my best friend.

Eva's probably pissed at me as it is. I sort of ignored her text earlier, not knowing what to say and not wanting to lie. I mean, really, at this point, why are we hiding?

Everyone will know soon enough. I keep telling myself this as I tap the phone against my bottom lip. My stomach rolls with my indecision, so I quickly make one.

I dial Eva's phone and hold my breath. When it rolls to her voicemail, I pout. She must be seriously pissed at me. Eva always answers my calls.

I think about calling back, but I'm suddenly exhausted. All of this worrying and thinking is taxing. I push the duffel bag to the floor and move to the center of the bed to curl into a ball.

I place my hand on my belly and make a promise to my little one. "Things will get better."

CHAPTER TWENTY-SIX

Not Yet

King

"I told you I wouldn't be ready to go," she groans from her spot on the bathroom floor next to the toilet bowl.

We've been trying to head out for two weeks now. That hasn't happened for a number of reasons. One, Misty's car is too small for all the shit she's insisting on taking back to South Carolina.

No, none of it can wait. I've tried to reason with her, but I've failed every single time as the tears start because she *needs* this or that. Of course, I give her what she wants.

Reason number two why we haven't been able to leave, this baby isn't having it. As soon as we act like we're going somewhere, Misty runs for the bathroom.

I give up.

I kiss the top of her head. "Yeah, I see that." I sigh. "I'm going to have to ride back in the morning. Let me see if Sugar can come stay with you for a night or two. Hang tight. I'm going to make a few calls, I'll be right back."

I kiss her forehead and stand to leave the bathroom. I hate seeing her like this. I feel like my heart is bleeding. I've never felt more helpless in my life.

"Hey, Prez," Sugar answers the phone, pulling me from my thoughts.

"Hey, Sug. I need a favor."

"You got it. Just let me know what you need."

"I need someone to stay with Misty for a few days. Eva's not around and Misty's not feeling well. You think you can head to their place in the morning and stick around for a bit?"

"Sure thing. I have a piece booked for the next two hours, but I'll head home and pack as soon as I finish the ink," she says.

"Thanks, Sug. I appreciate this."

"No problem. Mix has never failed me in a bind. I'd do anything for Mist. You don't even have to call in a favor for this one."

The knife twists. Mix has been there for all of us. He's been calling Misty to check on her nightly, and then he calls me to see if I know what's going on with her. I swear, it's like he knows I'm here. I keep telling myself I'm just being paranoid.

"Whatever you need, you ask for it, darlin'. It's yours."

"All right, Prez." She laughs.

I end the call and send a few texts. I need to get back to the clubhouse. I hadn't expected to be away this long. There are things that need my attention.

"Hey, Prez," Axel answers the line when I make my next call.

"Give me the facts."

"Some talk is coming in from New York and Alabama. Someone has been asking questions about us. You specifically. How the brothers feel about the way you're running things. How everyone feels about the changes you're making and how it's affecting all of the chapters," he rattles off.

"Who?"

"That's the thing. No one can give a name. I've just got drunken murmurs of some guy they ran into," he says.

"Well, I need someone sober to start talking," I bite out.

"That's it though. This guy is careful. He doesn't approach until the brothers are drunk and he blends in until they are."

I don't like this shit. It doesn't sit well with me at all. I grind my teeth as the wheels turn.

"I'm heading that way in the morning. Keep your eyes open."

"Got it, brother."

We hang up and the text I've been waiting for comes through. I move through the apartment, grabbing Misty's car keys. I loaded as much as I could in her little ass car.

I open the door and Teddy stands on the other side. I hand him the keys and he gives me a silent nod. He already knows what I need from him.

I close the door and turn back for my girl. I want to spend every second I can with her before I have to head out in the morning.

Misty

I groan as my stomach rolls again. I'm grateful that King is far away when my stomach decides to release its torture from the other end. I break wind hard and giggle at myself.

I'm a mess, but King hasn't left my side in weeks. Even while growling orders on the phone, he's been with me. I love him even more for that.

I lift to my shaky legs and edge over to the sink to wash my nasty mouth out. I make it through brushing my teeth before my stomach starts to quiver and roll again. I roll my eyes and return to my trusted spot in front of the toilet.

When nothing happens, I place my forehead to the cool edge of the bowl, not even caring at the moment. I feel like I've been through a train wreck. I think I nod off for a few.

The next thing I know, I'm in King's arms as he carries me into the shower. I lift my heavy lids to see he's still in his T-shirt and jeans. Before I can protest, he turns on the spray and we're both soaked through.

I'm placed on my feet and King drops to his knees to pull off my shorts, tossing them out of the shower. My tank top is next to follow. He looks up at me through his lashes, placing a kiss on my belly.

"Our baby," he says with a smirk. "I can see all the worry in your eyes, Misty. You're gonna have to let all that shit go. You and I both know I'll always take care of you."

"I know," I say softly.

King lifts his T-shirt over his head and tosses it out with my things. Creating a soaking heap of clothes in the middle of the bathroom floor. That's one more thing he better take care of.

My wayward thoughts are forgotten as King stands to his full height and starts to peel his jeans from his trim hips. I lick my lips as he springs forward heavy and loaded. King chuckles and wags his finger at me.

I pout as my pussy floods for him. I can't believe I can want him so much despite feeling the way I do, but I'd be a dirty liar if I said I didn't want to drop to my knees and swallow him whole.

After discarding his jeans, King grins like a fool, turning me in his arms to face the shower spray. I sag back into him as the warm water washes over me. It's the best feeling in the world.

My man's arms around me, the soothing water, and the calm that King's presence brings. I couldn't ask for more. On second thought, I guess I could. When King reaches for my shampoo and pours some in his palm, I'm done for.

"I love you," he says softly in my ear.

King does nothing gently, but somehow, he's found a way to be so tender and loving with me when I need it most. I relish in the feel of his long fingers as he massages my scalp. My entire back is cocooned in his heat.

"I love you too," I murmur.

"We'll give it a few days or weeks before we try to move again. I want you to make an appointment with your doctor to make sure everything's okay, before we head out," he murmurs close to my ear. "I'll be back as soon as I can. A day or two max."

"Okay. Mmm, that feels so good." I sigh. "I already have an appointment for next week."

"Why didn't you say something?"

"I figured I could see someone back home." I shrug slightly.

King releases a heavy breath but doesn't say anything. We both remain quiet; too lost in our own thoughts, I guess. I have a million things running through my mind.

Eva is going to lose her shit when she finds out what I've been hiding from her. However, it's my dad and little brother I'm more concerned about. Jacky is fragile, especially when it comes to me. I'm all he truly has.

Jacky respects Mix, but he'd prefer to stay to himself than show any emotion toward anyone other than me. Let's face it. Jacky and I have been through some fucked-up shit.

I may be older, but Jacky remembers that night just as clearly as I do. The only person other than me who has ever been able to get through to Jacky was Cage. Losing Cage just sent Jacky into a darker place than where he already was. I mean, he was only twelve at the time.

I was shocked to see him stick around after his eighteenth birthday and more shocked to see him start to hang close to King. I fear what this will do to the thin tether the club has on Jacky. How it will affect the trust he has given to King lately. I don't want to lose any more of my brother.

Now that he's eighteen, there's nothing holding him back at this point. I've watched for years, waiting for him to up and run away. I think King is the only reason he hasn't. He's the youngest of the Squad, which is one well-kept secret. I know because Jacky keeps nothing from me and, well, I pay attention to everything.

King's soft lips bring me from out of my musing. I look up into his eyes and get lost in their intensity. I watch as he takes a stroll through my soul with just a look.

"I'll talk to Jacky once things are squared away with Mix. He's becoming a man, Mist. It's very likely he's going to go off on his own for a while, but the Lost Souls are his home. He won't stay away for long," King says, as if reading my thoughts.

I close my eyes and nod. "But he's so angry at life. I don't want him out there angry and alone," I say in a pained whisper.

"Nothing you can do, darlin'. That there is a grown man. He has his own choices to make. Jacky is smart, he reminds me so much of myself at his age. He'll be just fine," he tries to reassure me.

"I hope so."

King covers my lips with his and delivers a soul melting kiss. I shiver in his hold as he walks me farther into the spray. The water washes the shampoo away as King continues to kiss me breathless.

I desire him. That's the only way to explain the way I feel. I crave him in every way imaginable. I wish I could crawl into him and make a place there forever and always.

He slides his hands down my sides, over my backside. I leap into his arms. King groans into my mouth as he holds me to him, and I settle my legs around his waist. My back is against the shower wall faster than I can think.

King breaks the kiss to look me in the eyes. "I don't know how I ever thought I was going to stay away from you. We're inevitable.

"Everything about you calls to me. The sound of your voice, the color of your skin, the way your hips sway when you walk, your eyes, I love your eyes and the way they look back at me. It was only a matter of time, baby girl," King professes.

"I was getting impatient." I laugh.

King slaps my wet ass. "You're always impatient," he grunts. "Like right now. You're rocking those hips, wanting me inside you. I'm not taking you here. You need to learn a lesson in patience."

"King," I whimper as I continue to rock my hips into him. He can't possibly be serious.

"No, baby." King chuckles darkly. "You will learn to wait your turn."

I know my face is one of pure shock when King takes a step back. Releasing my legs, he allows my body to slip down his wet front. His rock-hard erection glides across my skin. I go to reach for it, but he steps farther out of the way, shaking his head with a sexy grin on his lips.

"Seriously?" I gasp.

"Seriously," he says firmly and waves his finger in the air for me to turn around.

I cross my arms over my chest and pout. He narrows his eyes at me in warning. I huff and turn, obeying the unspoken demand.

I mutter to myself in my head as he washes first my back then my front, all while my back is too him. I'm so horny and pissed off by the time he moves me to rinse off the last of the body wash.

"Oh, God." I moan loud and long when he reaches around me to run his long fingers between my legs, teasing my soaked lips. "King."

"Yeah, baby, how can I help you?" he says into my ear with that deep, sexy voice.

I shiver and whimper, not able to form any real words. I just need him, all of him, in some way fast. However, my man isn't having that. He teases my lips repeatedly, never breaching the seam.

"Where's all that sassy mouth at now, baby girl?" he says in my ear. "Lost Soul got your tongue?"

"Shit, King," I cry out.

He drops to his knees behind me and pushes my legs farther apart. His large palm lands in the center of my back and he bends me over. I plant my hands on the wall and arch my back as he takes his first taste.

Damn right a Lost Soul has my tongue, and my soul as he eats the life right from me. The swirling, flicking, and slurping has my head spinning. My legs turn to jelly as I come, sagging into the wall.

"You wanted it, baby. You're getting it. I'm not done," King hisses out.

He turns the shower off and in the next motion, lifts me from my weak legs into his arms. Stepping out of the shower, he then wraps me in a towel and carries me into the bedroom. Once again, with a gentleness unlike King, he places me in the center of the bed.

He takes his sweet time drying me off, a little more thoroughly than I think is necessary. I just want him to finish what he started. I need him inside me. I ache for him in ways I've never ached for anything in my life.

King tosses the towel aside when he finishes his torturous pampering. Hovering over me, he looks down between my legs with a renewed hunger. He licks his lips as a thirst I've never seen before reaches his eyes.

"You're going to feel me in every part of your being," he says with a rasp in his voice. "When I'm done, you're going to know nothing but me. You won't have room for another thought outside of me," he breathes.

"Please," I plea. His words alone have me dripping wet with excitement and need.

King dips down like a snake and lifts my hips until my soaked offering reaches his lips. My mouth falls open and I start to thrash my head from side to side. He's showing me no mercy.

He's right, nothing else matters. Nothing else comes to mind. His determination is relentless and all-consuming. King has never gone down on me like this before. I claw at the sheets as I feel like I'm about to lose my mind.

It's not fair. This isn't normal, but I'm so not complaining. King eats my pussy until it feels like my heart is about to give out. I won't dare give in and admit I can't handle it.

I rock my hips into his face and bear down for the most explosive orgasm I've ever had in my life. This right here is magic of a new brand, and I will not be missing out on the final act. I cry out King's name at the top of my lungs as stars burst behind my lids.

"That's my baby," he croons and climbs my body.

He pauses to kiss each of my breasts before pulling the right nipple into his mouth. The sucking and slight bit of soreness sends me bucking off the bed. Only to convulse my way back into the mattress beneath me.

King smiles against my breast before moving the rest of the way up my body. I look up at him through my sex-drunk lids. I have a lazy smile on my lips.

"Don't tell me I tired you out already," he says with a sexy smile.

I shake my head, still not able to form words. He throws his head back and laughs. He pecks my lips as he lines up with my entrance and teases me with his shaft.

I moan and start to wiggle against him, but King makes sure I know who's in control. He doesn't give an inch. I pout up at him, but he only winks, then dips in for a drugging kiss. He kisses me long and deep, turning me into goo.

Just when I think I can take no more of this waiting and torture, he begins to slide into me. I swear, the feel of him gliding into me is like the completion of a loving promise every single time.

"King," I moan.

"Yeah, baby," he says, his breath fanning my face.

"I love you," I say and cup his face.

"Not half as much as I love you," he replies, then proceeds to show me through our lovemaking.

CHAPTER TWENTY-SEVEN

Friend sitter

Misty

"Damn, when Prez asked for this favor, it was not what I was expecting," Sugar says.

"I don't think this is what he was expecting to find when he came here, either. You have to keep it a secret for us at least until my dad gets back and we can tell him."

"You don't have to worry about me, this ain't none of my business. I love you and Prez together, I knew it would happen someday. I think Mix knows too. It will all turn out okay."

"I wish I could be so confident about it. I think he's going to wring both our necks."

"Nah, Mix will be the first one to bring me a pic of the kid, wanting a tattoo on his forearm," she says with a little grin.

"That would be so cool. I know you would make it amazing. I'm definitely going to come to you for one of those."

"Before or after you get King's brand?"

I tuck my head and blush at her words. Getting lost in thought as I eat the watermelon she brought for me. It's the first thing I've been able to eat and keep down in weeks. Thanks to Sugar, once she found out I was pregnant, she made sure I had crackers and ginger ale stocked up, both have gone a long way to help me stay out of the bathroom.

The morning sickness hasn't stopped, it just hasn't been as vicious. I'll take that over what was going on anytime.

She looks at me with her bright hazel eyes. They turn up in the corners and seem to be so large when she's excited. Her mixed heritage gives her a unique look. I swear you would think that she has on eye makeup, but that's just her natural lashes. Sugar is a mix of Latina, Native American, and Black.

Her hazelnut skin complements her jet black hair and makes her eyes pop even more from her face. She's gorgeous, gorgeous. Where am petite, Sugar is tall and statuesque. However, her curves could definitely rival mine.

She has always been the tallest out of our crew. And the oldest. At twenty-seven, she stands at six feet. Her hair falls to her knees when down. We've been trying for years to get her to model. Her tattoo sleeves are more interesting because of her darker tone.

Sugar once explained to me that the more pigment you have in your skin, the more the ink spreads. In other words, our melanin attacks the ink. So all of her pieces are done with wide strokes and shadowing so that they don't disfigure quickly.

It's quite interesting to hear her explain it. Not only is she one of the best tattoo artists, but she's one of the best for myelinated skin. I've watched her do some pieces that are just amazing. She'll tell you in a heartbeat to go big or go home.

"Does Eva know yet?"

"Nope."

Sugar releases along low whistle. I meet her gaze then give her a knowing look. I mean, we all know Eva. She may stick to herself and stay in her bubble, but when she knows something, she can't hold water. It's like she's not even aware that she's blabbering details.

"I can just see her talking about the baby in front of someone who shouldn't know and not being aware of it because her brain is preoccupied with some book or something. So no, I'm not telling Eva, not yet."

Sugar nods her head. "Yeah, I totally get that one."

She blushes a little and dips her head. The purple hue of her cheeks just makes her face even more beautiful. I can't help but wonder what she's thinking.

"Remember when we were little and all of us used to pick the brother we thought we would grow up and marry?" she asked.

I burst out into laughter and nod. "Yeah, it's always been King," I reply. I narrow my eyes on her. "Weren't you sweet on Vault for a bit?"

Her blush deepens and she waves a hand at me. "Yeah, but that was canceled in high school. We both decided we're better off as friends. He was older, more popular. The club was really the only thing we had in common. I'm not even sure I want to date a biker anymore."

I snort. Knowing two bikers who would really be upset to hear that. I've always wondered, does she really have no clue that Axel and Diggs are crazy about her?

In all honesty, I don't think Sugar has a clue how gorgeous she truly is. The bohemian-style clothes she wears go a long way to cover up her curves. with all the bangles on her wrist, sometimes, I wonder if she's trying to cover up.

Sugar is extremely shy and unless you're talking about tattoos, she's probably not going to open up too much to you. However, when she's comfortable, she will talk your head off.

Not many know Sugar spent some time in the military. I think that's why King chose her, of all people, to come sit with me. She's more than capable of keeping me and the baby safe and out of harm's way.

She's the closest thing to sending a brother to look after me. Sometimes, I wonder why we don't have a lady chapter of the Lost Souls with all the fierce women that are among the ranks.

I do believe Cage was on the way to letting Rose establish such a chapter before the accident. She would have made a great prez, just like her old man. I know I would have been one of the first prospects they had and not just because I had my eye on the future prez.

"*Qué estás pensando?*" Sugar asks.

Not many know that we're both Spanish speaking, not by looking at us. My father, being half Cuban, taught me the language before beating my mother to death. Sugar and I have always bonded over being able to speak the language to each other.

"I was thinking about how so much has changed," I reply. "Why don't you want to date a biker?"

"If I fall in love and choose to get married, my daddy won't be there to walk me down the aisle. Why? Because of club life. There was a time when I thought Cage would step in to do that, but he's not here. If I were to date a biker, I'm always going to worry every time he swings a leg over that chopper."

"Is that why you won't give Axel or Diggs a chance?"

She shoots me a confused look. "Oh, come on Sugar. You can't mean to tell me that you don't know," I groan.

"Don't know what?"

I tighten my lips. Knowing this really isn't my secret to tell, but at the same time as one of my best friends, I really want her to open her eyes and see the two great guys who are so deeply in love with her. Shit, I have one of King and it's amazing. I couldn't imagine having two Kings in love with me.

"Never mind, I have to go to the bathroom."

CHAPTER TWENTY-EIGHT

Finally

Misty

I scoffed down an entire breakfast of pancakes and bacon. I haven't had an appetite like this in weeks. I've been sitting here waiting for my stomach to betray me.

Thank God, it hasn't happened. I actually kept down dinner last night as well. King sits down on the couch beside me as he comes from the other room where he'd been fussing on the phone.

He pulls my legs into his lap. "How are you feeling? You look better this morning."

"I don't think I'm going to be visiting the porcelain god today." I grin.

"That's good." He rubs my legs. I can see the stress in his forehead.

He's ready to head back home. It's been a week since he left to check on things at the clubhouse. Sugar was actually a welcome guest. I'm still grateful she hipped me to some ways to settle my stomach.

"We can head back if you like. I think I can make the trip."

"You sure?" he asks, searching my face.

I shrug. "Yeah, I think I'll be fine."

He sits silently as he thinks. I know he wants what's best for me, but I also know he wants to get back to South Carolina as well. He twists his lips and runs a hand over his dreads.

Giving a nod, he says, "If you're still good in the morning, we'll head back tomorrow."

"Okay, I'm good with that," I reply.

Everything went well at my doctor's appointment a few days ago. I'll just find a new doctor in South Carolina when we get there. The one here looked like he was afraid of King anyway. I swear, I thought he was going to shit his pants.

"We'll be getting back just in time. Mix will be home soon," he says, keeping his eyes on me.

"Yeah, he told me as much. You know, sometimes I think he still sees me as that little nine-year-old girl he rescued on the side of the road. He doesn't see that I'm a grown woman."

King stares into his lap for a moment before those blues connect with mine. A world of conflict rests in their depths. I want to kick myself for bringing up my age.

It's still a problem for him. As much as we've moved past it, he still wars with it from time to time. I can see it in his face when he does.

"He loves you. Mix has always wanted the best for you. Like any father would.

"Since you were little, you always had to have things your way—not always a good thing. Mix has been there to clean it all up, even when you had no idea he was. There's a lot of love there, baby girl. He means you all the best. He's just making sure you don't have another mess for him to clean."

"That's just it. I don't need anyone to clean up after me. I'm fine."

He laughs and pulls a sour face. "Mist, you fell in love with the club prez and now you're saddled with my baby. What happened to all those big dreams? You wanted to travel the world."

"I can still travel the world. I'll just have a little person and my man to do it with," I say and smile.

He gives a slow smile in return. It lights his entire face. He shakes his head and kneads my thigh.

"If only shit were that simple."

"It can be… everything's going to change, isn't it?"

"Pretty much." He pauses for a moment. I watch as a wide range of emotions cover his face. I love that he's only ever this open with me. I've never seen him this expressive with anyone else. "When you're feeling up to it, I want you to look at a few of the places I like," he says finally.

I can't help smiling from ear to ear. I know he mentioned us moving in together before, but it's all becoming real. A baby, getting a place together, I'm still wrapping my head around the fact that he has said he loves me—hundreds of times.

This has to be love because he's putting his ass on the line for me. I scoot closer and cup his jaw in my palm. He leans in and kisses my lips.

"I can't wait."

King

She's sleeping so peacefully. It felt so fucking good to feed her ass all day and watch her keep that shit down. I can finally get her the fuck out of here.

The timing couldn't be better. Her bags in the corner catch my eye, there's no way we can get that shit back on my bike and I wasn't thinking when I rushed back here to her. I've had so much shit going on and I didn't know when we'd be able to head back.

Honestly, I needed to ride my bike back in case I needed to return to South Carolina again before Mist was ready to go. Now that she's ready, I need to figure this shit out.

I brush a hand over her hair. I'm still thinking about our talk from earlier. Mix doesn't still see her as his little girl. At thirty-one, I should be asking myself why I don't see the young woman she is?

I've lived. I've seen shit, done a lot too. I don't want to take that from her. Now we have a baby on the way. I'm feeling like a selfish bastard, but there ain't shit I can do about that at the moment. I need to get us home first and I can think about how to make this all right then. At least that's what I keep telling myself.

I get up and take my phone into the living room. I need to ask Brick for a favor to get the fuck out of here tomorrow. I want to leave as soon as possible, just in case shit turns south and Misty starts to get sick again.

"Prez," Brick answers the line.

"Hey, brother," I grunt. "How's my sister?"

"She's good, she'll be going to her first worksite tomorrow. I have a few clients who love some of her ideas and want to pull her in on their project teams already," he replies.

There's something in his voice… pride. Good. Eva must be doing well with her internship. I knew she would. She such a smart girl.

"Good, I need a favor, brother. I'll be by the worksite tomorrow to talk in person. Just give me the location," I say.

He doesn't respond right away. Actually, there's a long enough pause that I take the phone from my ear to look at it. When I see we're still connected, I place it back to my ear and grumble.

"Brick, you hear me?"

"Yeah, yeah, I hear you. I'll text you the address in the morning."

"Good." I sigh. "I need one more favor. I need to borrow one of your trucks. You can bring my bike to the club on the weekend. Need you in church."

It's time I call in the head of my Squad. I need facts and I know he'll get them for me. I'm not waiting for shit to find me. I'm gonna find it and squash it.

"Got it, see you tomorrow," he replies.

I grunt and hang up. I don't think I'll sleep much tonight. I have too much on my mind. I think I'll pack up the rest of this shit Misty has been mumbling about getting into the boxes I bought her.

"This is going to be a long night," I mutter to myself.

CHAPTER TWENTY-NINE

Conflicted

King

"What's on your mind, brother?" Brick asks as we make our way across the worksite to talk in private.

"I've fucked up. I've been seeing Misty and I haven't said a word to Mix about it yet," I blurt out.

Brick rocks back on his heels, his arms are folded across his chest. Something crosses his face before he quickly shuts it down. He's probably thinking of how fucked up I am to be dating not only my VP's daughter, but his daughter that's nine years younger than me.

"Is it serious?"

"She's pregnant with my baby. I'd say that's as serious as you can get. I'm in love with her," I reply, pulling a hand down my face.

He releases a low whistle. "Yeah, that's serious. Congratulations."

"Thanks." I start to pace as I think.

"You need to come clean with Mix."

"Yeah, I know that. I just don't know how he's going to take it," I say, blowing out a breath and tugging at my hair. "I'm nine years older than her. I should see her like a little sister, not someone I want to fuck."

"Misty's not a kid anymore. If you see her as your woman, you're not wrong for that. Now, if you were just in it for a quick fuck, I think Mix would have your balls, and rightfully so. Sounds to me like you care about her. Ain't nothing wrong with that," he says.

"Man, I feel like a bastard. This all went down wrong. We've been sneaking around. I've bent the truth on so much shit. If Mix wants the gavel and my patch, I wouldn't blame him."

"I don't think it's going to go that far. The old man has a soft spot for you. This may turn out to be a good thing. At least once you come clean."

I shake my head, pausing mid-pace to place my hands on my hips. "I just can't get over the age thing. I love her so fucking much, but I feel like I'm stealing time from her. You know what I mean? I'm taking some shit I have no right to."

"She probably doesn't see it that way."

"Fuck, Mist has been after me for years. All that flirting and shit just got out of hand at some point. Now, I can't breathe without her. It's like all of the torture in my soul and bones has been silenced by her light.

"Another reason I never should've let things go this far. She's so fucking innocent. You know this life. It will snuff that shit right out," I scoff as I think if the ass whipping Misty handed out to get in my bed in the first place. "Shit, it's already started."

"You know we're meant to be happy too. If that means making Misty your old lady, do what you gotta do, brother. You have a baby on the way. I think it's time you do what we do best. Shovel the shit and find the gold.

"This life may hate us every now and then, but we know how to make it work for us. Make this work for you. You want to love her, you love her. Fuck what may come your way. You two stick together, it'll work out."

"Thanks, brother. I needed to hear that," I say and pat him on the shoulder. "I'm going to head out. I need to get Misty's shit in the truck and get my ass back to South Carolina. I'll see you in church."

He opens his mouth as if he's going to say something, but clamps it shut and nods. I squint at him for a minute. There's something different about him. I go to home in on it, but my phone rings.

It's Misty. My heart leaps in my throat. I was afraid this would happen. Ready for her to tell me she's not up for the drive, I answer the call.

"Hello."

"Hey, babe. Can you bring me some of that French toast from that one place we went to? It was so good. Oh, and some strawberries and pineapples. Yeah, I want that and some ice cream," she rambles.

I chuckle. "Anything else?"

"Um, pretzels. Those thin ones."

"I got it. I'll be there soon."

"I love you," she says.

"Love you too, baby girl. I'm on my way."

Brick is right. Nine years apart or not. I'm in love with this girl and there ain't shit anyone can do about it. Not even me.

#

CHAPTER THIRTY

King

Misty's laugh fills the room and it's the sweetest sound I've heard in days. I wrap my arms around her from behind and bury my face in her neck. She smells so sweet.

"Is this the one?" I ask. "Shit, I hope so. We had to get up butt fuck early to get in here."

The realtor said the owner only wants morning showings, so we had to come in at damn near six in the morning. If I didn't have such a good feeling about this one, I would've said fuck it. From the way Misty's face has lit up since we walked into this place, I'd say I was right.

She turns in my arms and looks up at me. "This one feels like home. This is the biggest master bedroom we've seen, and all the other rooms are perfect. I like that it's a little secluded," she says with a sparkle in her eyes.

"This is it then. I'm buying you and our baby a house. You start thinking about what you want to put in here. We're getting out of the clubhouse as soon as we can. I'm tired of having to wait all day before you can come to my bed."

"It could take months to close," she says with a pout.

"What's my name, baby girl?" I grin and slap her ass.

"Whatever, King," she says and rolls her eyes.

"Yeah, but you know my name," I say and turn to find the realtor to get this shit rolling. I want to close yesterday.

I'm jogging back down to the first floor when my phone rings. It's Sal. She hardly ever calls me. I have to get on her ass about falling into her bubble, ignoring us all unless it's business.

Which causes me to stop in my tracks. I just talked to her about the financials I need yesterday. She's good, but she shouldn't be finished that fast.

"Hey, darlin'. What's up?"

"King, someone broke into my place. They stole my fucking bike," she panics into the phone. "Cage gave me that bike."

My head feels like it's going to explode as her words slam into me. My baby sister is in danger. I start to vibrate with rage.

"Wait. What the fuck? Where are you?"

"I'm on a bus heading for DC. I took off as soon as I noticed the break-in. I didn't know if they were still around. I grabbed what I needed and ran."

"Get off the bus at the next available stop and get on a plane. I want you to head for Lady, make a few stops, don't go straight. Text me when you arrive by bus. I'll send a Soul to pick you up there."

"I'm dumping this phone. I'll text you from a burner."

"Good, I'll send you the name of the Soul I'm sending. Stay low. If you run into trouble, call me ASAP."

"Okay, okay. I got it."

"It's going to be okay. I'm gonna get you home, kid."

"I know."

The trust in her voice chokes me up. This kid doesn't bother anyone. I tighten my hand around my phone. If something ever happened to her, I'd lose my shit. Bad enough I know she's hiding something from me.

We end the call and immediately I call the one person I can trust to bring her in. Gutter. He's the one brother that's not interested in pussy and is as loyal as you can get. He's also a big motherfucker and I happened to send him on a run to Seattle, where I just told Sal to head.

"Hello," his gruff voice comes through the line.

"Don't head back just yet. I need you to pick up a package for me. Hang tight and I'll send you all the information you need."

"All right. Got it."

"Keep your phone close. I'll have more details for you soon."

I hang up and shove my hands in my hair. This is what I've been talking about. I knew something was heading my way. Now that it's here, I'm ready to destroy a motherfucker.

"King?" Misty calls from behind me.

I look up to the top of the landing. She looks down at me with concern on her face. I wave her to come down the stairs, still unable to speak.

"Is everything okay?" she asks when she reaches me.

I grasp her hand and start the rest of the way down. The realtor appears and I remember what I had been going to do before that call.

"How did y'all like this one?" he asks.

"Put in an offer, $20k under asking, all cash, thirty days to closing, final offer," I say without breaking stride. "Make it happen, Walter. No is not an option."

"I've got it, Mr. Kennedy," he replies to our backs.

"King, what's going on?" Misty asks as I open the door to get her in the car.

"Shit just got real. I need you back at the clubhouse. We're about to lock shit down until I figure out what the fuck is going on," I say tightly.

Her face falls. I'm more pissed now. I hate that this day has been ruined for her. She was just so happy.

I pull her into me and hug her tight. "Everything is going to be fine. I'll always make sure you're okay. You and the baby will be safe. I promise."

CHAPTER THIRTY-ONE

Who We Are

King

My phone vibrates in my pocket while I storm toward my office. I pull it out, lifting it to my ear and answer.

"Speak."

"It looks like they ran through the place looking for something, Prez," Spider's voice comes through the line. He's the VP from the New York chapter. I had him go over to Sal's place to check it out.

He's one of the few people who knows I've been hiding Sal out there. Hell, I still don't know what I've been hiding Sal from. She asked and I made it happen, no question. Now I'm wondering if her past has anything to do with this shit that's going down.

I shake that thought off as Spider informs me her place was tossed. Most likely someone is looking for information. Somehow someone has found out about Sal's affiliation to the club. That shit boils my blood even more.

"Thanks, man. Do me a favor and put a few bodies on the place for a few days. Let me know if anything out of the ordinary goes down. I want to know if her neighbors shit one time too many. You feel me?"

"You got it. Are we still keeping this close?" he questions.

I know he's referring to his chapter prez. For now, I'm not trusting anyone. Spider grew up with me before he moved up North. He makes that small list of the few that I actually trust.

"To the fucking heart," I say and hang up.

I make my next call. Now that my gut is strongly telling me that this has something to do with me, I'm calling everyone in. That means Eva's ass is coming home.

"Prez," Brick's voice comes through as I pace my office.

"Get my sister home, now."

"Is there a problem? I got a text from Gutter."

"He's on the way to get Sal and bring her in. Her apartment was broken into and trashed. They took her bike," I say through my teeth.

I keep hearing her broken voice when she told me her bike was gone. I know what that bike means to her. Cage bought it for her. My old man had a real weak spot for Rose and her girls.

I grind my teeth and focus. I'm not taking chances. My Squad needs to be alert. If I have to put them into action, I want them on standby.

"I need all twelve ready. Get her here. I'm locking shit down until I have answers," I snap and hang up.

I dial the next two people I trust with everything I am. The most insane brother I know and his old lady. Where you find one, you always have the other. Even on the battlefield.

They got their shit together and now they're unstoppable. Grim is a fucking nutcase and his old lady, —who we affectionately call Reap—is the hinge that has come loose. Both badass and the fucking truth.

Let's just say the Navy threw them back. Rumor has it the CIA had their eyes on the two but took a pass. There's no controlling Grim and Reap.

I get the respect I get from them because of my old man and because we came up together. Our respect is from love. Other than that, they would both probably tell me to fuck myself.

Grim and Reap are exactly who I need from the sound of things. If shit's about to get real, then I'll make it as real as it gets.

CHAPTER THIRTY-TWO

Aftermath

King

Break-ins, car chases, crazy ex-wives on my doorstep—of all the fucked-up shit going on around here... I can't believe Brick has been fucking my sister behind my back. Yeah, I was and still am pissed as fuck at Gutter, but Brick... he's my best friend. That shit is cutting in a different way.

"She's pregnant, Eva's fucking pregnant," I snarl as I pace my bedroom.

"And so am I," Misty says dryly.

I turn and narrow my eyes at her as she stands by the door with her arms folded over her chest. I glare at the miniature Captain Obvious. She returns my glare with one of her own, moving her hands to her hips.

"It's not the same," I bite out.

"Yeah, you keep telling yourself that. You heard my dad. It's the same damn thing. How can you be such a hypocrite?"

"I asked my best friend, my brother, to do me a favor. That favor didn't include fucking my sister and knocking her up. You and I have been in a relationship. You're my old lady. It's different."

Misty's face softens. She closes the gap between us and places her arms around my waist as she looks up at me.

"I'm your old lady?"

I narrow my eyes on her. She has to be kidding. She's been mine since that very first night.

"You're tripping, baby."

"That's the first time you've called me that," she says, and gives me a goofy smile.

My anger calms just from the sight of that look on her face and her words. I cup her cheeks and brush my thumb over her lips. She so gorgeous.

"Is it?" I stare into her eyes.

"Yeah." She nods. She tilts her head to the side. "You do realize we don't have to hide anymore? I can move in here until we get the house."

"If I'm still alive after I go talk to your daddy, yeah."

"He didn't look so bent out of shape to me. I think we did all that worrying for nothing."

"I know Mix. He's going to have a few words for me."

She runs her hands up my chest. "Well, I think it's only right that you satisfy your old lady before you take off for battle," she purrs.

I move my hands to her ass, dipping in to taste her sweet lips. For the first time I don't feel like I need to look over my shoulder while we're together. It makes this kiss something I feel in my entire being.

My need to take her grows unbearable. I lift her thick ass onto my waist and carry her over to the bed. Reaching for the hem of my T-shirt she's wearing. I then pull it up over her head. She's showing. The little bump is cute on her. I bend to kiss her belly.

"I love your ass so much. I'll take whatever comes as long as I have you," I say and flick my tongue against her skin.

"I think Brick and Gutter feel the same way," she says. I lift my head and glare at her. "It's the truth."

"I'm not in the mood to talk about that shit."

"King—"

"Shut up about it, Mist. Or we can end this right here."

"Whatever," she mumbles.

I tug her sweats and panties down her legs and dive between her thighs. Once my mouth is on her fat pussy, all that attitude goes out the window. The topic of my sisters and their new love lives is forgotten.

Honestly, I need to get out of my head for a while before it explodes right off of my shoulders. As Misty cries out, I start to get lost in her juices and the press of her thighs against my ears. She tastes so damn good and the knowledge that she's forever mine and carrying our child only makes me hungrier for her.

This is life.

Misty

I bow off the bed as he devours my core. I'm on a high. He called me his old lady and now he's eating his way to my heart.

It feels so good, my toes curl as my legs dangle over his shoulders.

"King," I whisper into the room as if we still have to hide.

When it dawns on me that we're free to be us, I whimper louder. It truly sinks in that my dad knows and now we're free for King to let everyone know I'm his old lady.

He turns his head to my inner thigh and bites down before sucking the flesh into his mouth. My legs start to tremble as he pushes in and out of my core with two fingers.

"Come for me, baby. Stop holding that shit. You're not going to feel my dick until I have you sopping wet. Let go, Mist."

"Yes, yes, yes," I cry out as I ride his fingers.

He returns his mouth to my core, and I start to see stars. When he pulls his fingers from my pussy and lifts them to my lips, I immediately suck them into my mouth. He murmurs his pleasure into my center.

King presses his big palm to my stomach and the warmth from it sends tingles all over my body. Locking my leg around the back of his head, I ride his face hard.

My orgasm is so close, like a hook trying to reach the latch, straining for that last centimeter of space to catch. He growls into me and that's it. It's the last tiny push I need to go flying.

In true King fashion, he doesn't stop there. He continues to lap at my core, pushing his face in farther. My pleasure is heightened by the feel of that golden stubble.

I look down my body and lock eyes with those blues. The way he stares back up at me through his long lashes does something to me. It's as if a second hook catches and the trigger is relentless on my body.

I can't stop convulsing. I yelp in surprise when he flips me over and lifts my ass in the air. He parts my ass cheeks roughly and starts to devour me from behind. My eyes roll and I sink into the bed.

"Don't give up on me now." His voice vibrates through me, his breath caressing my skin. He flicks his tongue out against my ass. "You done already?"

I shake my head. "No."

"Good, that's my girl. Lift that ass for me and take this shit like I give it."

I lift my hips defiantly. I'm not going out like no punk. I can take all he's got.

And just like that, he turns it up to a new level. Pushing a thumb in my puckered hole, he puts his mouth to work on my core. I don't know whether I'm coming or going.

"King," I gasp. I try to suck in a breath.

I grab the sheets in a tight hold and bury my face. He slaps the shit out of my ass. "Work them hips. Come get all this. No lazy fucking around here. Put in that work for this."

I look back at him and scowl. He's lucky I don't smother him in my ass. I lift a brow. That doesn't sound like a bad idea.

He goes back to consuming me, but this time I clap my cheeks against his face. I rock and roll my hips, pulling groans of pleasure from him. I think he gets much more than he bargained for.

He fumbles behind me to get out of his jeans and cut. I silently scream through my next orgasm. He doesn't waste time with his T-shirt.

While my pussy ripples with my climax, he thrusts right into me. I bite the sheets to keep from screaming out. He's so hard. It feels so damn good.

The King that has been gentle with me since finding out I'm pregnant is gone. Savage King has returned with a vengeance. I wouldn't want it any other way. I needed this.

He reaches around my body and through my legs for my nub and starts to stroke it. "I must be doing something wrong. I can't hear you, Misty. I need to hear you. Stop playing with me and give me what the fuck I want."

Oh God, he's in one of those moods. Sometimes I wonder if I own any type of sanity. A sane person wouldn't provoke a beast. That's exactly what I did the moment I climbed into his bed for the first time.

"*King*," I scream when he shifts angles and taps right at my spot. He grabs a hold of my hair and starts to ride me hard. Throwing my hips back at him is becoming a task as I drown in his skilled fucking. "Damn it, King. Yes."

"That's all you got? What's my fucking name, baby?"

"King," I cry out.

"Louder," he growls in my ear as he presses his chest to my back. His cologne fills my nostrils, taking over my senses. I just want to eat him up.

I call his name mindlessly. "King!"

"Who's pussy is this?"

"Yours. It's yours."

He cracks a hand across my ass and thrusts deep. "Who do you belong to?"

"You, baby. I belong to you, King."

"Damn fucking right, Misty. Don't ever forget that. Now say my name for the whole damn world to hear who's property you are."

"King, King, King." I keep chanting his name until my throat is too raw to scream it one more time.

"That's my baby."

"Don't stop. I need more," I whisper through my sore throat.

"You better hold on. I'm about to put this ass to sleep."

And. That's. Just. What. He. Does.

CHAPTER THIRTY-THREE

Step UP

King

Dad slaps me on the back before he takes the seat beside me at the clubhouse bar. "What's on your mind?"

"They're calling for me to step up as the organization prez. I was trying to hold out until Uncle Kevlar is released, but a few of the clubs are in a bad way. I just don't know what to do or if I'm ready to take on all that responsibility. I'm not you and I'm not Uncle Kevlar," I reply.

"I don't think that anyone pushing for you to be prez is asking you to be me or my brother. You're a smart man, King. You've done some amazing things while I've been gone. I think you should step up. It's your birthright, your destiny."

"Yeah, but what if that's one thing too much for Misty. With the baby on the way, everything has changed."

He grunts. "So, I guess I didn't run things for years as a single father."

"Dad, that's different," I say. "I had to call in a favor with the senator to keep the DEA off the New York chapter's doorstep. There are too many knuckleheads causing a whole lot of trouble.

"New York is a weak point, Pop knows this, that's why he went there to recruit people to help him with his BS. How long before other MCs realize they're our weakness and go to take advantage of that? The system Sal has built for us, that's something we don't want out there. She and I worked hard on an algorithm that would serve us.

"All it would take is one jealous or envious clown to pull it all apart. And I'd be left standing on the top of the hill with the severed head in my hand covered in blood. Do I really want to put my neck out like that?"

"All good points, but as a leader, you always take risks. At the same time, you do what's best for everyone you're leading. The New York chapter needs you, there're still some good brothers there. Stepping up isn't a bad thing, King."

I mull his worries over. he could be right. Things have been heading in this direction for a long time. I take a deep inhale. my decision is made. I'll do what I need to do.

CHAPTER THIRTY-FOUR

Taunting

Misty

Two months later…

I stand at the door of King's office, peeking out at the main area. It's packed with people we know. Brothers from other chapters, friends, and family. There have to be over three hundred people out there.

"You look so pretty," Rose coos.

She's one to talk, she looks like an angel. I was so happy when she was willing to be a part of the wedding party. I'm surrounded by a loving family. The way the MC life is supposed to be.

The yellow gowns they're all wearing make their wide range of brown skin tones radiate. The spaghetti strap dress complements each of their figures, it was the perfect choice. Everything is perfect.

"You're getting married," Eva squeals.

I place my hand over my belly and smile as I tighten my grip on my bouquet. The feel of the layers of lace scrape against my palm, making this moment surreal. Yes, I'm getting married.

"Hold that thought," Reap says before she runs off holding the hem of her dress.

I stifle my laugh. I think we'll be getting another Lost Soul around here soon. That's the third time this morning. It will be so awesome to get to raise our kids together.

"I can't believe he did this for me," I whisper to no one in particular.

The clubhouse has been transformed into a floral wonderland. There are roses and lilies everywhere. At first, I didn't think they'd be able to pull it off. I was concerned about getting married in the clubhouse, but King reassured me that they would make everything perfect, and they have.

I don't know where to rest my eyes, everything is so breathtaking. I look down the aisle at my handsome, soon-to-be husband. He looks great in his suit, the crisp white shirt causes his tanned skin and blond beard to pop. I'm vibrating with happiness.

Mix holds out his elbow for me and it hits me we're going to do this. All my life I've been in love with this man waiting at the altar for me, and here we are. I'm about to be his for life. My son kicks from inside my womb, bringing tears to my eyes.

I look up at my dad. "I want you to know how grateful I am for all you've done for me and Jacky," I choke out.

"This is all I've ever wanted for you. To see you happy. You couldn't have picked a better brother. I know you'll always be protected and cared for."

"I hope you find your happily ever after, someone to make you happy after all that you've sacrificed to raise us."

Mix throws his head back and laughs. "My old ass ain't finding shit, but I'm happy to see all you young people find it."

"Never say never, Dad."

He gives me a warm smile that lights his entire face. Mix has always been a handsome man. His hazel eyes are sharp and have a sparkle to them. They speak of so much wisdom. Wisdom he has shared with me and Jacky throughout the years. I don't think I could have been loved more by my actual father.

Mix has given us love unconditionally, without asking for anything in return. All in all, I'd say I've lived a blessed life. I turn my attention back to King, impatience filling me.

"Let's get you to the altar before that man tears this place apart," Mix says.

I inhale deeply. "I'm ready."

King

I'm nervous but completely calm at the same time. With all that's going on, now probably wasn't the best time to have a wedding. However, I couldn't wait another day.

I want to be married to my son's mother when he arrives. So here we are. Jacky, Brick, and Grim stand beside me as I wait for my bride to walk down the aisle.

Jacky is full of nervous energy. I'm not sure what's going on with him, but as he pulls his phone from his pocket to look at it again, I turned my attention to him. He has a scowl on his face as he looks at whatever is on the screen.

Rage ignites his green eyes. He's been excited for his sister, so it throws me to see him so distracted and angry today. I know it has nothing to do with us. Although I didn't need it, he gave us his blessing.

"Everything all right?" I lean in to ask.

He purses his lips and shakes his head. "Yeah, I'm good. This is your day. Don't worry about it."

I know right away something is wrong. Once I get this ring on Misty's finger, I'll get to the bottom of it. He'll be heading for New York in a few months, so I want to make sure his head is right before he goes.

He goes to put the phone back in his pocket, but fumbles and drops it on the floor. I chuckle and go to pick it up for him. Rage fills me the moment I see the screen. Without asking, I start to scroll through the pictures before me.

"How long has this shit been going on?" I hiss low enough for him to hear.

Misty stumbles a few steps and almost comes to a stop. Causing me to realize I need to gain control of my expression. I try to reel it in, but it's hard as my gaze turns back to the phone.

"Answers, Jacky. I need answers."

"It's not important right now, it can wait."

"Bro, this motherfucker is so dead," I say, handing him back his phone.

Brick pats me on the back. "That may be, but you can let it go for now. We'll take care of it. Here she comes."

Mix and Misty stop before me. I want to kick myself when I see the worry in her eyes. I take her hand as she searches my face with her gaze.

"What's wrong? What happened?"

"It's nothing."

There's no way I'm going to tell her that her biological father has been sending pictures to her brother with the word *bastard* scrawled across them. Old photos of Jacky as a baby, no more than five. Probably all from before Pop disappeared out of their lives after killing their mom.

I'm sick to my stomach as I understand the hurt I see on Jacky's face. Hasn't that man hurt him enough? Why taunt him like this? The kid is just trying to find his way through his anger, he doesn't need this bullshit.

As if sensing he needs him, I spot my dad out of the corner of my eye as he steps up to Jacky's side, placing a hand on his shoulder to give it a slight squeeze as he dips his head to his ear and whispers something to him. My temper settles as a smile comes to Jacky's face. Dad steps closer to me and slaps my cheek.

"Whatever it is, you both let it go. This is your day and nothing can ruin it. Cherish this moment," Cage says before returning to his seat beside Rose, who's beaming at me and Misty.

I nod my head and licked my lips, focusing all my attention on Misty where it belongs. I place both my palms on her belly as we make our way through this ceremony. Happiness floods me. Even with all the crazy shit going on around us, this is our peace. Each other.

"I love you," I say against her lips before I kiss my bride.

When she comes up for air, breathless, everyone cheers around us. She gives me that smile I love and replies.

"I love you too and always will."

CHAPTER THIRTY-FIVE

Warning

King

As we stand in my office, with the door closed for privacy, my father's face turns tomato red as he scrolls through the pictures on Jacky's phone. I thought he should know what was going on during the wedding and, being that Jacky is his son, and not a bastard, I figured he could calm my brother down because he's been furious for the last few hours.

If anybody can talk some sense into him, it'll be Dad. Although now, from the look on my father's face, I don't know if that was such a good idea. If either one of them could get their hands on Pop right now, they would finish him.

"Jacky," Cage chokes out. "Your mother was sort of a friend to me. She understood there could be nothing between us, so she chose to keep you a secret from me, but I promise you if I would've known, there was no way any other man would've raised you but me. A bastard you are not. You're a Kennedy, nothing but strong men come from my loins. I'm proud to be your father.

"Don't let this maniac take anything away from you. He's nothing but a dead man talking," Dad says. "A dead man I intend to shut up."

Jacky nods with tear-filled eyes. I know this is weighing on him. Watching this go down is tearing me apart. He's a good kid, he doesn't deserve this. It's like I'm watching him fight to climb out of a barrel and Pop just keeps pulling him back in.

"Thanks, Dad," he says after swallowing hard.

Dad pulls him into a bear hug and slaps his back hard a few times. I knew telling Dad was the right thing to do. This is what Jacky has been missing, what he needs. If anyone can help him heal, it will be Dad. Although it's going to be a long road. We're talking thirteen years of damage here.

I pat my brother on the back and nod my head. Thinking to give them a moment, I turned for the door to go get a few beers so we can celebrate. When I step out of the office, the party is in full swing. Misty is on the dance floor with Mix and Rose.

We catch eyes and she gives me a blinding smile. I hate that all of this is happening on her special day. If I can keep it from her, I will.

I head straight for the bar and hold up three fingers to old Jacks, signaling for the brother to hand me three beers. He pops the cap off three longnecks and brings them over. I grab one and take a long pull.

As soon as I turned toward the crowd to people watch, I regret it. Toothless is headed straight for me. I'm not avoiding the brother. He's a good guy, loyal and very protective of the club. He does everything by the book. As I've heard it, he had a part in writing the bylaws.

He's also the member of the club that always knows when something is going wrong. Every time he opens his mouth, it's to tell me that something is about to blow up in my face. It's a gift and a curse. He just has a nose for sniffing out shit. I groan because the last thing I want is to hear some bullshit today.

"Hey, Toothless."

"Hey, King. This is a beautiful spread. Gorgeous wedding, brother. I'm happy for you. I'm also glad you decided to step up and take over as the organization prez. Wanted you to know that the brothers really appreciate it," he says.

I groan again internally. None of that is supposed to go into effect for another week or so. I wanted to go on my honeymoon and live a normal life before stepping into that role. The last thing I need is for Misty to find out how much more I've taken on, especially with the baby on the way. A lot is going to change, and I plan on keeping all club business as far away from my wife as possible.

"I mean no disrespect, brother. I'm not trying to bring you club business on your day I just thought you needed to know this," Toothless says.

And here we go. I brace myself for whatever is about to come out of his mouth. Rumor has it he lost his teeth because he's always bumping his gums. He paid a fortune for the replacements that are in his head now. He has one of the whitest, most perfect smiles I've ever seen.

"A lot of our ATF problems weren't our own doing. The Falcons are involved, they want our territory. I think someone is trying to finish the job they started with your uncle up north."

The Falcons. I've been hearing their name buzzing a little more than I would like. I'm going to have to phone a friend. Trip and I are still friends. While a lot has changed with his MC, our relationship hasn't.

If the Falcons are trying to pull some shit, I'm sure Trip has distanced himself from it as much as he can. Trip and I have an unspoken agreement. We watch out for each other.

He's the one who called to tell me to watch my back. However, I may have to call a sit-down with their prez and figure out what the fuck his problem is. We've had a truce for years, things have been settled. We don't bother them, they don't bother us, but now every time I lift my head, I'm hearing their name out of someone's mouth.

It's simple, you want war with me, say that shit and I'll bring it. There's not a brother around me scared to knock some heads. Actually, there's a few who have been a little bloodthirsty, waiting for some action.

Toothless continues as I muse through my thoughts. "All we need is a new prez that's wise enough to pay attention to the little shit. That's what's been getting us in trouble. Nobody is watching our backs, too many dumb mistakes. I'm sure that will change as you get ahold of the club.

"However, I'm hearing you're about to run into a similar problem. You have something Castro is looking for. You're doing something right and Castro wants to know how. He's still a player on your board, whether you know it or not. And Pop is bending any ear that will listen to get help," he finishes.

"Thanks for the heads-up, brother. You're right, this ain't the day for that and I don't want my new bride hearing any of this. You come see me before you head out. We'll talk then."

There are brothers from several of the chapters here, so I do intend to call a meeting to get updates on everyone's status before they return back home. I need to know what's been going on behind my back. I already know that we have big issues in New York, which is one of the reasons why my brother is going up there, I need someone on the ground to tell me the truth. Jacky is just the Squad member for that.

Misty

"Hey, you," I sing as I walk up to my big, strong husband.

I wrap my arms around his waist. He pulls me into his embrace. There's a smile on his lips, but it's not in his eyes. King has been stressing for weeks and I know it's not just about the wedding.

However, I refuse to ask him about club business, I know better. I'm here if he wants to talk, if he needs me, but I won't press him.

"You all right?"

He kissed my forehead. "Yeah, I'm good."

"Then come dance with your wife, Mr. Kennedy." This time, his smile does reach his eyes.

He places a hand on my belly and escorts me out to the dance floor. "I'm Glad You're Mine" by Al Green begins to play as we get out onto the dance floor. I spot my brother dancing with Sal. Cage and Rose are out on the dance floor together as well. I can't help thinking that this has turned out to be the perfect day.

CHAPTER THIRTY-SIX

Facts

Pop

"Wax, you better have something for me I can use," I snapped at my little brother.

I'm getting tired of his shit. Everything I asked him to do, he manages to botch. No one around me seems to be able to do their fucking job. I'm so close to losing my shit.

I still don't have that operating system that Castro wants. Not to mention I think he's turned into a pussy after some little message the Lost Soul sent him.

That ex-wife of Bricks was an unexpected hitch in my plan. I had no idea she was connected to Castro and could blow things up so badly for me.

If one more thing blindsides me, I'm just gonna set fire to that compound and watch it burn. Enough with all the games.

My daughter means nothing to me today, she married that spawn of my enemy. She's a traitor.

My daughter. The jury's still out on that one. What I need is some solid concrete information.

"Yeah, I found something out for you. She's yours. The DNA test pans out," Wax informs me.

I made it his job to get some of Misty's DNA and prove she's mine. This is good news, I guess.

"Well, I guess that's a game changer. Wedding or not, she's my actual blood. Change of plans, fellas. I need to get my baby girl out. Then we destroy those motherfuckers. It's time to call the Falcons."

I look around the room at my makeshift crew, they'll do for now. The Falcons have some real muscle I can use. That's who I need to finish this. Once I take over the club. I'll get me some members worth having. You're only as strong as your weakest link.

CHAPTER THIRTY-SEVEN

All The Family

Misty

"Hey, Uncle Bear," Eva and Sal chant as the handsome older man walks over with open arms and a wide grin on his face.

Bear is a Lost Soul from the old days. He's been around as long as Cage. He's as old school as it gets. He has a daughter, Frankie, who used to come around. She was on a softball team when we were younger. I can't remember the last time I saw Frankie.

However, when Bear pulls me into a hug, his scent is so familiar and welcoming. It reminds me of the few good times I had memories of.

There are so many Lost Souls here that I remember from my childhood. Of the fifteen chapters, I don't think there's one that's not represented here today. There's New York, Tennessee,

Chicago, of course South Carolina and Georgia, along with California, Nevada, Texas, Alabama, Louisiana, California, Pennsylvania, South Dakota, and New Mexico.

"Look at you girls all grown up. Looks like I'm going to have to start coming around the club again. I'll have a bunch of grands to spoil."

He pulls me into a hug and whispers into my ear. "Damn proud of you, young lady, damn proud. Congratulations." he pulls away and releases me.

"I remember when you all were snotty nosed little brats running around with Frankie," he says.

"Speaking of Frankie. Where is she?"

He pulls the pained face. "Things change, baby girl. Things change."

As we stand around, the photographer continues to take pictures and more people come to congratulate me. My feet are starting to swell and I'm getting so tired. My lower back aches. I say a prayer for my son not to try to make an early appearance today, we still have a few months to go.

Reap ambles over with a scowl on her face. "Everything okay?" I ask.

"Will you and Eva babysit while we handle business?" she asks and rolls her eyes.

"You're pregnant?" Eva asks.

Reap stomps her foot. "This is the last thing I need. They were just talking about patching me in and letting me get my reaper. Now Colin's going to lose his shit. There is no way he's going to allow me to remain an enforcer with a baby on the way."

"You don't know that for a fact. No one else will have his back like you do," Sal says. "You two are to the point of breathing as one. I've watched it with my own two eyes."

"Ugh, I never thought about this part when we hooked up and got married," Reap mumbles.

"Have you told him yet?" Eva asks.

"Not yet, I'm just confirming for myself," she replies.

"Looks like apple juice for everyone around here," I cheer.

"Not me," Sal sings. "But I'll go get you guys some."

"Where's Sugar?" I ask and look around the yard.

"I saw Axel pushing her around in her chair not too long ago," Eva says.

"I think Diggs took her inside to go to the bathroom," Reap says and shrugs.

"The brothers from the other chapters were so bummed out, they were looking forward to getting pieces from her, but she's just not up to it yet," Eva adds.

Yeah, I think it's going to be awhile before Sugar is ready to get back at it, she's been up for about a week and it has been a big adjustment for her. Thor has been hopeful and said she should fully cover after some therapy. Diggs and Axel have been by her side the entire time.

"I'm glad Colin and I didn't make such a big fuss like this," Reap says with a frown on her face. "I mean, it's gorgeous and you look stunning, but this just isn't my thing. I know he felt bad and wanted more, but the money we saved was enough to buy our condo. I'll take living in our own place over living in the clubhouse any day."

"Yeah, that makes sense," I reply. "I guess I got lucky. King already purchased the house before he proposed."

"The prez is always on his shit. You're so lucky. That man is going to take such good care of you. You know you moved up the priority list?"

"Are you kidding me? I don't need the Squad to look after me. I mean, how much trouble can I really get into?"

Reap gives me a pointed look. We both burst into laughter. Just then, Sal returns with our juice. However, our attention is drawn by the rumble of bikes.

The reception is still going, and nobody seems to be leaving yet, so it's odd to hear so many bikes running. I look outside the compound, and I don't recognize any of the bikers that are out there.

"Oh boy," I mutter as Reap pulls her guns from under her dress.

I draw my brows as I realized the cuts of the bikers outside the gate are Falcons. My husband is going to lose his shit. Of all days to pull this, this is not the one. As soon as I have the thought, I see King fly from inside the clubhouse. Spider, the VP from New York, hot on his heels.

King

Someone got the fucking memo mixed up. Somehow these motherfuckers think I'm a pussy. To show up here at *my* compound, on *my* wedding day, they must have lost their motherfucking minds.

Up until this point, everything was going so smoothly. I was just inside talking to one of the senators who happens to be a Lost Soul. I was explaining to him some of the changes I intend to make that will make it easier and more prudent for him to have an affiliation with us.

A lot of the brothers have been getting on board as I've been talking to them today. Yeah, yeah, I'm not supposed to be doing club business on my wedding day, but when else am I going to have so many brothers in my grasp all at one time? I need them to understand how important these changes are for all of our livelihoods.

Business will increase, ownership will increase, and affiliation will increase. Sal is building a system where we can see how our businesses run across the board. We will be able to help one another to grow and understand each business's bottom line.

We ride together, we thrive together that's my main focus. No one has to want, no one has to be left behind. We have enough brothers in the ranks with brains that are phenomenal. Many are borderline geniuses. We can do nothing but win.

Just as I'm ready to pull my piece and light shit up, one of the bikes comes closer to the compound gate. I recognized the rider right away. It's Trip.

We grew up together, went to school together. In our world we should have been enemies, but we began as friends before we even understood the life. It's then that I realize that this is a friendly gesture, because Trip would never disrespect me like this. Falcon or not.

The formation behind him opens up and a flatbed truck pulls through with two bikes on back.

I wave for Teddy to open the gate. The tow truck and the bikers with Trip roll in and park alongside the rest of the Lost Souls. This wedding has just become a lot more interesting.

As the person who called me a few months ago to warn me about the trouble heading my way, I get the feeling that Trip is coming to bring me more than a bike as a wedding gift.

***

"My feelings were hurt when I didn't get an invitation, brother," Trip says.

"No offense, I just didn't want any drama at my wedding."

"Shit, and here I am rolling up with Falcons and a tow truck. All unannounced."

I chuckle. "It wouldn't be you if you didn't. Been bringing drama into my life since kindergarten."

Trip rumbles with laughter, his gray eyes sparkling as he runs a hand through his dark hair and gives that mischievous smile of his.

"No, but I'm here to give you some information I think you should have. They're getting ready to send in an undercover cop to infiltrate you.

"Pretty boy, rich kid. I know you and I know you can work this in your favor. Show them who you really are, brother.

"You're the best there is. What you do for your club is more than anyone has ever done.

"You make honest men out of these brothers. Your families are all fed, every one of your men is taken care of. Don't let them come in here and try to destroy that. You're setting up a blueprint for the rest of us," he warns.

"Thanks, Tripp. That means a lot."

"Not a problem," he says, reaching into his cut and pulling out a thick envelope.

I take the envelope from his hand and give him a nod. Like I said, we've been thick as thieves since we were young. Colors mean nothing between us. My daddy welcomed him in with open arms when we were kids, even though his dad blew a gasket until I saved Trip's life and he had to eat humble pie.

Just then Misty walks over with a curious look on her face. I reach for her waist and pull her into my lap. Trip gives her a friendly smile.

"I remember you," Tripp says. "You finally got his full attention."

Misty ducks and bows her head. "Yeah, I guess I did."

CHAPTER THIRTY-EIGHT

Debt owed

Castro

"Who the fuck do they think they're playing with?" I bellow.

I throw my glass across the room into the wall. I grow tired of all this deceit. That crazy biker has dragged me into the middle of some shit I never intended to be involved in. Yes, there is bad blood between myself and King Kennedy as well as Brick Mason.

Two names I will never forget. They owe me, but it's a debt I've chosen to ignore. I'm a wise man and I've lived this long knowing which battles to choose. There's something about those two, they're just not right in the head.

However, Pop is a different story. I very well plan to collect that debt and pop his head right off his shoulders.

He hasn't bought me the operation system I've asked for and he's brought me into the middle of some private war. Not to mention Magdalena, who has cost me millions of dollars that's now in the hands of King Kennedy.

I have two options here. I can go after my money and seek the revenge I'm owed. Or I could turn my attention to the man who came to me for my help but has yet to deliver a thing on his end. Then there's the matter of my cousin who thinks that I don't know that he was involved with Magdalena and the theft of my millions. I wish King would have sent me his head along with Magdalena's.

For now, I plan to send a message to Pop.

Pop

"I think that meeting went well," I say to Wax as we walk toward the cage I parked in the back parking lot.

"If you say so."

I glare at him and roll my eyes. I'm getting tired of his attitude.

"You know, I'm not forcing you to be here, just know that when you pick a side, you better pick a winning side. I have no problem making sure you're found in a body bag just like the rest of them."

"We're all going to end up in body bags anyway," he mumbles so low, I just barely hear it.

"When I left, I should have taken you with me. Now you're just a little pussy. Go ahead, run back to Cage and the rest of them. See how they treat you when they find out that you betrayed them." I get heated and start to pound my chest. "I'm your family. I'm your flesh and blood. We share the same daddy. Cage ain't never did shit for you, but your loyalty lies with him?"

"Why can't you see that this is crazy? What did Cage really do to you? From what I remember, he was always there for you. Cage and Mix cleaned up the mess that you made with your wife."

I swing at him so hard I spin in a circle, my chest is heaving when I come to a full stop.

"Don't you ever mention Jewels. You were too young to know anything about her or the situation. You've been fucking brainwashed. Cage is all about Cage everything he does for everyone is to benefit him, you'll see."

"Man, fuck this. You have a death wish. You see to that shit by yourself," Wax grumbles and walks off.

"You'll need me before I need you," I yell after him.

I pull on my cut to straighten it and start for my car once again. I'm muttering under my breath about that ungrateful brat when I hit the key fob to unlock the cage. As soon as I press the button, I fly back and land on my ass. The explosion is so hot my brow immediately breaks out into sweat.

Some type of paper or something is floating in the air. I wait for a piece to land beside me and see that it's cards. Jokers in particular. I groan and run a hand over my hair. Castro, I guess he's sending a message.

I need to figure out how to get that operation system. Maybe that info Wax bought me on Kodak is the key. I'm almost positive the youngest girl is the connection. If I can get to her, I can get to that operation system. That big motherfucker she's dating now who rescued her from my guys might just be who I need to target.

Phone in hand, I start to dig for more information. I'll get Castro what he wants so he can get the fuck off my back and then I can handle the Lost Souls.

CHAPTER THIRTY-NINE

What's Mine

Cage

Since we told Rose that accident had happened on the back of my bike, she's been wary to go with me for a ride. I don't blame her. After all, she almost lost her life the last time she rode at my back. Doesn't mean I don't want her on the back of my bike as bad as I want her to remember me.

There's just something about the feel of your woman pressed against your back as you're riding down the road. It's something I've been longing for, for a long time now.

I figured since it's such a nice day, maybe I can get her to go for a ride. Maybe a picnic or something. Some time for us to get to know each other once again.

I walk into the kitchen to find Rose at the stove. I walk up behind her and place a hand on her hip, placing a kiss on the top of her head. She looks up at me with that scared rabbit look in her eyes, as if she's not sure if she should turn and run.

I hold in a sigh, I know it's going to take time. It just feels like it's been forever since I've been able to really hold my wife.

"Would you like something to eat?"

I look over hungrily. "Sure, I wouldn't mind." She blushes and turns back toward the stove and piles eggs and bacon on the plate with some toast.

She then walks over to the dining table where we've been eating every morning. I think I might be getting somewhere. I've seen more looks of interest in her eyes than fear lately.

We're silent for a bit as we both start to eat. I look up and find her staring at me. I lift a brow, allowing her to realize she can ask me whatever she wants.

"Cage, that's not your real name, is it?"

"No, my birth given name is Christopher."

"Oh."

"I've always been good with my hands. There was a time when I would prefer to work on cars more than motorcycles. So, they started to call me Cage."

"That makes sense."

I wipe my mouth with a napkin and push my plate aside. "I was thinking maybe we could take a ride and have a picnic, you can ask me anything you want. I know there's a lot you don't know about me."

She looks down and starts to wring her hands. "The picnic sounds nice, but I don't think I'm ready to get on the back of a bike just yet."

I nod my head. It's better than nothing. At least she's agreeing to go with me.

"We can take the Shelby, no problem," I say. "I'll make us lunch."

"You? You're going to make us lunch?"

I look over and lick my lips. "Baby girl, I was taking care of me and my boy for a long time before you finally stop running from me. I know how to survive on my own. I can cook, clean, do laundry. You be surprised all the shit I'm able to do."

"Well, excuse me, Mr. Kennedy. I truly am learning something new every day." She gives a small chuckle.

"I have so much I want to teach you," I say, dropping my voice and giving her a heated gaze.

It's becoming harder and harder not to flirt. Especially when she's always so breathtaking. I loved her in that yellow dress at the wedding the other day. It took everything in me to keep my hands to myself.

She surprises me with a wicked smile and a wink. "I'm no spring chicken, and I might remember more than you think. It's like riding a bike, boo."

I let a low growl rumble in my chest. We're going to end up in each other's bed sooner or later. Although she still seems a bit skittish, lately she's been flirting back. I can't wait to have those thick hips in my hands once again. She doesn't have to remember me, we've been building a relationship outside of what she remembers. Hopefully she'll fall in love with me all over again.

"You go get ready, I'll get the basket set up and grab us a couple of blankets to bring along."

"Okay," she says shyly. "And, Cage?"

"Yes, darlin'?"

"Thank you. Thank you for everything and thank you for being so patient."

I give her a broad smile. "I'm no stranger to chasing you. I've loved you from the first time I set I eyes on you. If I have to wait another hundred years to have what's mine, I will."

Rose

I stand at the kitchen island with my hands pressed to the countertop, bouncing nervously from foot to foot. This big, strong man is making sandwiches for our picnic. I watch as he cuts the grilled chicken and roasted pepper sandwiches he's made for us into triangles.

My heart warms, I realized that I don't like the large sandwiches, so I do believe this is something he's doing because he knows me well. He wraps each portion in cellophane and places them in a basket. I'm overjoyed when he turns on a pot of chocolate and proceeds to dip over a dozen strawberries into it.

Next, he grabs two blankets and a bottle of champagne from, I don't know where, placing the champagne and a few bottles of water into a cooler. I have to say this man is impressing me. He's not at all who I assumed he was when we first met, or should I say, reunited.

My husband. That sounds so funny. Yet as I stand here, I'm thrown into a memory.

Cage and I were sitting on a blanket in a Meadow. Eva, Sal, and Misty's little giggles filled the air as they chased after one another on their little legs. They were all so small.

Cage had one hand on my belly and the other cupped my throat as his lips were pressed against my ear.

"Darlin', all you have to do is say yes," he rumbled. "I'll take care of you and protect you. I'll make sure the girls are always cared for."

Warmth spread through me and the words were right on the tip of my lips. Just as I was about to answer, Sal ran over and stood at the edge of the blanket.

"Daddy, are there any more pineapples?"

"Sure, baby girl," he replied, digging into the basket to pull out the container to hand to her.

She took it from his hand and dropped to her knees on the blanket as she started to munch on the fresh fruit. Her big brown eyes fixed on the two of us as a huge, happy smile graced her face.

I turned my face up to look at Cage. "When did she start calling you daddy?"

"I don't know, but in my heart, they've been my baby girls since the day you walked into my life."

I'm brought back to the present by Cage's hand splayed on my lower belly. His fingertips so close to my heat. My stomach flips and I stifle a groan.

He dips his head and leans into my ear. "You've been remembering things, haven't you? You get this look in your eyes," he murmurs low.

I shrug it off and go to step out of his embrace. My nerves are a mess. I wonder if he knows what he does to me every time he's so near?

***

This picnic has been amazing. I didn't know Cage has such a sense of humor. I've been laughing so much my stomach hurts. Man, it sounds like we were totally in love and enjoyed everything about our lives.

I drop my gaze to his lips, they look so soft and kissable. I bite my own lip to keep from leaning into him, from pressing mine to his. I can't help wondering what he looked like before the accident. Even with the scars, Cage is a very handsome man. Judging by King and Jacky, he was a striking man, I can see why I fell for him.

"Any champagne left?"

"Nope, we're all out. Judging from the basket, you enjoyed lunch," he says.

"Can you blame me? It was delicious. You have skills."

"More than you know," he says, with a wicked grin and a naughty wink.

I scoot closer and go to lean in to kiss him. However, something over my shoulder grabs his attention. He shoots to his feet so fast I can only look up at him in confusion.

"Do me a favor, stay right here, don't move," he says tightly.

I turn to look in the direction that has his attention. A brown-skinned man dressed in jeans, bike chains, and a cut that doesn't seem to belong to the Lost Souls stands by the car we came in. It looks like he's keying the car. My chest tightens as anger starts to fill me. Who is this person and why is he damaging our car?

Cage storms over toward him like a Raging Bull. I know he told me to stay here, but my gut is telling me that if I don't go, I could end up needing to bail him out. I quickly race in their direction. They're already in the middle of a shouting match when I arrive.

"You piece of shit," Cage bellows. "You know that car belongs to her, you motherfucker."

"Does she remember that you built it for her? I hope she does. The blow will be that much more powerful. I plan to fuck up everything in your life. That grandbaby you have on the way. Your son's business. The entire club. And there ain't shit you can do about it but watch."

"That grandbaby is yours too. The fuck is wrong with you?" Cage rages and lunges at him.

I jump between them, pushing at Cage's chest. "No, don't, he's goading you. Let it go, it's just a car. We can paint it, or you can build me another. New memories can be made, but I can't get another you."

Cage freezes and looks down at me, a wide range of emotions run over his face. Reluctantly, he lets it go, tugging me into his arms to hold me close.

"I'm going to see you again and next time you won't be so lucky," Cage says. "Stay away from what's mine. I so much as hear your name and I'm coming for you."

CHAPTER FORTY

Text

Misty

There's been a ton of activity around the club. However, King hasn't shared with me any of what's going on. I'm not surprised. I'm just concerned.

My husband comes home looking so stressed out daily. I wish there was more I could do. Although, I know the majority of it is club business. I'm taking on more responsibilities at Soul Expressions to take some of the weight off his shoulders. Yet there are only a few months before the baby is due and I have to slow down a bit as well as get the house ready. Eva and Sal have been a great help.

Rose and Cage paid to have the entire nursery decorated. My son isn't even here yet and I know he's loved.

"Hey, Misty," Diggs croons as he walks into my house carrying Sugar.

Axel brings up the rear, pushing her wheelchair. The girls are all coming over so we can have a girls' night. Board games and laughter, that's the goal. Sugar looks up at Diggs with a blush on her face as he sets her down on the couch.

My mouth falls open when he leans in to peck her lips and to my surprise Axel goes over and repeats the same gesture. I have no idea what's going on with these three, but it sure looks like they finally told her how they feel. From the look on her face, I don't think she objects.

"I'm starving. My husband eats all the food in my house. Where's the meat?" Reap calls out as she enters through the front door. "If you try to feed me some finger foods, I'm out, this baby wants food."

Sugar and I snicker at Reap and her antics. She and Colin have been hilarious during her pregnancy. Her bump isn't showing yet, but she sure can eat. I don't know where she packs it all.

"Yo, Reap, where's Grim?" King calls from upstairs.

"I Left his greedy ass in the car, Prez. If I didn't, me and this kid would never get to eat."

King cracks up. "Tell him I need him inside. Don't worry. I'm grilling out back. You ladies will have plenty of food."

"I'm staying," Diggs shouts.

"You're welcome to, brother," King replies. "But know your ass is helping with this crib."

"No problem."

I shake my head. I should have known better. I knew this was going to turn out to be more than girls' night the moment I saw King heading for the grill with a platter of steaks.

Soon the house is full of Lost Souls and their ladies. The women and I gather in the living room, sitting around as we joke and laugh. I look at Eva and frown.

"You don't look like you're going to make it to your wedding," I say as she sits and rubs her back.

Her eyes widen in horror. "Don't say that. Between the discomfort and the fact my fiancé is trying to dig them out every time we have sex, I'm afraid I'm not."

We roar with laughter. Suddenly, Eva bursts into tears.

"Brick," Reap yells through the house.

That big man comes running. "What? What? Where is she?" he asked, looking around wildly for his fiancée.

When his gaze lands on her, he stops and folds his arms across his broad chest. A smile comes to his lips as he saunters over and sits on the edge of my coffee table. I get ready to curse him out for sitting on my furniture until I watch what he does next.

There isn't a dry eye among the pregnant women. Even Sal tilts her head to the side and gives an *aww* face.

As Eva sniffles. Brick reaches for her feet and pulls her shoes off. I'm not even sure where he pulls the honey massage oil from, but he brings her feet to his lap in starts to massage them.

"Aww," I coo.

Grim enters the room with a large plate and sits down beside Reap. I burst into laughter and fall over to my side when she snatches a rib off his plate and starts munching on it. she has barbecue sauce all over her face as he scowls at her.

"What?" she says, holding the rib to the side as she shrugs her shoulders.

Grim drops a kiss on her sticky lips. "You're lucky I love you so much I'll stand in front of a bullet for you. If anyone else snatched my rib, I'd bite their hand off. "

"Whatever. Who made the Mac and cheese?"

"Cage," King replies as he walks into the room with a plate in his hands.

"Oh, give me that," Reap says and snatches Grim's plate.

Something catches my attention at the corner of my eye, and I hold my breath. Sugar scoots to the edge of the couch, grabs ahold of her wheelchair, and tries to stand. King quickly hands me the plate and goes to try to help her. Before he can get to her, Diggs and Axle both pop up out of thin air.

Sugar frowns as each one of them takes an arm. "I'm going to have to learn to do this on my own at some point," she says.

"Not really, what do you need, where do you want to go?" Axel says.

"I have to go to the bathroom."

"No problem. You want to walk or do you want one of us to carry you?"

"I'd like to try to walk if you don't mind."

"Cool, we've got you."

I turned to look at King and lift a brow. He shrugs his shoulders and lifts his palms. I think that's his way of saying it's none of his business. Therefore, it's not mine. I look to Sugar and she gives me a tiny grin. I plan to get to the bottom of this before the night is over.

Right as I have that thought, my phone chimes and I pull it from my pocket. Yes, my sundress has pockets. I place a hand on my belly as I looked down at the text.

Unknown: *we need to talk.*

Me: *who is this?*

Unknown: *your father.*

Me: *what do we need to talk about?*

I tighten my hand on the phone and get ready to block the number. I have no intention of communicating with this man. I remember what he did to my mom, how could I forget?

Unknown: *I'm still your father. There's so much you don't know or understand. What happened between me and your mother was a mistake. I'm a changed man. You and the baby you have on the way are the only family that I have left. I want to get to know you both.*

My heart squeezes. In all honesty, I've dreamed of the day this would happen. I take a peek up at King as I chew on my lip. I wonder how he would feel about this?

Me: *But you're causing trouble for my husband, how can we reconcile when you're threatening everyone I love?*

Unknown: *Things change. Let's call all that water under the bridge. My grandson or granddaughter needs to know where they come from.*

Me: *grandson.*

Unknown: *Oh, a boy. Oh, that's wonderful. What do you plan to name him? Would you consider Alejandro?*

Me: We're going to name him Prince. Sorry, Dad. I don't think we're there yet to name him after you.

Unknown: *But I would love if we could get there. maybe you're next born? Either way, I want to be in your life. It's what your mother would want. We need to talk.*

"What's up with you?" King asks as he chews.

"Nothing, just looking at some last-minute items online," I lie and feel like trash.

However, if I tell him it's my father, he'll stop the calls now. If there is a way a truce can be made, and I can get my father back at the same time. I want to at least try. My heart tugs. I hate that I lost my mother and my father. Mix has been everything, but it's still not the same.

Who wants to know their father is out there, but he just doesn't want to know you? This text gives me hope. Maybe he does actually want to know me.

CHAPTER FORTY-ONE

What's going on

Misty

We've moved outside to the Jacuzzi. Diggs and Axel thought it would be good for Sugar to sit in the warm water for a while. The girls and I all have nonalcoholic beverages. Our bellies are full and the laughs and entertainment keep rolling.

It's a good thing that our property is secluded because King is blasting rock music through the house. I guess we should enjoy it before we have a little one here and we can't make any noise. Rose is sitting in the Jacuzzi with Sugar.

She's so cool. I love having her around. Eva and Sal are so lucky.

"So," I say, looking pointedly at Sugar. She blushes that deep purple blush of hers. "I was wondering, would you like to share with us what's going on with you, Axel and Diggs?"

"I knew that was coming," she says.

"Okay, I wasn't going to ask, but I want to know too," Reap says.

"They may have both told me they're interested in me and we might be giving it a try to see if we can all work it out," Sugar replies.

"Oh my," I croon. "Things are getting spicy. No, seriously, how do you feel about all of that?"

"At first, it was a lot, but I can't say that it doesn't have its benefits or appeal."

"So, wait. Let me get this straight. You guys are sharing? Like sharing, sharing?"

"Okay, let me stop you all there. I think you all have the wrong idea. We all have something to offer and we each provide something to make a healthy relationship. Like a team. We each have a position to play in order to win the game."

"Owww, girl, I like the way that sounds. You play your position. I'm not mad at you," I say. "But damn that's a whole lot of fine."

"Right," Sal, Eva, and Reap say in unison.

Sugar sloshes water at us.

"What? I'm just saying," Reap says. "I see why you're in a rush to get back to yourself."

We all burst into laughter. I totally agree with Reap. Axle and Diggs are two fine ass men. I'd be in a rush to get back to one hundred percent too.

"You know, you and Grim would look crazy good on camera, I'm just saying. Since we're throwing things out there," Sugar says.

"All right, all right, I don't think King would approve Sensual Souls as a business," I say.

"Sensual Souls, I like the sound of that," Reap chimes in. "I'll have to bring that up in church."

We all giggle. This is exactly what we needed. Even King has seemed more relaxed tonight. Family and good food will do that to you.

CHAPTER FORTY-TWO

Church

King

I bang the gavel, bringing church into session. We have an extensive list for tonight. All things that I need to get in order before I send my brother out there into the world and before I truly step up as the organization prez.

"First on the list, does anyone know where Pop is? Has anyone gotten a hit on his location since he showed up at Dad's picnic?"

I look around at all the grim faces as they all shake their heads. Not one person able to lift their eyes to look at me out of shame for not being able to pin down this bastard. I don't blame them, I'm disappointed, but I don't blame them. Pop is one slippery SOB.

"I was able to get the scratches out and repaint the car for Cage," Ashton answers.

"Thanks, brother, send me the bill."

"Next item. We've all seen the file on what's going down in New York."

The room fills with grumbles. Everyone here has seen what's in those reports Gutter presented to us. The New York chapter has fallen to shit.

They've been infiltrated by snitches and rats. The chapter is pretty much eating itself. After their chapter prez had a stroke about a year ago, things have since fallen apart.

Spider has been trying to keep the chapter on the up-and-up, but there are a few resistant members who have made that difficult for him. Not to mention the acting prez is no good.

"The first order of business in New York is to remove Thorax."

There's an actual FBI investigation open against them. If it weren't for Clayton Hennessey, they'd all be locked up by now. As a good friend of Brick's, Hennessey has been doing all he can to block what's going on there since my requests a few weeks ago.

"We're sending Jacky up north. We're hoping he can back Spider up. They're going to need a major clean out. Which means a whole lot of changes for their chapter.

"Some of that may blow back since we're the mother chapter. There's always been a conflict between South Carolina and New York because while my uncle started New York, my daddy started the one here. New York has always felt that it was the first. And there are a lot of brothers who'd argue this fact."

"Everyone here needs to keep their nose clean. That means not a single out-of-pocket activity. If it's not your business, then it shouldn't be your business. I'm taking any patch that goes against this order. No exceptions. You feel me?" I finish.

"Prez, what about those guns we have coming in?"

"Find someone to dump them on. As a matter of fact, Brick, see if Trip is willing to take them."

"Got it."

"Are you sure you don't want me to go up with Jacky?" Grim says. "I can make the transition very easy."

"I thought about that, brother, but it's best if we let Spider establish himself. If we roll in and do things our way, then he doesn't establish the power he needs to."

Grim nods his head with a thoughtful expression. I've thought about this and the best way to do it. Jacky is strong enough to establish authority as a second while still allowing Spider to rise as the head.

"Jacky also understands the Squad system. He'll be able to recognize the leaders there and help Spider to establish his own twelve."

"How about the other chapters?" Mix asks.

"I need to make a trip to Tennessee. I believe I have a prez for them in mind, it's just a matter of whether the brother wants to move out there or not. Give me some time on that one.

"However, the other chapters seem to be stable. One or two have some financials that could be doing better. I'll help with that. Unless anyone else has anything they want to share with me?"

They respond with grunts. I look around the room.

"Okay, if there are no other issues, let's hear from the treasurer and the secretary and then this meeting is adjourned."

"Oh, one more thing. Pop threatened my unborn son. Find him."

CHAPTER FORTY-THREE

Jacky

"My dad and King think it's best for me to move to New York. I'm going to move into Sal's old apartment. In a way, I'm glad. I need this change," I say to my sister.

We're sitting out in the clubhouse's backyard while she sunbathes. I'm about to leave her right here. This sun is frying my white ass. I run a hand through my curly locks to push them out of my face.

"You sure you want to do this?" she asks with tears in her eyes. "You can at least wait until after the baby comes."

"But they need me there now. I'll be back to meet him."

"What's the hurry?"

"Things are volatile in New York, they need the stability of a new president and a VP. They need their own squad. All things King is depending on me to help them make happen."

"But you're only eighteen. Can't Vault or Axel or one of the other brothers go?"

"I'm not a baby, Misty. King can count on me as much as he can one of the others. I'm going because I'm the right person for this."

She sighs and rolls her eyes. "I'm not saying you're a baby. I'm saying you're *my* baby brother, and I don't want you to leave."

"You had to know that I was going to leave sooner or later. I've never found my place here and I need to do this for me. Please, Mist, try to understand."

"All right. All right, but you have to promise to call me at least once a week."

"That's your way of allowing me to grow up?"

"It's the best you're going to get. Take it or leave it."

"All right, I'll take it. Once a week. I want pictures as soon as that kid is born."

"Is it weird for you?"

"What, being the kid's uncle? Yeah, it is kind of weird that you married my brother and you're my sister."

"In all fairness, you're half brother to both of us."

"Not making it better, Misty. You will always be my entire sister there isn't a part of you I won't claim. Just put yourself in my shoes, I want to find that in my own life. To be someone's person, for them to accept all of me."

"I hear you, Jacky. It was a bad joke. I'm sorry."

I narrow my eyes at her as I whip my head back to get my long hair out of my face. Gathering my hair together, I pull it back into a knot. Misty reaches to brush back the fine baby hairs around my temple.

It reminds me, I need to stock up on my shampoo and ship it to New York. It's a hard brand to find and the only one I use. I actually lose my shit when I can't find it. Old issues.

"Do me a favor, whatever you do, don't cut your hair while you're gone. It's you."

I kiss my sister on the cheek. "Never." I wink at her.

"Oh my God, I hope Prince is as handsome as you. I can just see it now. The honey-blond hair. The silky curls. Remember when you were little? You were so cute."

"Nah, you're cuter than me. He'll probably look just like Cage and King."

"Oh, shut up. Like you don't look just like them." She cups my face and shakes my head back and forth. "You've always been handsome. The ladies adore you."

"Ladies, I don't have time for that shit. I'll leave all that love stuff to you and King."

"You say that now, but once you meet the one, she's going to have you wrapped around her finger, I know it."

"That will be the day."

"I'm proud of you Jacky, we've come a long way. Don't let that night destroy who you are. Let it go, forgive and move on, become to the man you're meant to be," she says.

I purse my lips and squint at her. I can understand her not wanting me to kill her father, after all, he is her father. However, that man owes me something. I'm taking his life sooner or later. For now, she can believe that I'm letting it go. The last thing I want is to hurt my sister.

I nod my head and pull her into my side for a hug. "Don't worry about it."

Misty

I've tried my best to mind my business, but enough is enough. I'm not happy that King is sending Jacky away. I walk into King's office at the clubhouse and sit on the edge of his desk.

"What aren't you telling me? What's so important that he has to go now? I get that things are a mess in New York but I feel like there's something else you're just not saying."

"Mist, I'm going to need you to leave this one alone. There is a ton of shit going on right now that I just can't share with you. Can't you just trust me as your husband?"

"I trust you, but I get this feeling like… I don't know you're holding back information, information that I should probably know."

"And if you needed to know, I would have told you."

I roll my eyes and cross my arms over my chest. King pulls me to him and places his hands on my belly.

"Come here. You know I would never send him into harm's way, don't you? Everything's going to be fine. I've always got you, Misty, every part of you. Your brother, our son, I'll take care of it all. Sometimes you don't need to know because you don't need to know how far I have to go to get it done. I'm handling it."

Something about the conviction in his words causes me to relax. I truly do believe that King will do everything in his power to make sure our families are safe. Jacky included.

CHAPTER FORTY-FOUR

Still Don't Get It

Misty

Present, Six months later...

"Am I wrong, Misty?" King growls.

"No." I pout.

"Do you remember any of that shit?" he continues.

"Yes," I mutter. "But King. I had to do this. You don't understand."

I'm pleading a lost cause. He's totally pissed off. There's no calming him down at this point. I should just shut up.

I look into his heated glare and sigh. He's not done. I know this is just the beginning. I might be better off sitting in a cell.

He hasn't spoken a lie. I'm always finding my way into trouble. I have a hard head and a need to defy. I challenge King every chance I get.

I know I drive him crazy. I just can't help myself. Although, this time, I can honestly say I did what I thought was the right thing to do. I had to.

"Why, Misty?" King snarls. "Why do you need to get your ass in the middle of shit? You know what? I should just keep your ass pregnant. It's the only time you listen and do as you're told."

I frown at him and his words. I can't help myself. I let a snarky smile touch my lips as I think of when I was pregnant. I wasn't that obedient.

"Are you fucking kidding me? Is she smiling?" King tugs at his dreads.

"I'm not smiling," I protest.

"Yes, yes, the fuck you are," he points a finger at me.

"Brother," the detective speaks up, seeming to remind us both we're still in this apartment and others are here with us, witnessing all this. "Whatever you're going to do, we need to move. I'm not going to be able to hold this off much longer."

King turns to him and glares. He turns his head back to me, narrowing his eyes. I can see him thinking. The tears burn the backs of my eyes.

I truly think he's going to let me go to jail. He looks that pissed off. I'm so fucking screwed. King's next words sink my heart. He confirms my worst fears.

"Put her in your car. She still doesn't get it," King grunts.

"Wait, I get it. Please, King. Don't do this," I plead.

"You don't get shit," he snaps. "I'm tired of it. Time and time again, you stick your nose in places it doesn't belong. You defy me every step of the way, and you keep shit from me that I need to fucking know."

"King," I try.

King cuts his hand across his throat. "No, when will it end?" His eyes fill with hurt. "When I lose you? When our son loses his mother? Fuck, Misty.

"Every brother in the club would put his life on the line for you, but you pull this shit. I don't know what's worse. This shit or that bullshit you pulled with Pop. I'm done. I can't," King growls, turning to leave the apartment.

His words sting so much, I can't even say a word. I know how much I've already hurt King. It was the reason I tried to handle this more smoothly this time. *Shit.* I feel like crap. For him to equate this to *that.*

I guess he has a point.

King is right. I haven't learned my lesson. I look around as the detective lifts me to my feet. Eva hangs her head low as Brick has an arm wrapped around her. Grim has a tight hold on Reap's waist.

All four of them have somber looks on their faces. Yeah, we've taken some hits in the past year. Prince and the other children were such welcome blessings by the club and everyone around us. Then we had those moments that shaped who we all are today.

It's my reason for being here tonight. I had a reason for doing everything I did. I just didn't think about how that would hurt King, *again.*

The detective walks me out of the apartment and helps me into the back seat of his SUV, still in cuffs. I'm surprised to find King in the front seat. I lick my dry lips, trying to think of the right thing to say to him.

We pull off and I still haven't found the words. I can see King's jaw ticcing as he stares out of the window. He's so mad.

That vein in his temple that pops when he's ready to explode is pulsing.

"If you'll just let me explain."

"How can you possibly explain this? Do you know how fucking lucky you are? You could've been killed in there or worse, it could've been someone else that responded to the scene.

"Everyone's putting their necks on the line for this one. You fucked up this time, Mist. You fucked up bad."

"I know." I start to sob.

He sighs. "Go on, Misty. I want to hear this. Explain."

I lick my dry lips again as I stare down in my lap. "It all started the week after... after I had that meeting. About six weeks ago. You were already so stressed out."

Here we go again.

CHAPTER FORTY-FIVE

How It Started

Misty

Seven weeks earlier...

"Hey, babe," I say cautiously as I stand in King's office doorway.

He lifts his head and grunts. He's still pissed at me. I can't blame him. What I did was sort of stupid.

I saunter to his desk and slide onto the edge. He's watching me closely. I cup his face and kiss his lips.

"I'm sorry. Please talk to me."

"If I talk to you, I'm going to yell. I'm not ready to talk," he says and pulls his face from my hand.

"Then listen," I say. "He's my dad, King. My flesh and blood father. I thought I could reason with him."

"Are you fucking kidding me?" he roars. "You have to be kidding me. Pop wants me dead. He wants my father dead. He wants our son dead. How are you reasoning with that shit, Mist? Do you not realize he's the one that sent that guy after Terry and that rapist after Sal for a second time?

"Come on. You're smart as fuck. How do you go and do some shit like that? You know what, don't answer that. Smart has nothing to do with sanity. Your fucking little ass is crazy."

"I didn't know that. King—"

"Misty. I told you I don't want to talk to you. Respect that shit and get out of my face."

"Hold on. You don't have to talk to me like that. I know you're mad, but don't make me curse your ass out."

His entire face turns red. I think I just pushed too far. King talks to everyone just the way he feels.

He points a finger at me. Baring his teeth, he shakes his finger at me as if in warning for me to stay put. He marches to his office door, slams and locks it and storms back over to me.

I place my hand against his chest when he returns to hover over me. It's no use. I can't hold him off. He's all up in my face.

"Tell me what you don't understand about you being every fucking thing I live for? Go on, I'll wait."

I lower my eyes. I feel like shit. I didn't mean to make him so mad at me. I really thought I could help. I was nine the last time I saw my dad. How was I supposed to know the man was truly sick in the head? He used to beat the shit out of my mom, but he was never abusive to me.

"I… I'm so sorry."

He tilts his head. "Sorry? Sorry for what? For taking my son where that maniac could've harmed him. Sorry for going to see that lunatic behind my back? For taking his calls for months and not telling me. What exactly are you sorry for?"

"Prince was in the car with Eva. He was safe—"

"Bullshit," he bellows.

"If Cage and I didn't get there when we did, he would've been gone with you and our son. That motherfucker was plotting on you. I've taught you better, baby. You've learned this life in and out. You knew better."

"He's, my dad. I didn't think—"

"Exactly! You didn't think. You got emotional and let that fucker in here." He taps my temple. "He's a master at that shit. It's why Cage warned you to stay away from him. But *no*. You go and try to hand that motherfucker my life.

"He wouldn't have had to pull the trigger, baby girl. All he had to do was take my wife and son. I would've been shit to the world. I'd be the walking dead. You don't get to hand people that kind of power over us. You feel me?"

"Yeah." I nod as the tears fall. "I feel you. I was wrong."

He throws his head back and blows out a breath. "Stop crying, Mist. That shit guts me."

I try to stop the tears. I start to sniffle and my breath catches. He groans and takes my face in his hands, pressing his forehead to mine.

"I love you. Stop crying," he murmurs and kisses my lips. "Only time I want you crying is when I'm inside you, knocking them walls down. Hush up. I'm pissed but you're still everything to me."

This time, for the first time in a week, he takes my lips and kisses me deeply. I fumble with his belt and jeans. I need to feel him. I need him to show me his words are true.

He's been so mad at me. I haven't been sure we'd make it. Wife or not. I was sure he was going to divorce my ass.

I get his pants down his hips as he pushes up my sundress. He shifts my panties aside and thrusts inside me. I allow my head to fall back, and my mouth falls open.

King starts to kiss and suck his way down my neck as he rocks into me. He grunts as if he's not getting deep enough. Tugging me closer to the edge, he thrusts harder. My teeth chatter.

He wraps his hand around my throat and squeezes firmly, tilting my head back. "Fuck, I've missed you. Your hardheaded ass drives me so crazy. Let me take care of you, baby. Stop trying to do my job for me. You hear me?"

"Yes," I gasp as he thrusts into me repeatedly with strong strokes.

King

I could've killed Misty for that shit last week. Eva was suspicious of the guy she'd been sitting in the diner with. Eva also didn't like that Misty wouldn't let her go inside with her.

It turns out Eva doesn't remember Pop, since she was only about nine when he disappeared. The truck started to get too hot for the three kids and Eva texted Brick to send him a picture of the guy Misty was sitting with in the diner.

Cage and I lost our shit and jumped on our bikes to finally get our hands on Pop and keep him from harming my family. That motherfucker has been threatening my son, my father, and anyone close to my father, which includes me. I had no idea he was messing with Misty's head, making her think he wanted to resolve things so he could be in her and Prince's life.

All hazards of not telling your woman what's going on in club life. If I told her all the shit going on around here, she wouldn't have gone within ten feet of that motherfucker. Pop is taunting me and Cage. The only question we have is which one of us is going to put him to ground first.

I look in Misty's eyes and my heart bleeds for the little girl who lost her daddy and wants to believe he's still a good human. He's not. He's a piece of shit that's going to meet his maker.

"I love you, King," she moans as her walls squeeze around me.

"Then act like it. Stop making me crazy," I grunt, and bury my face in her sweaty neck. I lick her skin and savor her taste. "I'm going to spank your ass next time."

"I thought you wanted me to behave," she pants.

I growl. "See. Straight crazy and I'm right there with you because I love your ass so much."

I push her back down on the desk and throw her legs over my shoulders. Pulling her ass over the edge of the desk, I go crazy in her pussy. Coming close to losing her was too much to bear.

I can't control my need to take her hard against my desk. We said we'd wait for Prince to turn one before having another baby. That shit ain't happening.

"King," she cries out as if she can't take another single stroke, but take she does. Every single stroke I give she takes.

"Fuck," I roar as my own release sneaks up on me and floods her pussy. "Damn."

I drop my head between her breasts. I tighten my jaw as I remember why I was so pissed at her in the first place. I lift up and pull out of her body.

She looks up at me with a plea in her eyes. "Don't."

"I'm not. I'm still pissed though. That's not going to just go away because we fucked."

She sighs. "I know. Maybe we can…"

She trails off when a knock comes at the door. I fix her clothes before fixing mine. Kissing her forehead, I say, "We'll talk at home. I got shit to get done around here. We good?"

"I hope so."

"We're good."

CHAPTER FORTY-SIX

What To Do

Misty

"Oh my God, you smell that?" Reap gasps. She looks down at little Colin strapped in the carrier on her chest and frowns. Then she whines. "Why? And he's smiling. He's just like his father. I need to find someplace to change his stink little ass. Ugh."

I can't help laughing at her. He is smiling with all his adorable little stink self. Thank God Prince is fast asleep in his stroller.

"I'll come with you. These two are probably soaked by now," Eva says.

"I'm going to run into this store. I've been eyeing a skirt and some shoes in there," I say.

I just changed Prince before he fell out. We'll have to head home soon, and I want to get to this store before my son wakes and demands we leave. Lord, the boy has a set of lungs on him.

Reap grumbles and marches off to find a bathroom. Eva follows behind her, giggling to herself. I walk into the store and head for the rack with the skirt I'm looking for.

Reap has been whipping all of our asses back into shape. I think I have a more toned and fit body after having my son. Reap can be a little hardcore.

"They were just saving you all for themselves, I guess," someone snarls behind me.

I turn to find a greasy-looking guy standing behind me, glaring at me and my son. I squint and it hits me who he is. He looks like shit.

"Striker?"

He licks his teeth. "So, you remember me. I always wanted a piece of that ass, but I could tell Prez had a thing for you. He was always watching you when he thought no one was looking. You and Eva were on the top of my list. Bitch got me thrown out the fucking club."

"No, you got yourself thrown out of the club. Did you really think it was a good idea to grope the prez's sister?"

"I had too much to drink. I wasn't thinking," he snarls.

"Why is this my problem?"

"Because my life turned to shit because of your old man. I know shit. I know shit that can take the entire club down. I have a connect with the ATF. One call and it all goes up in smoke."

I ball my fists. King will beat the shit out of him. I want to watch when he does.

"What do you want?"

He moves forward and runs a finger down my cheek. It feels like my skin starts to crawl. I jerk my head away. I'm so not about to fuck this guy. He's out of his fucking mind if he thinks that's what's going to happen.

"If you never would have opened your big fucking mouth this would have gone away. I would've apologized to the brothers and King never would've had to know," he says tightly.

"You're delusional. You're lucky you're still breathing."

"I was just about to move up in the ranks. That money was so fucking good. Then poof. You opened your mouth, and it was over."

"You still haven't said what you want."

"I want reparation. You're the prez's old lady. You have access to the cash. You can get me what I want."

"You're insane. How in the world am I supposed to get you cash? I don't have access to any money to give you."

"You're going to find it or else that kid and all those other little bastards you whores have been pushing out will be fatherless. They're all going down. Every Lost Soul, cop, politician, businessman, runner— I'm taking them all down," he hisses.

Why the hell didn't King kill him? I tighten my fists. King isn't stupid. There's no way Striker's threats can be valid. He doesn't have a leg to stand on. I get ready to tell him to go fuck himself, but his words give me pause.

"Before you start thinking you're smarter than me or that I can't make good on my word, know this. I was a cop. Internal affairs tore into my ass and took my badge after I lost my patch. I was kicked off the force, but I still have friends that are salivating to take the Lost Souls down," he warns.

"Take this shit to King. It has nothing to do with me."

"It has everything to do with you. I'll make your life miserable if you don't do every fucking thing I say. That pretty job you have at Soul Expressions… it ends if King gets locked up. All the assets of every single company will be frozen. You and your pretty little friends will be jobless and whoring to feed your brats.

"That is, if you're not thrown in jail with your man. Just think, your little boy will be raised in foster care, or better yet, don't you have a crazy-ass daddy that's looking for revenge? What if he were to end up with your boy?

"After all, I got shit on your little brother too. He's old enough to go to max as an adult now," he says with a slimy grin.

I bare my teeth and growl at him. Totally a King move, but I feel that shit in my soul. This motherfucker is threatening my family. *My* family.

"You're digging your own fucking grave."

"You say a single word to King and all bets are off. My boys will blow the whistle."

"You dirtbag. You won't have to worry about my husband."

"That shit is sexy. We may need to get to know each other better before this is all over. I'll be in touch."

He takes off without another word. I pull my phone out to call King and pause. What if he does have something on the club? I close my eyes and bring my phone to my chest.

"Hey, you all right?" Reap's voice causes me to open my eyes.

"Yeah, I'm fine. I need to get home."

"Did you get the skirt you wanted?" Eva asks.

"No, they don't have my size." Just then Prince wakes and starts wailing. "Let's go."

King

"Why can't anyone find me this motherfucker?" I snarl as I look around at my brothers.

Pop has fallen off the map again. I want this fucker dead so I can move on with my life. That shit he pulled with Misty was the final straw. When I find him, I'm putting my boot in his fucking neck.

"He's playing mind games. The sick bastard," Mix says.

"He's pissing me the fuck off. That's what he's doing," Cage adds.

My father has been just as livid as I have. Pop has turned his world upside down once again. First, all the shit with the accident, then that bullshit he pulled with Jacky, now this shit with threatening me and Prince. My dad is like a caged animal ready to explode out of his confines.

"He's going to make his next move soon. He's too arrogant not to. He knows he pissed you off. I say we continue to wait him out. Going on the attack is only going to expose us. That's what he wants."

I look at Brick and clench my fist. I know he's right. Pop needs us to make wrong moves. I'm not that kind of asshole. I'm smarter than that. I think that's why he went after Misty. He needs me to lose my head and fuck up.

Not gonna happen.

"Find him," I bark. "We don't need to press him before he moves, but I want to know where the fuck he is and how he's moving."

"We'll get him," Grim says.

I grunt and drop the gavel to end the meeting. I want to get home to my wife and son. I've been missing them since they left to go shopping.

I wouldn't have let them go if Reap hadn't been going along. I'm tightening the reins around here. Too much going on.

I get up to leave, but my father gives me a look. I sigh and remain in my seat. Obviously, I'm not going anywhere.

"You heard from your brother?" he asks when everyone has filed out.

I purse my lips. "No. He's still in New York. Spider says he's all right. Working in the financial district. Clayton is keeping an eye on him."

"Hennessey?"

"Yeah."

My dad pulls a hand down his face. I can see the stress lining his features. This thing with Jacky has been weighing on him.

"You and Misty good?"

"She drives me crazy but we're fine."

He chuckles and sits back in his seat with his arms folded. "I remember when Rose was wild and sassy. Boy, did that woman make me chase her."

"You loved every minute of it. I remember. You would get this look in your eyes when you were getting ready to run after her." I laugh.

"Might be a family trait. We like us some crazy ass women."

His eyes turn distant for a moment. Probably thinking of a life that has passed. Everything has changed for Dad and Rose. I sigh, not wanting to dive into that.

He turns his focus back on me. "Go home. Kiss my grandson for me. Enjoy every moment while you can, King. It goes by so fast."

He reaches over and pats my cheek. I give him a nod. That's just what I plan to do. Go home to my family.

CHAPTER FORTY-SEVEN

Tired of This

Misty

"What's my name?"

"*King.*"

"Whose pussy is this?"

"It belongs to you, King. Only you."

He's being exceptionally rough. Much rougher than usual. His hold on my hips is so tight, it feels like he might break the skin. He's pounding into me hard as his sweat drips onto my back. When he reaches for my arms to hold them behind my back, I start to sob loudly.

My phone starts to ring, and I roll my eyes in frustration. I'm on the cusp of my fifth orgasm. Fuck that phone. I'm going to die this death by orgasm in peace. Somehow, we haven't managed to wake Prince, so we're not stopping. Besides, I have a feeling I know who that is on the line.

A loud growl rips through the room as King releases into me. He collapses beside me and pulls me onto his chest. My phone chimes with a message and I go to check it.

"Where are you going?" King asks as I scoot to the edge of the bed.

"I need some water after that," I turn to him and wink.

I get up on shaky legs and head downstairs, my phone clenched in my hand.

"I can't keep doing this," I mutter to myself and push a hand into my hair.

I'm getting so tired of this shit. Striker calls at least once a week, asking for more money. I've been giving him cash out of my account. King doesn't monitor my bank account. He just sends an allowance and extra if I ask. My paycheck also goes there.

I'm sick of giving Striker my money, I'm sick of sneaking around, and I'm sick of him threatening my man and my family. I want this shit over.

I pace my kitchen as my mind races. That bastard called in the middle of King fucking my brains out. I didn't answer because I'm not stopping sex for no one but my crying son. Prince is fast asleep, so there was no way I was answering shit.

"I hope you're not up to anything stupid. You answer my calls or I'm going to hand you all over to the ATF. You keep trying me," Striker says when I call him back.

I find out what he wants and quickly end the call. I'm *so* tempted to run right upstairs to tell King about everything. He'll put an end to all of this. My phone buzzes in my hand just as I have the thought.

Unknown: *Don't get any ideas. Your brother is so young. Would be ashamed for him to get locked up.*

Unknown: *Have my money by tomorrow. Same time, same place.*

I scowl at the phone and grind my teeth. I'm going to beat his ass until blood pours out his mouth. I promise I am.

I have to figure something out. I need to know how valid this threat is. I'm done wondering.

I need facts. I need to know if Striker can be touched without harming my family. I won't continue to live like this. If I can just get the answers I need, then I'd know if I can tell King without this blowing back on everyone.

Someone has to be able to help.

"Here she is. Here's mommy," King croons.

I turn to find him shirtless, in a pair of sweats, with our son in his arms. Prince has red cheeks and a pout on his face. I can tell he was crying. My heart squeezes at the sight of my man and my son. I can't let anything happen to King or any of the rest of our family and friends.

I release a heavy breath. I have to figure out what to do. I'm not going to be able to sustain Striker's demands for much longer.

"Hey, little guy, what's the matter?" I coo at my son, plucking him from his father's arms.

"We're missing our girl," King says, wrapping his arms around us. "I thought you were just coming down for some water. I was trying for one more round before this little guy woke."

"Sorry, Eva called."

The lie tastes like shit in my mouth. This… this is the part I hate the most. I never lie to King. This shit has me lying to him and it's not sitting well with me at all. It's getting harder to get away and not lie. King always wants someone around to watch me. I've had to get creative.

"You guys working out tomorrow with Reap?"

"Yeah, are you working from home? I wanted to go get my hair and nails done."

He kisses the top of my head. "I'll stay with Prince so you can have some girl time. I'll give you some cash, make a day of it. Just make sure Reap's with you. She can bring Colin over if she doesn't have a sitter."

Yup, I feel like complete shit. Lower than shit. I've been lying for a month, and he's been nothing but the perfect husband.

"How does that sound, Prince. You want to hang with your old man and your little buddy? We can get into all kinds of trouble. Titty milk and TV for everyone," he coos at our son.

Prince squeals at him and bounces in my arms. I love them so much. King dips his head to blow a raspberry against the baby's neck.

"Do you need me to help with that job? I can work on some of the graphics tonight if you need."

"I'm good, baby." He releases me to move over to the refrigerator.

"Maybe we can take a trip up to the cabin. I think Prince would like it up there," I say.

King shakes his head as he closes the door after taking out some grapes. He pops a few in his mouth and leans against the kitchen island. When he levels those blue eyes on me, I see that shift in his mood instantly.

"Nah, we can't take off that far yet," he says.

I frown. I should've known that. I was just thinking about getting away from all of this.

If I have King alone away from here, maybe I could tell him what's going on without him being reactive. If he reacts right away, that could set Striker off. I won't be the trigger to that gun.

"You okay?" King's voice brings me back from my musing.

"Yeah, just tired." I kiss my son's head. "I'm going to see if I can get him back down. You coming?"

"Need to make a few calls."

"See you upstairs."

King

"Do me a favor, brother," I say into the phone once I know Misty is out of earshot.

"Name it," Grim says.

I've never been a fool in my life. I know my wife too well. Something ain't right.

"Have Reap glue her ass to Misty until further notice. Some shit ain't fitting. If it's Pop fucking with her, I want his head."

"You got it. I'll talk to her tonight."

"Thanks."

I hang up. Staring in the direction Misty and my son just left in, I narrow my eyes. She's not crazy enough to go behind my back with that fucker, Pop. I know she's not.

So, what are you up to, Misty?

CHAPTER FORTY-EIGHT

Crossing Paths

Misty

"Okay, you're going to need to tell me what the fuck is going on with you," Reap says.

I've been trying to find a way to ditch her all day. I just barely pulled it off last week when King gave me that spa day. I stare ahead at the road, ready to make a decision.

I lick my lips and turn for the park. She doesn't take her eyes off me. I can feel her staring a hole in the side of my face.

I park the car at the little park we take the babies to sometimes. Erica goes to say something, but I shake my head. I've become so paranoid. We get the boys out of their car seats and head for the swings. Once they are settled and swinging, I start to talk.

"I need help."

"What's going on? Should I call Prez?"

"God, no. He can't know about this until I find out how serious this shit is. Do you remember that brother, Striker?"

"Yeah, personally, I never liked him. He had this creepy way of looking at us. I can count the number of times I almost throat punched him," she replies.

"I wish you would've," I grumble. "He's been blackmailing me. He says he has shit on the prez and the club. I've been giving his dirty ass money."

"You have to be shitting me."

I huff. "I wish I were. I need to find a way to see if this shit he has is legit. If he runs to the ATF, will they have enough to harm us."

"You leave this shit to me. I'll see what I can find out."

"You have to be careful, Erica. He said if I said anything, he'd blow the whistle. I want to know if he can hurt my family without hurting my family. And if he's full of shit, I want to put his ass to ground for putting me through this bull," I hiss.

"I've got it. How long has this been going on?"

"Too long. Almost a month and a half. I'm running out of money. If King looks into my account, he's going to have a lot of damn questions."

"Don't give him another dime," she snaps.

"If he truly has something, he'll ruin our lives if I don't cough up the cash. Actually, I've been trying to ditch you to drop off a payment all day."

She turns to me and places her hands on her hips. "Then I'll put his ass to sleep now."

"No, he says if something happens to him, his boys will blow the whistle for him. I need to know facts. We can't just react to this. I need to know what course to take."

She glares at me. I can tell she's not happy. Reap would rather place a bullet in his head and be done with it.

"We go make the drop. Then I'll do some digging. You're not going to keep paying this fucker. You need to talk to Prez. He's going to lose his shit."

"I know. I just need to make sure it's safe to tell him."

"All right. Fine."

King

"You're one bold motherfucker," I snarl as I find this piece of shit leaning against my bike.

Pop grins at me, blowing smoke out this side of his mouth. I can't believe this is the same dude I grew up looking up to as an uncle. I was eighteen when he killed his wife and took Misty and Jacky's mom from them.

"I come in peace," he says with a smug grin. "How's my baby girl? She still slumming with your filthy ass?"

"Fuck you."

He chuckles. "You clean up nice for your little business. I wonder what they would think of the real you."

He looks me over from head to toe as if his appraisal is worth something. His worn jeans and leather jacket don't make him a fashion expert. I'm dressed for the business meeting I came here for.

I just finished closing a major account for Soul Expressions. My dreads are in a neat bun on top of my head and I have on a three-piece suit. My dress boots are shining, as are my cuff links.

I go to slip my hand into my messenger bag for my piece. Pop shakes his head as he glares at me. "All these cameras and people around here. You're not leaving my baby girl out here on these streets while you sit in a cell. No, I want you dead, that way she can at least have the insurance money."

"You can kiss my ass," I growl.

"You get your affairs in order, King. Your end is coming."

"You want to threaten *me*. You have some huge balls. I promise you, I'm not the one that's going to be kissing dirt, motherfucker. You picked the wrong man to have a hard-on for."

"You're big talk, kid. Just like your old man. You two have turned that club into shit. I'm going to take it all from you. I'll restore that shit to its former glory and bask in the fact that I did it while pissing on your bones."

"I'm a whole different animal from my old man."

"You and I agree on one thing. You are all animals that need to be put down."

I step forward. "Mr. Kennedy." I turn to find the assistant of the CEO I just met with. His hazel eyes bounce between me and Pop. "I'm so glad I caught you. Mr. Daniels has just a few more questions. Do you have time to come back inside?"

"Yeah, sure," I grumble.

"I'll see you around, King. You take care of business."

My muscles are coiled so fucking tight. I'm ready to say fuck everything and blow his damn head off. However, he's right. If I kill him here and now, I'll ruin more lives than just mine. I'm not doing that shit to my wife and son.

"I'll see you soon," I call over my shoulder, not looking back. *This shit is going to end. Very soon.*

CHAPTER FORTY-NINE

Never Mind

Misty

I should've said something to Reap weeks ago. After making the drop, she was able to get the answers I needed within less than five hours. I could jump with joy and kiss her.

We stand in one of the bedrooms at Cage and Rose's place. Reap filling me in as fast as her lips will allow, while changing Colin on the bed.

"It turns out Striker does have cop friends—well, a couple of ex-cop friends and one still on the force—but they're all scumbags like him who are no longer on or once tried and failed to get on the Lost Soul payroll. According to Reap, King's connections run so deep these guys would be spitting in the wind if they tried to blow the whistle.

"They can say whatever they want. It won't stick. It may just be a thorn in King's side that he doesn't need right now, but I say tell Prez," Reap says after she finishes telling me all she's dug up.

"They've been taking your money and having a good time among the five of them. One guy has gambling debts, another is facing a divorce, and the wife is getting everything. Striker is a bum that never tried to find a job after losing his badge.

"He actually ran to Philly to his baby sister's house right after until her husband got fed up and threw him out a few months ago. He's been off the grid because he became a couch potato in their basement. Good for nothing," she continues.

"King has the brothers watching for his return. If you don't say something soon. He's going to figure it out. Listen, the other two are just plain assholes and junkies to boot," she says.

I can't wait to tell King about this shit. I thank Reap and rush to my car.

I ask Eva to watch Prince while I go have a talk with King. She and the twins are hanging with Rose this evening. Rose always loves having the kids around. Today has been an emotional day.

Rose called me Izzy. That was my mom's nickname. Rose is starting to remember things. Small things, but they're coming back.

I get home in less than fifteen minutes. I take a deep breath as I reach my front door. I know King is going to hit the roof when I tell him all of this. I'll never get all that money back. I'm sure they've blown through every dime already. Including the drop from today.

"I don't give a fuck," King roars.

His voice carries through the house. I move past the foyer and up the stairs. I find him in our bedroom pacing. He's full of rage, bouncing on his toes with it. He stops barking at whoever's on the phone when he sees me.

"Where's Prince?"

"With Eva at the grans' house. What's going on?"

He looks at me for a few beats, then turns. "Lockdown. This motherfucker wants to show me he can get to me. We end this now. Call everyone in."

He pauses to listen to the other line. "Do I sound like I care? If they ain't family, send them packing. I want everyone at the clubhouse within the next hour."

This isn't the right time for this. He's already ready to blow. If I tell him now, there's no telling what he'll do.

My phone buzzes in my hand. I look down and see red. I've dropped off ten grand once a week. Ten fucking grand.

Unknown: *I need another drop. Tonight. Make it happen.*

King comes over and lifts my chin. I quickly close the text and shove my phone into my pocket. He searches my eyes with those blues.

"You have any contact with your dad?"

I frown. "No. Not since that diner. I'm not stupid, King. I get he doesn't mean me any good. Or at least not when it comes to you. If I hear from him, I'll tell you immediately."

He continues to search. The words are right on the tip of my tongue, but I can't bear to put this on his shoulders. Not tonight.

"What's going on, baby girl?"

"It's nothing," I say, pasting on a smile. "I just hate lockdowns. Especially now with the baby."

He pulls a face and runs a hand through his loose dreads. He's barely containing all the anger and rage within. I don't know what has happened, but it couldn't have been good. I know it has to do with my dad for sure.

"Shit. You sound like Brick." He pauses to think for a minute. "How about this? You and the girls can stay at the grans' house with the kids. After we get through with church, I'll have a few of the brothers put on the place. You guys should be fine with just Reap for a little bit."

"Okay, I think that will work."

His fingers fly across his phone as he sends off a text. "Pack your shit and whatever you need for Prince. We'll head out in twenty. I'm going to follow you there. I want you to have your car in case if an emergency. Pack your piece. I'm not taking any chances."

"King." I tip toward spilling it all.

"Yeah, baby?" he says it so gently, my heart squeezes. I can see the stress in his features.

Yeah, I can't dump anything else on him. A plan starts to form in my head. King has enough on his shoulders. I can take care of this.

"Never mind."

King

There are souls crying tonight. I can hear them. Someone's about to die. I'm ready for it to be Pop. I'm banking on it being Pop.

However, the bona fide reaper in me knows it's not. Which is what has me on edge. I'm responsible for every Lost Soul that follows me. I'm not losing one tonight.

"You feel it too," Grim says as he stands next to me outside the clubhouse.

I give a nod.

"Ain't one of ours, brother. I know that in my bones. This one is long overdue though. Someone has wronged us and they're about to pay," he murmurs.

"You call Jacky?"

"Talked to him an hour ago. He's on his way home. Once Squad, always Squad."

I nod again. I squint at the sky above. It's even red this evening as the sun sets. Some shit is going down.

"Alert all our guys. If they hear something out of the ordinary, they need to be the first to respond. If it's one of ours spilling blood, we need to cover the tracks."

"Got it, Prez."

I pull out my phone and stare. I should call Misty and check on her and our boy, but I can't afford to be distracted. Not just yet, and I'm sure to be distracted if I talk to Misty. Something is still going on with her.

The last two bikes we've been waiting for roll into the compound. Mix and my dad pull up together just like old times. For a moment, I feel like I'm ten all over again, waiting for them to return.

"Retired my ass," I mutter and turn to go back into the clubhouse.

CHAPTER FIFTY

Elbows Deep

Misty

"Are you kidding me?" Reap nearly shouts when I pull her in the bedroom upstairs to tell her Striker has been texting me every ten minutes demanding a drop tonight. "That greedy bastard is about to pay. You leave this to me. Stay here with my son. If anyone looks like they don't belong, shoot first, ask questions later."

"You can't go alone. Besides, this is something I need to do. I'm going to call him on his shit. I'm not giving him another dime."

Eva pushes into the room and we both turn to look at her. "What's going on?"

"That douchebag that felt you up has been blackmailing Misty and taking her money. That shit stops now."

"Wait, what? Striker?" She moves farther into the room. I groan. I was trying to keep her and Sal out of this.

"Yeah, that son of a bitch."

"Reap," I hiss. "I don't want to involve anyone else in this. King is going to lose it as it is."

"You have to tell him," Eva says.

"Not with all the shit he has going on." I rub my temples.

Reap shakes her head. "I told her the same thing. Either way, this shit gets dealt with tonight."

"Yeah, by me."

Reap throws up her hands. "Fine by me. If you want to be the one to do the dirty work, I'm good with that, but I'm going with you."

I palm my face. I should've known she wouldn't let me go do this by myself. It was hell getting her to stay in the car when I made the drop this afternoon. If it weren't for the boys with us, she wouldn't have let up.

"I'm going too."

I look at Eva like she has lost her damn mind. Brick will kill us all. "This is getting out of hand. I'll handle this. You don't need to come along."

"I don't need to, but I'm going," Eva says, placing her hands on her hips.

And this is why Brick has been grumbling that she hangs around Squad members way too much. I shove a hand in my hair. If I'm going to do this, I need to make a move now. I can't sit here arguing about it.

"Going where?" Sal asks as she enters the room with Eva's little girl, Destiny, in her arms.

"Oh, no. It's better you have no clue. Please, you can stay here and help Rose with the babies."

"If it's going to cause a fight between me and Gutter, I'm good with that. We have enough problems," she mutters, placing a hand on her bump.

"Okay, that's settled. Let's go," Reap says.

King

"We found our boy boarding a commercial flight to Brazil," Diggs announces.

"It seems he's calling on old *friends.*"

I work my jaw as my arms rest across my chest. Pop has decided to go to war, for real. The child's play is over.

"Castro is mine," Brick says.

"Ours," I say through my teeth. "His pass is revoked. Call Armando. Let him know I'm about to make his dreams come true. Negotiate the terms and conditions."

"As good as done," Brick says.

Cage lifts to his full height and leans on the table with his knuckles. "This is between me and Pop. It's time I settle the score. That motherfucker is mine. When he steps foot back in South Carolina, I want to be the first to know.

"I'm not stepping on your toes, King. There's just some shit you can't let go as a man. This shit is mine."

I nod. Although I want to be the one to put a bullet between Pop's eyes, my old man has way more reasons to be the one to pull the trigger.

"Why wait for him to come back?" Grim says. "I have the connections we need to take this shit right to Castro's door. If they are together, let's kill two motherfuckers with one blast."

"He has a point," Mix says.

"Brick, you think the Squad is up for this? You guys can get me and Dad in?"

"The Squad is always ready," he replies. "I can get you, Cage and me inside."

"Add me to that list. I want to see that motherfucker take his last breath," Mix rumbles.

I think it over for a bit. With a nod, I say, "Let's get rolling. We're going to Brazil."

Misty

Striker is too eager for this money. When I texted him I'd meet him at the spot, he gave me the address to an apartment. Reap didn't like that one bit. She wanted to make sure the location wasn't a trap. Eva and I are waiting in the car for her to return.

I parked a few blocks away so she could scope things out. I jump a little when she opens the back passenger door and slips back into the vehicle. Eva and I turn to look at her expectantly.

"All five of them are in there. Just like I thought," she fumes. "They're drinking but I don't want to underestimate the situation."

"So, what are we going to do?" Eva asks.

"Misty, you're going to knock on the door as planned. When they open the door, you both be ready. We have to be quick. This isn't going to be a little sit-down like you planned," she says pointedly to me.

"I don't know. We didn't come here for this," Eva says. "I say we call the guys now. They have every intention of Misty coming by herself and harming her."

"Exactly why I'm not waiting." Reap snorts. "You stay here if you don't think you're ready for this. It'll be better that way. You can be the get-away driver."

"Wait," Eva rushes to say. "It's two of you and five of them. No one in this car is over five-five."

I actually laugh. That shit is the truth. She's being kind. I don't think any of us are over five-four, although Eva likes to claim her quarter of an inch.

"My height ain't never stopped shit," Reap says.

"Everyone relax," I say. "We have to do this and do it fast. If King gets back to the grans' house and we're not there, we're all in a load of shit."

"Fine," they say in unison.

"As I was saying. You knock and when they open the door, I'm going to kick that motherfucker in, and we all start blazing. We use the element of surprise, and our height won't make a damn difference. In and out," Reap says.

"Got it. Let's go," I reply.

Eva and Reap get low and I drive closer to the house Striker's apartment is in. I park out of sight of the house's windows, but somewhere with a great sight advantage for us. I see just when someone pulls the curtains back and peeks out.

We all pull our pistols and head for the apartment, staying out of view of whoever's watching. Reap nods at me once we're in position and I ring the doorbell. I have one hand behind my back nervously.

A voice in the back of my head tells me how insane this is. Three black women standing out here with guns, knowing at least one person inside is a cop. There are so many things that could go wrong.

"You're a Lost Soul. You were born into this shit. Chin up, baby girl. My guns don't miss a beat," Reap whispers.

Only seconds after the words are out of her mouth, the door opens and all hell breaks loose. It all happens so fast. Reap moves past me and kicks the door in. She puts a bullet between the eyes of the guy that answers.

He's not Striker. I want Striker's ass. I move into the house and aim. Eva steps in behind me. Reap has taken down two more guys just that fast.

It's the two that are out of sight that throw everything off. Striker comes rushing out of one of the rooms, throwing his arms around Eva. She drops her gun to the floor. Another guy jumps out of nowhere, charging at Reap. They get into a scuffle, and she drops her weapons.

However, I think that's intentionally. Reap loves hand to hand combat. She's about to kick this dude's ass.

I aim at the guy Reap is putting the breaks to, then at Striker. Eva is holding her own and has gotten his arms from around her. He throws a punch at her face, causing her to stumble back. Eva growls and starts to kick his ass with some of the moves Reap has been teaching us.

"Shit," I mutter.

I don't know if I can pull the trigger. It all sounded good in my head. Now, this is a life. I take it, I can't give it back.

I jump when a shot is fired, I swing my gun back toward the other guy and Reap. She has a foot on his back with her gun aimed at his now open head.

"Fucking bitch," Striker snarls. I turn to see him holding his balls. "I'm going to kill all of you whores and then have everyone you know placed behind bars."

And just like that, I pull the trigger. We turn to run out but there are two cops standing in the door looking at us with wide eyes. I drop my gun and get down on the ground before they can even tell us to. We never have a chance to get away. I didn't even hear their sirens.

CHAPTER FIFTY-TWO

Lost Soul

King

Present

"You see. I was only thinking of my family, King."

I close my eyes against the rage. I know her heart is in the right place, but she just doesn't get that I've got her. I will always have her. Shit can be burning down from here to New Mexico, but I will have her and my son.

If I hadn't had a gut feeling to put our boys on high alert, her ass could be in jail in a cell. A few of our guys were on patrol in the neighborhood. They heard the shots and called in Dice once they recognized Reap. That's the only reason they're not going to jail tonight. This shit will never be repeated. The calls from the neighbors were explained away as firecrackers.

"No matter what's going on in our lives, you come to me first. I don't care what they tell you they can do to me."

"Okay," she murmurs from the back seat.

I look at Dice and nod for him to head to our place. As pissed as I am, I'd never let the mother of my son sit in a cell. Misty is my woman. I love her crazy ass. I still can't believe the shit they did tonight.

Reap murmured to me that Misty was the one to pull the trigger on Striker. I need to get her home alone to see where her head is at. Once the shock wears off, my girl could be in a world of hurt. She took a man's life.

I turn to look into the back seat when her pleas die down. She's passed out. Fast asleep. I look at her gorgeous face and wonder, how can I not love the fuck out of her? She did that shit tonight for me. She's officially the badass old lady she's always wanted to be.

"I'll clean all this shit up," Dice says as he stops in front of the house. "Striker and Hanson were stirring shit for themselves with a few fuckers on my shit list. I'll just point things in that direction. I'm due for a big bust."

"Thanks, brother."

He tosses me the keys to the cuffs. I nod and get out of the SUV. Opening the back door, I lift my wife out of the car and start for the house. Once inside, I take her up to our bedroom.

I grin as I think of the lesson I plan to teach little Miss Misty. Placing her on the bed on her side, I uncuff one of her hands. She begins to stir, but I move quickly to cuff her to the headboard. She blinks up at me. As she gains consciousness, she looks around to find her bearings.

She visibly sags in relief when she takes in our bedroom. "Thank God," she sobs. "Can we go get Prince?"

"He's staying with his grandparents for the night," I reply as I take off her shoes and work her jeans down her hips.

"Why am I cuffed to the bed?"

"You're about to learn a very important lesson."

"King, I'm exhausted. I don't want to fight about this anymore. I know I was wrong."

"Nah, you don't. You think you can take on the world by yourself. I want to show you that you need me more than you know."

"King," she whimpers.

I push her shirt up to expose her breasts, tugging the bra cups down beneath them. Her nipples bead, enticing me, but I won't touch them. I want her on the edge, needing but not receiving.

"One of the problems is, I've never told you no and meant it. You take advantage of that shit. You get away with murder because of it."

Her eyes widen. I see the hurt that fills them. Poor choice of words on my part. I go to soothe her but restrain myself. I'll get to that later. This will be like peeling an onion. There are layers to the shit going on between us.

I ghost a hand over her skin, from her torso down to her thighs. She starts to pant, her belly quivers. I move up her body to her ear.

"I need you to see what you mean to me, Mist. I need you to feel me when I say I've got you. I need you to see you need *me*," I whisper into her ear.

Misty

He pulls away from my ear and looks into my eyes. I can't still my racing heart. I want to feel his hands on me, but I know he's purposely not touching me. He leans in as if he's going to kiss my lips, but he doesn't make the connection.

Instead, he pulls away and gets off the bed. Reaching in his pocket, he pulls out his phone and swipes at it until music starts to play from it. Soon he has it hooked up to the bedroom's Bluetooth system and Jodeci's "Cry For You" spills out into the room.

He puts the phone down and starts to strip from his clothes. He pulls his hair up and places a band around his locks. The entire time, his eyes are on me.

I squirm on the bed as need builds inside me. His taunt muscles flex and ripple with his movements. The beard he's been growing and keeping trim is sexy on him. It adds to all things delicious about King. His dick points straight at me as he moves to climb back on the bed beside me.

"There's a difference between me and those boys you tried to tease me with. I'm a man, Misty. A man that loves you with everything I am," he says as he looks down at me.

"I love you too. I was only protecting our family."

"Yeah, I know that, little mama," he says with a grin. "I'm proud of you, baby. But that shit wasn't yours to do. I told you before, I'll tell you again. Never give anyone that kind of power over us. They can't take me from you, and they can't take you from me if we're one."

He moves his hand over my breast and shadows it across my skin, not touching me the way I need. Goose bumps rise across my flesh. He licks his lips as he watches the trail he creates with his hand.

"Please."

"Ah, you see. You can't touch yourself, can you? You need me, don't you? You see how this works."

"Oh God, King don't."

He chuckles. "Now you see how I feel. I ask you not to pull this crazy shit and you do it anyway." He lifts, shifting his big body until he settles between my legs.

Yet he still doesn't touch me. Not more than parting my thighs with his, before getting face-to-face with my pussy. His breath fans my folds. I wiggle my hips and rock them up toward his face, but he doesn't give in.

"Please."

"I've begged. I've pleaded with you to understand I need you safe. I need your hardheaded ass to do what I ask you to. We have a son, Mist. Don't make me raise him on my own. Don't make our son me."

I gasp and my heart breaks. I close my eyes as the tears start to fall. I'm thrown back in time to one of the random times King and I spent alone time together as friends.

"What are you doing here, kid?" he said.

I was fifteen, but it still stung so much to have him call me kid. I remembered what day it was. I waited for him to come to the clubhouse, but he never came. I took a cab to his apartment. Eva, Sal, and I all had a key to his place, in case of emergencies.

That day was an emergency. It was the anniversary of his mother's death. The day that haunted Cage and King. King's birthday.

"I came to see if you were okay," I replied as I took a seat next to him on the couch.

Beer bottles were everywhere. He was taking it hard that year. King's place was never a mess. The disarray of his appearance and that of the apartment spoke volumes.

"I'm fine."

"No, you're not."

"Go do some kid shit, Mist. You don't need to be around me."

I folded my arms over my chest. "You need a friend. I'm here to be that friend. I know what it's like to lose a mama. That shit hurts years later, even after you can't remember her face, when her voice is gone, and you can't remember her scent. It hurts forever."

King's mother was killed in a store robbery when he was four. She forgot the Spiderman candle he wanted and he cried when it was time to sing "Happy Birthday." Cage had, had too much to drink.

King's mom promised to go and come back quickly. She never did. He felt like that shit was all his fault.

That day, King wrapped his arms around my waist and cried into my belly. He let me see him in a way no one else ever had. It was the day he told me that he blamed himself for not having a mother. It was also the day I vowed I'd be his old lady.

King's mouth on my core brings me back to the present. I finally get it. King takes loss personally. Losing me would fall on him, so would caring for our son. I need to let him protect me so he can know he did his part.

It all falls into place. His needs, my needs, our son's needs. I protect our family by taking my hands off and allowing my man to do it. That's all he's asking for.

"I feel you, King. I get it, baby." I moan.

He looks up at me, his eyes filling with a mix of love, triumph, lust, and… peace. He really starts to devour my core. I tug at my restraints, wanting to touch my husband. I come, crying out his name and bowing off the bed.

I blink away my tears as he climbs up my body. He looks down into my eyes. "Finally, you're with me, finally."

He takes my lips and kisses me deeply. My essence bursts on my tongue from his mouth. He slides into my body and starts to make love to me the way only he can.

"I need you so much," I whisper when he releases my mouth.

He places his forehead to mine, still rocking into me steadily. So many emotions stir inside. This isn't like our usual lovemaking. This is the grown-up us. The King and Misty that have grown to love and be there for each other.

"Fuck, baby," he pants. "You will always be where my soul belongs."

"My soul has always been yours."

And for the rest of the night, we prove it. Cuffs and all.

Changing Tides

Cage

"Have you found your peace?" she says as she looks me in the eyes.

Have I found my peace? Pop is dead and he can't harm those I love so...

"Yeah, darlin'." I nod. "I've found it."

Rose turns to look at our kids with their children in the backyard. The place is filled with loud conversations, laughter, and the cries of little ones. I'm proud of our kids. King did good with the girls. I'm proud of him too.

"What now?"

I focus on her gorgeous face. I love this woman more today than I did when I chased her down to marry me in the first place. I brush my fingers across her cheek.

"Now… now I can focus on getting you to remember me. Remember us. I need you to stop being so scared of me, darlin'."

She shakes her head. "I'm not scared of you. I'm… I'm afraid of the way you make me feel when I'm around you. You say you're my husband, but I don't remember you. I would think I'd remember a man that makes me feel… feel like this."

I slip my hand around her neck and do what I've been dying to do since I laid eyes on her for the first time in six years. I kiss my wife. She grabs a hold of my forearm as she melts into me. It feels so fucking good. I deepen the kiss and draw her body into mine.

She jumps back, startled. She drops her gaze to my growing erection. "Oh," she murmurs.

I can't help the grin that comes to my lips. "Don't worry. You've never had a problem taking all of it," I say huskily.

"Um… wow. Um." She lifts her eyes to mine. "You can move into our bedroom. Maybe that will help me remember."

"Thank fuck," I growl and tug her back to my lips.

I nearly carry her up to our bedroom right now. I back her into the counter and shove my thigh between her legs. Her moans are music to my ears.

Someone clears their throat and a giggle sounds. I break the kiss to look up. King and Misty are standing at the sliding door watching us.

"About damn time," King says with a grin on his smug ass face.

He goes to the icebox as Misty leans in the doorway, watching us. "You guys have always been perfect together. You two made me believe in love."

"Did I wear black and lilac to our wedding?"

I snap my head toward my wife. She's looking up at me with a distant look in her eyes as her brows furrow. I cup her face.

"Yeah, baby, you did. You sure fucking did."

King

"Oh my God! She's remembering," Misty squeals to the girls at the picnic table.

"I think we all should leave. I don't believe those two are coming back out anytime soon."

"Yeah," Misty laughs, holding her round belly. "I think Cage is going to spend the rest of the night jogging her memory."

"Everything's changing again," Mix says with a smile. "It feels right this time. No more shadows, no more bullshit."

"Finally," Brick grunts.

"I don't know. All is fair in love and war. We may get to see a different type of battle," I say as I watch my little brother nurse a beer.

Little brother.

That shit still sounds weird, but it feels right. Jacky is my little brother and I'm here for whatever he needs. Even if that means bringing his future to him.

"I know what you're thinking," Misty whispers. "He's torn. If you can figure out a way to fix this for him, I'll wake you every morning with head."

I take a long pull from my beer and grin. "Consider that shit done."

ACKNOWLEDGMENTS

Oh my Lord! This book was a 3 year pain in my butt, plus two more weeks to rewrite it. I had so many angles to tell it from and they never wanted to work with me. Finally! I have a book I love. From here we have seven and half new Lost Soul books to go.

Thank you to all of my readers for following me and my many worlds. It's so much fun to get to create and find the story the characters want to tell. It can also be taxing, so thank you for understanding that each book needs time. Thank you for every email, message, and post. Love you guys to life!

Thank you to my husband. He has to sit through the tears when I'm not sure I'm doing it right. Which is all the time. He keeps pushing me when I'm ready to give up. Thanks, Boo.

Someone stand up and give God praise! If you only knew. To God be the glory. If you ask, be ready to receive. There's no shortcut, but Grace and Favor can get you through. Preeeeessss! New blessings for team Blue. Thank you, Lord.

Next! Cage and Rose. Back to work.

ABOUT THE AUTHOR

Blue Saffire, award-winning, bestselling author of over thirty contemporary romance novels and novellas, writes with the intention to touch the heart and the mind. Blue hooks, weaves, and loops multiple series, keeping you engaged in her worlds. Blue is a hybrid author, writing her own publishing company Perceptive Illusions and for Sourcebooks, as well as Dreamspinners Press as Royal Blue.

Blue and her husband live in a house filled with laughter and creativity, in Long Island, NY. Both working hard to build the Blue brand and cultivate their love for the artists. Creative is their family affair.

Blue holds an MBA in Marketing and Project Management, as well as a MED in Instructional Technology and Curriculum Design. She is also an NLP Master Practitioner.

Wait, there is more to come! You can stay updated with my latest releases, learn more about me, the author, and be a part of contests by subscribing to my newsletter at
www.BlueSaffire.com
If you enjoyed Always, I'd love to hear your thoughts and please feel free to leave a review. And when you do, please let me know by emailing me TheBlueSaffire@gmail.com or leave a comment on Facebook https://www.facebook.com/BlueSaffireDiaries or Twitter @TheBlueSaffire

Other books by Blue Saffire
Placed in Best Reading Order
Also available....
Legally Bound

Legally Bound 2: Against the Law

Legally Bound 3: His Law

Perfect for Me

Hush 1: Family Secrets

Ballers: His Game

Brothers Black 1: Wyatt the Heartbreaker

Legally Bound 4: Allegations of Love

Hush 2: Slow Burn

Legally Bound 5.0: Sam

Yours: Losing My Innocence 1

Yours 2: Experience Gained

Yours 3: Life Mastered

Ballers 2: His Final Play

Legally Bound 5.1: Tasha Illegal Dealings

Brothers Black 2: Noah

Legally Bound 5.2: Camille

Legally Bound 5.3 & 5.4 Special Edition

Where the Pieces Fall

Legally Bound 5.5: Legally Unbound

Brothers Black 4: Braxton the Charmer

My Funny Valentine

Broken Soldier

Remember Me

Brothers Black 5: Felix the Watcher

A Home for Christmas

Be My Valentine

Coming Soon...
Ballers 3: His Team
Brothers Black 6: Ryan the Joker
Brothers Black 7: Johnathan the Fixer

Blue Saffire Exclusive on the
BlueSaffire.com Site

The Lost Souls MC Series
Forever

Never

Always

The A Million to Blow Series

A Million to Blow

A Million to Stay

A Million Blown Coming soon...

Other books from Evei Lattimore Collection

Books by Blue Saffire

Black Bella 1

Destiny 1: Life Decisions

Destiny 2: Decisions of the Next Generation

Destiny 3 coming soon...

Star

Other books from Royal Blue Gay Romance

Collection written by Blue Saffire

Kyle's Reveal

Beau's Redemption Coming October 22, 2019